Praise for Ellie Rollins:

"Pure whimsical delight. Magic does blow throughout the world, and *Zip* proves it!"
—Lauren Myracle, *New York Times* bestselling author of *ttyl*

"A clever novel with a bright and spunky heroine. Readers will root for her and empathize with her search to find her place in the world."
—*School Library Journal*

"Slapstick humor and a sense of magic help maintain this affecting story's levity as Lyssa learns to overcome her fears and accept change."
—*Publishers Weekly*

"Totally enchanting! I loved this book every step of the way! Lyssa's journey is a once-in-a-lifetime odyssey, where seeds sprout in front of your eyes and the winds of change blow you to runaway rock stars and glass-skinned monsters alike."
—Shelby Bach, author of *Of Giants and Ice*

"Zip, zap, and zoom with Lyssa as she races against the clock!"
—GirlsLife.com

Snap

Snap

ELLIE ROLLINS

An Imprint of Penguin Group (USA)

razOr
bill

A division of Penguin Young Readers Group
Published by the Penguin Group
Penguin Group (USA), 345 Hudson Street
New York, New York 10014, U.S.A.

USA / Canada / UK / Ireland / Australia / New Zealand / India / South Africa / China
Penguin Books Ltd, Registered Offices: 80 Strand, London WC2R 0RL, England
For more information about the Penguin Group visit penguin.com

Published simultaneously in Canada

Library of Congress Cataloging-in-Publication Data is available.

ISBN: 978-1-59514-515-4

Printed in the United States of America

1 3 5 7 9 10 8 6 4 2

This is a work of fiction. Names, characters, places, and incidents either are the
product of the author's imagination or are used fictitiously, and any resemblance to
actual persons, living or dead, businesses, companies, events, or locales is entirely
coincidental.

For Summer,
best friend and honorary sister

CHAPTER ONE

The Cat Has Eyes

Danya woke to the sound of thumping on glass and blearily blinked the sleep from her eyes. Golden light filtered into her room. All around was muffled morning silence.

Another thump came from the window, followed by a loud, sudden snort, like someone revving the engine on a lawn mower.

"Hold your horses," she said, rubbing her eyes. She sat up and let out a laugh that was half snort. Could a *horse* hold his horses?

She hopped out of bed, crossed the room, and pulled back the curtains—revealing a long brown nose pressed up against the window. The nose belonged to her pony, Sancho.

He was a tiny Shetland pony, just over three feet tall—short, like Danya. He stood on his back legs, his front hooves propped against the window ledge so that Danya could see his golden-brown belly with its big black heart-shaped splotch in the middle. His chestnut mane hung down over his eyes.

Danya unlatched the window and swung it open. The Kentucky air was heavy, and already hot for summer. It smelled like freshly cut grass and the daffodils her neighbor, Mrs. Harrison, grew in her front lawn.

Sancho pushed his head into her room and pawed at her window ledge with his hooves, like he wanted to climb inside and curl up in bed with her. Danya tickled Sancho beneath his chin, and the pony let out a light, breathy grunt, his lips flaring up around his teeth. "What is it?" she asked, following Sancho's gaze. It was then that she noticed the time. *Oh no!* It was already eleven A.M. Danya had stayed up late reading again and must have overslept . . . which meant she was late to help her father out at the farmer's market, like she did most Sunday mornings. "Let me grab my book and pen, and we can get going," she said.

Danya's room teetered between lovably messy and totally chaotic. An emptied dresser drawer stood on its side as a makeshift desk, clothes strewn around it in knee-high piles. The framed photographs on her wall were all a little askew, and a few of the posters had scribbles in the corners because Danya had been testing her pens for ink. The pens themselves were hiding *everywhere*—they poked out of the flowerpot on Danya's windowsill and peeked from underneath the tangle of sheets on her bed. Her lucky purple gel pen stuck out of last night's half-eaten cheese sandwich, which sat on her bedside table. It wasn't that Danya was a messy person; it's just that her mind always seemed to be focused on something more interesting than cleaning. She grabbed the gel pen from the sandwich and stuck it in her pocket.

The book she'd been reading last night was now half-buried under the rumpled covers of her bed. It was one of her favorites—the third book in the Adventures of Ferdinand and Dapple series. Out of habit, she flipped to the last page and smiled at the photograph of an old woman with wildly curly white hair and a dark, deeply wrinkled face. The name beneath the photograph read ANGIE RUIZ. Angie Ruiz was the author of all the Ferdinand and Dapple books. She was also Danya's grandmother.

Danya reread the description of Angie, her famous *abuelita*, for what had to be the hundredth time. Angie had been everywhere—Italy, Bali, Peru—and done everything.

She'd climbed to the very top of Mount Kilimanjaro and learned to craft authentic clay pots at a gallery in New Mexico. She'd run with the bulls in Barcelona and perfected the art of sushi-making in Japan. Danya had never met her grandmother, but sometimes her father would tell her stories about his great adventurer of a mother.

Ever since Danya was born, Angie had lived in a tiny village in Cuba where she didn't have access to a phone and was twenty-four miles from the nearest post office. She'd written the stories about Ferdinand on an ancient typewriter in her tiny, one-room house and sent them to her publisher on the back of a donkey.

Sticking the book under one arm, Danya grabbed her bag of pens, notebooks, and writing supplies and headed back toward the window, where Sancho still waited, pawing the ground impatiently.

"What's up, buddy?" Danya said. "Is Mom mixing grass in your good hay again? You know she only does that to make it last longer."

Sancho cocked his head and fixed Danya with one dark eye, letting out a huff of breath from one nostril.

"Fine, don't believe me," Danya said, grinning as she ruffled his mane. She grabbed her gray T-shirt with the purple heart on the center from a pile on the ground and slipped it on over the tank top she'd worn to bed. Then she slipped into her favorite pair of jeans, folding the cuffs up so they didn't drag on the ground. Most jeans were too long for her short legs.

Just before climbing out the window, Danya placed a letter for her *abuelita* on her pillow, where she knew her mother would find and mail it.

A few minutes later, Danya rode Sancho into the farmer's market. Her T-shirt already stuck to the sweat on her back, and the summer air was just growing warmer.

Dozens of people wove in and out of the brightly colored stands, carrying canvas bags piled high with fruits and veggies. Lemon and honey smells filled the air, along with the scent of her mom, Maritza's, delicious cookies, which Danya balanced on the saddle in front of her. She rocked gently back and forth on Sancho's back as the pony trotted, and only once or twice did she have to tug on his ear to keep him from stepping on someone's toes.

Danya got Sancho when she was only three years old. Back then their house had been almost like a farm. Her dad, Luis, often brought home new cows and goats and sheep so he could experiment with all different varieties of cheese for the fancy wine and cheese restaurant he owned downtown. One day he arrived with a full-grown Shetland pony and her tiny Shetland foal, Sancho, a runty little pony hardly bigger than a puppy. Danya had always been small herself, and she'd been just the right size to climb onto Sancho's back.

Then three years ago, Sancho's mom—Jupiña—died in a fire that destroyed the stable in Danya's backyard, killing a few chickens and their old cow, Henrietta, too. It was the worst day of Danya's life. She still had nightmares about the fire sometimes, and she couldn't think about it without remembering the crackle of flames and all the smoke she'd inhaled. Her throat squeezed up at the memory, like she was trying to swallow a fist, so she tried to think about it as little as possible. Then her dad lost his restaurant. They had to sell off the surviving animals one by one. Now only Sancho and Bess, the mean old goat her dad kept to milk for cheese to sell at the farmer's market, were left.

Danya gave Sancho's ear a double tug to get him to go left and Sancho turned, waiting patiently for an old man on a motorized scooter to cross before he started trotting again.

Luis Ruiz's arms were propped on the cheese stand as Danya and Sancho approached. He wore his usual flannel shirt and jeans, his hair tidily combed back from his forehead. But something about him seemed *off* this morning, though Danya couldn't quite put a finger on what.

He gazed off into the distance, as though staring down an invisible foe.

Sancho whickered softly, and Danya patted his neck. "I think you're right," she said under her breath. "Dad does look tired." She pulled Sancho to a stop in front of her father's stand and said, louder, "Hey, Dad. Sorry I'm late. Sancho troubles. He's been acting antsy this morning."

Her dad gave Danya a sideways smile that didn't quite reach his eyes. "I'm glad you brought him along, actually. He's . . . well, he can help me carry some of the extra cheese and desserts home today."

Danya searched her dad's face. In her *abuelita*'s stories, Ferdinand could always tell whether someone was lying just by looking at them. They'd wink or twitch their nose and Ferdinand just *knew*. Danya watched her father, but he didn't wink or anything. He laughed and leaned forward to ruffle Danya's curls.

"You okay, Snap? You look kind of serious." Everyone had taken to referring to Danya as Snap because ever since she was a kid, she was known for getting lost in books. She used to think she wanted to be a writer someday. She loved making up stories in her head, but she had a hard time organizing her thoughts enough to get them down on paper. People were always telling her to "snap out of it," and the name just stuck.

"I guess," Danya said. "But . . ." The buzzing static from the walkie-talkie she always kept in her back pocket cut her off.

"Hold on a second," she muttered, digging the walkie-talkie out. She switched on the talk button and groaned into the speaker. "Mom, I'm coming but—"

A familiar voice cut through the static, interrupting her. "The cat has eyes."

"Pia? Is that you?" Danya clenched the walkie-talkie so tightly her knuckles turned white. Pia had her other walkie-talkie? The only way that could be possible was if Pia was at her house! Danya's mom hadn't mentioned she'd be coming for a visit today.

"The *cat* has *eyes*," Pia said again, "and the wind is blowing north-northeast."

Danya frowned. The air around her grew warmer by the minute. She wiped her sweaty palms on her shorts before pushing the talk button again. "I heard you the first time. But that's not part of our code."

Pia hesitated. "Er . . . the cat has *teeth*? No, wait, I've got it—the cat has a tongue!"

"You're supposed to say 'the cat has *my* tongue,'" Danya said. "I can meet you in our secret place in five! Over!"

Danya switched off the walkie-talkie, but her dad was

helping a customer now: a bald man in a fancy black suit with shiny, shiny shoes. Luis's back was to Danya as he wrapped a stinky wedge of blue goat cheese that smelled exactly like his favorite sneakers before her mom insisted they be thrown away.

"Help me down, buddy?" Danya said, giving Sancho's back a pat. Sancho knelt in the dirt, and Danya scooted off his back. She slipped his reins through the fence post and tried to get her short fingers to work the ropes into a knot.

Suddenly Sancho tugged on his reins, his pupils wide and black. He yanked again, harder, and the reins slid from Danya's fingers.

"Whoa there!" said a deep voice behind her. Danya turned, hoping it was her dad. Instead the bald customer her dad had been helping approached, his shoes kicking up clouds of dust. Now that Danya could see him better, she noticed his slim-fitting black pants still had a crease down the legs, like he'd just bought them at a store, and his shoes were so shiny she could probably make faces at herself in their reflection. The man wore dark sunglasses even though clouds filled the sky, covering the sun.

Danya glanced at her dad again, but he was busy with another customer. Sancho snorted into her neck and backed up against the fence. Danya knew that snort. It meant Sancho was *scared*.

"Is he always so ornery?" the bald man asked, kneeling next to them.

"Only around people who make him nervous," Danya said. The man smiled at Danya, but something about his smile seemed wrong, like his lips were pulled too tightly over his straight, white teeth. He tried to pet Sancho's nose, but Sancho pulled away and shook his mane violently. Danya reached out to calm him, but he trembled beneath her fingers.

"Are you feeling okay, buddy?" she asked.

"Well, there's your problem. You shouldn't talk to him like he's a person," the man said. "I work with horses, and you have to show them who's the alpha, let 'em know you're the boss."

Danya frowned—she wasn't Sancho's boss, she was his friend—but before she could say as much the man grabbed Sancho's reins and in a single fluid movement steered the pony's head around so Sancho was forced to look him right in the eye.

Before Danya could open her mouth to tell the man to get his dirty mitts off her horse, Sancho whinnied and reared back, pumping at the air with his hooves. He was a tiny little pony—but he was strong, and he struck the man's hand, *hard*. The man shouted in pain, dropping the reins like they'd burned him.

"What's *wrong* with you?" Danya yelled at the man, grabbing for Sancho. Sancho dropped back to all fours and chomped down on his bit with his front teeth. "You shouldn't mess with other people's pets!"

The man smiled again—that strange, stretched-out smile that almost didn't look like a smile at all. He held up his hand and Danya could see the beginnings of a dark, purple bruise forming where Sancho struck him.

"That horse needs to be broken," he said. Then he turned on the heel of his shiny shoe and stalked back over to Danya's father.

Anger and nerves clawed at Danya's throat as she watched the man go. Her father would be furious that Sancho struck one of his customers, even if the bald man was pestering them. Sancho snorted again and kicked the dirt. This time Danya didn't need to ask what was bothering him.

"Don't worry," she whispered, patting Sancho's neck. "There's no way I'm leaving you behind with that creepy guy hanging around. I don't care what Dad says."

Nervously, Danya glanced over her shoulder. Her dad was busy talking with the man in the suit. Any minute she was sure he'd storm over and demand to know what happened, and she and Sancho would both be in a heap of trouble. The injustice of it made her cheeks burn. If they left now, it'd be worse, but at least that man wouldn't get another chance to bother her pony. Swallowing her nerves, Danya untied Sancho's reins and climbed onto his back.

"Let's go," she whispered. "Quickly."

Sancho whinnied in agreement, licking her pant leg with his scratchy tongue. Together they rode off toward home.

CHAPTER TWO

The Secret Mailbox

"Keep quiet," Danya hissed into Sancho's ear as she steered him behind the large oak tree next to her backyard patio. Sancho nodded and placed his hooves carefully down on the grass to keep from stepping on any twigs.

The Ruiz family's backyard was bigger than their entire house. They weren't great gardeners, so crabgrass and dandelions covered the ground, leaving only a few spots of lush green grass left. Danya thought it looked awesome, like a patchwork quilt. A row of tall, leafy-green oaks separated the patio from Sancho's pen, and to the east were the shed, Bessie the goat's pen, and a now-empty coop that'd once been filled with chickens. The toolshed was in the far western corner, next to the remains of the old stable, the one place in the yard that made Danya's stomach coil.

That old stable was where Sancho's mother, Jupiña, died. Even though the terrible fire that took her life had been months and months ago, Danya was convinced the thick smell of smoke still hovered in the air around that spot. She held her breath whenever she walked past.

Danya slid off Sancho's back, and he let out a soft, breathy snort that was little more than a hot puff of air against her neck. She peered through the branches. Her mom sat on the patio, her forehead damp with sweat from the Kentucky heat. Danya was a slightly smaller carbon copy of her mother—she had the same big brown eyes and crazy curls, and she even had a widow's peak on her forehead that made her face look like a heart.

Pia's mom, Danya's *tía* Carla, sat at the table across from her mother. The two women sipped coffee from tiny, ceramic mugs and spoke in low voices. An old shoebox sat on the table between them. Danya frowned at it. Her mother usually kept those shoeboxes in the back of her closet.

"This is going to be tricky," Danya muttered, watching her mom and aunt. She'd decided on the way home that she and Sancho should hide out for a while—just until after her dad got home. Then Danya would brew a cup of his favorite tea, explain everything, and apologize for leaving the market when he needed help. But if she tried to lead Sancho around the house to his pen, it would bring them directly into her mom's line of sight. Danya's mom would be furious that she'd left the market with Sancho after she'd been told to leave him behind.

Suddenly a staticky, fuzzy voice sounded from Danya's writing bag, interrupting the silence in the yard.

"Danya? I've been waiting, but . . ." Static crackled from the walkie-talkie, interrupting her cousin's voice. "Hey, can you hear me? Snap?"

Pia! Danya grabbed for her bag quickly, digging around for the walkie-talkie. Sancho blew breath from between his lips, telling Pia *"shh!"*

"Snap?" Pia said again. "Snap, you there?"

"Hello?" Maritza called from the patio. The chair creaked as her mother stood.

Danya fumbled nervously, dropping her bag before she could find the walkie-talkie. She threw her body over the bag to muffle Pia's staticky voice. From somewhere beneath her, she thought she heard her cousin say, "Over."

"Danya? Is that you?" her mom said. For a moment there was silence. Danya inched forward on her hands and knees and peered around the tree to make sure her mom hadn't seen her. Sancho mimicked her, pulling himself forward on his hooves. His breath warmed Danya's neck as he, too, tried to peer around the tree.

Maritza stood at the edge of the patio, shielding her eyes from the sun as she scanned the yard. Then she turned and snatched the box from the table.

"Better put the mailbox away," she said to Tía Carla. "Before Danya finds it."

Danya frowned. Her mom was being pretty weird about some old shoebox. Why didn't she want Danya to find it? Maritza adjusted the box in her arms and Danya inhaled sharply. The word *Angie* was written across it in large block letters.

Angie Ruiz? Danya's *abuelita*, the famous novelist adventurer? Danya's heart leapt into her throat, like it always did when she thought of her grandmother. She leaned in closer, as though it would help her see inside the box, but Maritza slipped into the house. Above her, Sancho whickered in frustration, blowing a thick curl over Danya's eyes.

Though she was still curious about the box, Danya seized her opportunity to make their escape. She gathered her things as quietly as she could and led Sancho around the house, behind the old toolshed.

As they approached the remains of the stable, however, she froze. There were still a few blackened boards lying across the grass, and the ground below was scorched and dead, with just a few tiny shoots of grass starting to grow up near it. Danya edged around the boards and burned grass, holding her breath and keeping her eyes clenched shut. She felt like she was walking on a graveyard. Sancho seemed anxious, too. All of his muscles tensed up—it made Danya feel terribly guilty. He trotted faster, anxious to put the spot behind him. Neither of them liked to be reminded of what happened that day.

Beyond the toolshed, her dad had set up a faded orange tent that was now Danya and Pia's secret hideout. Christmas lights twinkled from the tree branches above, and a shadowy figure moved inside the orange canvas. Danya pulled Sancho along, racing for the tent. Every step she put between herself and the burned grass and boards made her feel a little better.

She tied Sancho's reins to the nearby tree, where he would be safely out of view of the house, and was just lifting the canvas flap of the tent when Pia shot out, knocking her over with a hug that was really more of a tackle. The girls rolled backward into the grass, laughing as they tried to untangle themselves. Instantly Danya was happy again.

Danya and Pia liked to say they were practically twins, even though they didn't really look much alike. They were both eleven and three quarters, though—their birthdays only three days apart—and they'd been celebrating them together for as long as they could remember. Pia had the same deep, golden skin and chocolaty brown hair as Danya, but she was tall and gangly, almost entirely made up of sharp elbows, pointy knees, and limbs that seemed to stretch forever. Her hair was curly like Danya's, but Pia wore it so short that it stuck out of her head in angles and spikes and gave her the look of someone who'd stuck her finger in an electric socket.

"You're here you're here you're here!" Pia hooted. She leapt to her feet and pulled Danya into the tent, yanking so hard that both girls toppled back onto the ground. "Secret handshake?"

Danya bumped Pia's fist with her own, then the girls tapped elbows and leaned back to slap their feet together, causing the orange tent to shake around them. The tent was small and already crowded with books stacked along its sides in wobbly towers. Half the books were old library copies from the school where Maritza worked part time as a librarian. She got to keep the old, crumbling books for Danya when the school replaced them with new copies.

"How're things in Danya Land?" Pia asked, plopping on the ground. Her lips widened into a smile, showing off the hollow space where her last baby tooth had been. Danya's baby teeth had fallen out early on, but Pia's last baby tooth had stayed put, like it was staging a protest, until Pia's dentist finally had to pull it out himself. Her grown-up tooth still hadn't come in, and Pia liked to make up stories about how she'd *really* lost her tooth in a motorcycle accident when she tried to perform a triple flip through a ring of fire.

Danya thought about the weirdness of the morning—the man at the farmer's market and how her mom was hiding an old shoebox. But the weirdness was more a feeling than anything else, and she didn't know how to explain it, so she simply shrugged.

"Good," she said. She didn't like to look in Pia's eyes when she lied, so instead she focused on the hollow space in Pia's smile. "How 'bout you? Where's your dad? I just saw your mom out on the patio."

"He's visiting his sister or something," Pia said. "Oh! I finished that book you gave me." She grabbed the very first Adventures of Ferdinand and Dapple book out of her overnight bag and handed it to Danya. "It was pretty cool. I liked the part about the heroic tasks."

Danya took the book from Pia's hands and ran a thumb over the cover picture of Ferdinand on top of his horse. In the first Ferdinand and Dapple book, Ferdinand realized he wanted to be a great hero, so he set out with Dapple, his trusty steed, to complete the Fifteen Heroic Tasks. Danya used to daydream about completing the tasks herself, with Sancho. But that kind of stuff only happened in stories.

As usual, she flipped to the very last page and studied the black-and-white photograph of Angie Ruiz.

"Something kind of weird just happened," Danya said, looking up from the book. Then, before she could stop herself, she blurted out what she'd just seen: her mother gripping the shoebox, saying she didn't want Danya to find it. The name, *Angie*, written in black letters.

"Dude! A *secret box!*" Pia bounded to her feet and nearly knocked over a wobbly stack of books. Her mouth twisted into a smile again, showing off her missing tooth. "What are we waiting for?"

Danya couldn't help grinning. Pia made everything an adventure.

The girls left Sancho safely hidden in the trees (even though he grunted and pawed at the dirt—Sancho *hated* being left behind) and crept toward Danya's house, sticking to the shadows and darting behind trees to keep their mothers from seeing them. Danya and Pia's moms were once again sitting at the patio table, sipping their *café con leche* and talking in low voices. Just as Pia and Danya ducked behind a clay pot filled with herbs, Maritza leaned across the table and wrapped Tía Carla into a hug. For a second, it looked to Danya like her aunt had tears in her eyes. But before she could get a better look, she felt a yank on her arm.

"Now," Pia hissed, dragging Danya forward. They darted across the patio, slipped into the house, and eased the door shut with a barely audible *click*. Once inside, Danya pushed aside the curtain covering the back door window and stared out onto the patio. Her mom and Pia's mom were still hugging. It definitely looked like Tía Carla was crying.

"Is your mom okay?" Danya asked, watching Maritza pat her *tía* Carla on the back.

"She's fine. Come on. If you don't hurry, they'll see us." Pia grabbed Danya's arm and pulled her down the hall.

Light filtered into the bedroom from around the curtains over the window, giving everything a dusty gray glow. Danya pushed the door shut behind her, feeling a shiver that was part guilt, part excitement. She wasn't supposed to go into her parents' bedroom without being asked, and she definitely wasn't supposed to go through their closet.

But then Pia glanced over her shoulder, grinning her wide, gap-toothed smile, and Danya shivered again. Maybe this was against the rules, but Danya just couldn't shake the feeling that her parents weren't telling her something. Ferdinand would have figured out what the secret box meant—and so would she.

Danya tugged on Pia's sleeve, motioning to a set of

folding doors in the corner. Pia nodded, and the girls crept across the room and pushed the closet doors open.

"Bet it's up there." Pia pointed to a row of shoeboxes lining a shelf at the top of the closet. Danya recognized the red one from the patio table. The "mailbox," her mom had called it. She went up on her tiptoes, but the closet shelf was too high. Her fingers were a good two inches from the bottom of the shoebox. "Give me a boost?"

"Let me try." Pia jumped—once, twice, three times. She caught the box with her fingers, causing the whole thing to tumble off the shelf. The shoebox hit the floor and the lid popped off, spilling photographs, letters, and postcards everywhere.

"Oops!" Pia said. She and Danya dropped to their knees and started gathering the photographs from the floor. Mostly they were old, faded pictures of Danya's parents back when they were very young. Danya pushed them aside. Beneath a few dozen more photographs was a stack of old letters bound together with a faded green ribbon.

Danya slid the ribbon off and studied the first envelope. It was her mother's handwriting again:

Angie Ruiz c/o The Palace Retirement Community
1869 West Cervantes Street, Lake Buena Vista, FL
32830

"Wait . . . what?" Danya studied the letter, confused. This couldn't be right. Her *abuelita* lived in *Cuba*, not Florida. She didn't own a phone, and she was too busy traveling around South America to write or visit—that's why she'd never answered any of Danya's letters. Danya's heart beat wildly in her chest. She tore the letter open. Inside was a photograph from Danya's first birthday, when she got frosting up her nose from the birthday cupcake her mother had made.

Intrigued, Danya opened another letter. A second photograph fell out: this one of Danya learning to ice skate with her dad at Christmas. She wore red-and-white-striped mittens and was laughing because her dad had just slipped and fallen.

"They're all marked *return to sender*," Pia said. Danya barely heard her. She'd just noticed a thick, manila envelope underneath the stack of letters. This one didn't have an address written on it at all. She picked it up and dumped its contents onto the carpet. Several dozen folded letters fluttered out. Unlike the return-to-sender letters, these hadn't been stamped by the post office. They'd never been sent at all.

With shaking hands, Danya unfolded the first letter and stared down at her own crooked handwriting. She'd written it months ago, right after finishing the second Ferdinand and Dapple book.

"I wrote these," she said, almost in a whisper. "My mom and dad always said they'd send them to my *abuelita* in Cuba, but . . ."

Danya's voice caught in her throat, along with the thick, sour taste of tears. No wonder her mother called this box the *mailbox*. Every time Danya asked her to send one of her letters to her grandmother, *this* was where she'd put it. Her parents never mailed anything she'd written. Her *abuelita* didn't live in Cuba. She swallowed hard and shook her head.

"They *lied* to me," Danya said. "About *everything*."

"Danya Marie Ruiz!" Danya's mother's voice echoed throughout the small house, surprising Danya enough that she jumped, dropping her *abuelita*'s letters. The patio door slammed shut.

"She sounds mad," Pia said, glancing at the mess surrounding them. Photographs and postcards covered the floor. "We need to get this all cleaned up. . . ."

Danya knelt on the carpet next to Pia, mechanically sweeping the letters back into the shoebox. But her mind was still on her *abuelita*, her letters. The lies.

Footsteps thudded in the hall, and the bedroom door swung open.

"Danya, what—" Maritza started. Danya stood, the

letters to her *abuelita* still clenched in her fists. Maritza stared at the letters, and the anger drained from her face.

"Where did you find those?" she asked in a gentler voice. Before Danya could explain, her father's voice drifted in from the front porch.

"Maritza? You in here?"

"Come with me," Maritza said quietly. Danya followed her mother into the hallway, moving numbly. So many emotions tumbled around inside her head that she felt like it might explode. There was guilt over sneaking around and anger at her parents for lying to her, but also confusion. What did this mean? Why had they lied?

But when Danya saw her father, she froze and her mind went blank. Her dad wasn't alone—the bald man from the farmer's market was right behind him.

"What's he doing here?" Danya asked, surprised by the anger in her voice.

Her father didn't answer her question. "Danya, where's Sancho?"

"Why?" she asked. The bald man smiled his strange, stretched-out smile, and all her other confusing emotions faded away. Sancho was alone in the yard outside, without her there to protect him. She itched to run to his side.

"He's out back, by the tent," Maritza cut in. Her dad

gave Danya a sad smile, then led the strange man through the back door.

Danya moved to follow her father and the man outside, but her mother took hold of her shoulder and pulled her back. "Why does that man need to see Sancho?" Danya asked, trying to wiggle away.

Maritza took a deep breath. "Sweetheart, when your dad lost his restaurant, there was lots of money we couldn't pay back. Things have gotten harder lately and now we're overdue on loan payments to the bank. We've all had to make sacrifices, and it's just getting too expensive to keep Sancho. This way, we can pay the bank back, and that man can give him a better home, with lots of fresh hay and plenty of space to run around."

"Wait . . ." Danya said, her voice strangely hollow. "You're not . . . we can't *sell* Sancho."

Something in her mother's eyes caused a cold chill to sweep through Danya's body.

"*Mija*," she said. "We already did."

CHAPTER THREE

The Hero's Journey

"That man offered to buy Sancho," Maritza continued. "He came by early this morning to look at him, but your father and I didn't have the heart to wake you and tell you what was happening. First thing Friday morning all the paperwork will be finalized, and he'll come by to pick him up."

"No." It took Danya a second to realize she'd said that word out loud. She opened and closed her mouth a few times, but she couldn't think of what else to say. That one word echoed through her head. *No no no no no.*

Finally, she found her voice. "But . . . you can't . . ." Danya couldn't finish her sentence. She squeezed her eyes shut. Sancho! No wonder he'd been so upset this morning—it wasn't about the hay at all—he'd been try-ing to tell her about *this*, and she'd completely missed it. She wanted to collapse on the floor and scream and cry, like she used to do when she was little and didn't get her way. She tried to hold back the tears, but when she opened her eyes, her cheeks were damp anyway. "Why would you . . ."

Before she could finish her sentence, the patio door swung open and her dad walked back inside. He paused to wipe his boots on the doormat.

"Daddy! Tell Mom we can't sell Sancho." Danya raced into the kitchen and grabbed her dad by his sleeve. "Tell her I need him. Tell her!"

The bald man with the sunglasses stepped into the kitchen just behind Luis. He smiled at Danya, and she took a step backward, wanting to put as much distance between them as possible. She remembered what he'd said back at the farmer's market. *That horse needs to be broken.*

Danya knew with a sudden certainty that Sancho could *never* go live with this man. He wouldn't care that Sancho didn't like the stiff brush or that he hated grass mixed with his alfalfa hay. He wouldn't know Sancho sneezed when he got a splinter or that he needed a haircut every two weeks or his mane would grow so thick he wouldn't be able to see.

"Mr. Howard, this is my daughter, Danya," her dad

said, ruffling Danya's hair. "She loves her pony, you know? Come with me and we'll finish up all the paperwork."

Luis led Mr. Howard over to the dining room table. Panic rose in Danya's throat.

"Dad!" she shouted. Maritza took Danya by the shoulder and ushered her down the hall. As they drew near her bedroom, Danya yanked her arm away.

"I . . . I know everything," she said in a shaky voice. "I know you lied to me. Abuelita Angie doesn't live in Cuba. You never sent her my letters."

"Danya . . ." Maritza lifted her hand to her head and pinched the bridge of her nose between two fingers. "Listen, *mija*, we never meant to lie to you. Things between your dad and his mom are just complicated. I didn't send your letters because I didn't want to risk you getting hurt, too."

She reached out to squeeze Danya's shoulder, but Danya pulled away roughly.

"You never meant to lie to me? You told me the reason Abuelita Angie and I could never meet was because she lived so far away. But she lives in Florida! And you said you sent her my letters, but you didn't. And now . . . now you're giving away my best friend." Danya's voice cracked, and she had to work hard to hold back her tears. She felt like everything she thought she'd known was crumbling beneath her, like sand.

She opened her mouth to say it wasn't fair, but the only thing that came out was a choked sob. Panic set in, and the room around her began to spin. Without looking at her mom again, Danya raced into her room, threw herself onto her bed, and let the tears come.

Hours later, after refusing to come to dinner, Danya rolled onto her back and stared at the horseshoe pattern she'd helped her mom paint on her wall years ago. As the sun set outside her window, shadows covered the horseshoes, slowly growing so dark that Danya couldn't see them at all. She felt numb all over, like crying had drained her of every single feeling. She almost didn't notice her stomach growling from missing her dinner. Almost.

When the sky outside was completely dark, the bedroom door creaked open, casting a wedge of light across the room. Pia slipped inside.

"I figured you'd need some space. But I brought you leftovers." She flicked the light on and set a plate down on the dresser, easing onto the edge of Danya's bed.

Danya wiped her nose with the back of her hand and sat up, pulling the dinner plate onto her lap. Pia had brought her a piece of lukewarm chicken and some green beans.

"Look, we're not going to let them take Sancho away,"

Pia said firmly, reaching out to squeeze Danya's hand. "We need a plan, that's all."

Danya stuck a green bean in her mouth, barely tasting the food as she chewed. "Yeah . . ." she said. "A plan." She sniffled, trying to think. "Maybe . . . maybe your parents could take Sancho for a while? Just until my dad gets a better job."

Pia frowned, considering this. "We might be able to hide him in the bathtub," she said. "He's small, and my mom mostly uses the shower in her room. Or maybe—" Pia was cut off by the sound of arguing coming from the other room. The girls fell quiet. Danya motioned for Pia to follow her as she crouched near her bedroom door, pushing it open an inch.

Danya's parents spoke in rapid Spanish. Pia leaned in close to the door, screwing up her face in concentration. Like Danya, Pia had picked up bits and pieces of Spanish from her family, but neither of the girls was fluent enough to translate a whole argument. Danya lifted a finger to her lips.

Danya's dad was talking. His deep voice was rumbling and quick, making it hard for Danya to understand what he was saying.

"*. . . barco ha navegado . . .*" Danya heard. She frowned.

It sounded like he said the *ship* had *sailed*?" . . . *esperanza* . . . . *hundió* . . .

"Something about hope? And something was sunk, I think?" Pia whispered.

Danya knelt closer to the door just in time to hear her dad rumble," . . . *la fortuna!*"

Danya and Pia turned to each other, eyes wide. "The fortune!" they translated together. In the kitchen, her mom and dad fell quiet. The girls glanced at each other nervously, and Danya's heart thudded in her chest. Had her parents heard them? Did they know she was listening in?

Danya scooted closer, holding her breath so she wouldn't make a sound. Finally, her mother spoke. In English, this time.

"You know Angie might help. Just ask her," she said.

"I can't," came her father's firm reply.

Carefully, Danya pushed the door closed. Before she knew it, she was on her feet, pacing the length of the room. She stopped next to her dresser and picked up *The Adventures of Ferdinand and Dapple, Book One: The Hero's Journey*. Turning it over, she stared at Angie's photograph on the back cover. Her *abuelita*'s kind face looked back up at her.

"What happened between you and my dad?" Danya wondered out loud. But Abuelita Angie just stared, silently, from her photo, refusing to reveal her secrets. Sighing,

Danya flipped absently through the book, as though it might yield some clue. Just before she reached the back cover, a piece of paper fluttered from the pages and drifted to the floor.

Frowning, Danya bent over and picked up the paper, wrestling back the thick fall of curls that dropped over her forehead. It was the list of fifteen heroic tasks Ferdinand had to complete in order to become a true hero. Danya had read the list so many times the page must've come loose from the binding. She'd long since memorized every item, but she still ran a finger down the words on the page as she fitted it back into its proper spot in the book.

1. *Be called to action*
2. *Receive a "sign"*
3. *Rescue someone suffering an injustice*
4. *Act in the name of love*
5. *Suffer a great sadness or loss*
6. *Offer your service on a royal mission*
7. *Give chase to the enemy*
8. *Taste of the forbidden fruit*
9. *Receive supernatural aid*
10. *Experience a profound shock*
11. *Face a personal demon*
12. *Speak to a prophet*

13. Reconcile past harms
14. Make the ultimate sacrifice
15. Win the coveted treasure

She felt her eyes filling with tears again. She'd always had a secret dream that one day she and Sancho would go on an adventure like this. But the adventure in the story wasn't real, and in a week Sancho would be someone else's pony. His adventures with Danya were over.

"Wow," Pia muttered, her face inches from Danya's ear. Danya jumped. She'd been so lost in the comforting words that she hadn't realized her cousin was behind her. Pia reached out and snatched the book from Danya's hand. "One . . . be called to action for a mission." She looked up from the list, her lips all pursed together, eyes shining. "Danya, don't you see? *This* is your call to action. Saving Sancho is your mission!"

"What do you mean?" Danya said.

"This is *just* like Ferdinand and Dapple, right? Ferdinand's mother lost all of her prizewinning cattle to that bandit at the beginning of the book, but instead of just letting it happen, Ferdinand set out on an adventure, and he got them back! That's how he became a hero."

"It's just a book, Pia." Danya pressed her face up against

her window, trying to see Sancho in the yard outside. But the sky was too dark for her to make out much of anything.

Pia grabbed Danya's arm and spun her around. "It's more than a book. It's a guide. If you follow all of the steps in the book, you get to be a hero. *You can save Sancho.*" Pia waved the list excitedly in front of Danya's face.

Danya stared at the book in Pia's hands, doubtful. She thought back to the fire-blackened grass in the yard outside, and a shiver ran up her back, like a thousand spiders dancing over her skin. Pia might think this was a sign—Pia might think Danya could be a hero, but Pia still believed in make-believe and magic and fairy-tale adventures. Danya knew better. Danya and Sancho had been close enough to the fire that took Jupiña to hear the horse whinny and kick in her stable, but they hadn't been in the backyard when it started. Sometimes Danya remembered that sound, and it always made the hair on the back of her neck stand on end. Pia hadn't been here on the night of the fire. If she had, she'd realize that sometimes bad things happened and there was nothing you could do to stop them.

This book wasn't a magical guide to saving Sancho—it was just a story her *abuelita* had written.

Just as she opened her mouth to protest, a lightbulb in Danya's head switched on.

La fortuna, her mother had said. The fortune. Angie Ruiz had made a small fortune writing the Ferdinand and Dapple books. And her mother said they couldn't keep Sancho because he cost too much money.

Danya grabbed the book from Pia's hands and stared down at her *abuelita*'s picture. They couldn't follow a list of tasks in some book and expect to become a hero—that didn't make any sense. But they *could* figure out how to find her *abuelita*. Her mother said it herself—Angie would help. Danya's father didn't want to ask her, but that didn't mean Danya couldn't.

"Pia," Danya said, a smile spreading across her face. "I think I have a plan."

Pia grinned, the hollow space in her teeth peeking out from beneath her lips. "I knew it! We're going on an adventure, right? We're going to become heroes, just like Ferdinand?"

"Not quite," Danya said. "But I think I know how to save Sancho."

CHAPTER FOUR

Rescue Someone Suffering an Injustice

"We need to find a map to get to Florida," Danya explained, her words tumbling over one another in a rush to get out of her mouth.

"*Florida?*" Pia repeated.

Danya nodded. "We're going to Florida, to find my *abuelita*. Since she's really famous, we can just ask her to borrow the money to keep Sancho and pay back my dad's loan. I know she'll want to help."

Pia screwed up her face, thinking. "We should have kept one of those return-to-sender letters," she said finally. "That way we'd have her real address."

"1869 West Cervantes Street, Lake Buena Vista," Danya

said, reciting the address from the envelope she'd found in her mom's closet. "I memorized it. And the name of the housing community she lives in is called the Palace."

Pia blew air from her cheeks. "Okay. A map, then. You guys have a computer, right?"

Danya hesitated. They did have a computer, but it was in her parents' room, and she was only supposed to use it for schoolwork.

"Let's check the bookshelves in the living room first," she said. "My dad used to have all these map books there."

Pia nodded, and the girls snuck out of Danya's room and past the kitchen, where Maritza was doing the dishes. The radio was cranked all the way up, and Maritza sang along in a quiet voice as she scrubbed pots and pans. Pia raised an eyebrow.

"Singing makes her feel better," Danya explained in a whisper. "It's what she does when she's upset about something. Come on. The books are over here." Danya led Pia to the bottom shelf of her dad's bookshelves, where he always stashed thin, spiral-bound atlases of the world. She sat cross-legged on the floor and pulled a stack of the map books onto her lap.

"We need to find one that'll show us how to get from Kentucky to Florida," she said, quickly shuffling through them. Pia crouched next to her and did the same.

France . . . Italy . . . Danya read silently. *West Coast . . . World Atlas . . .*

"Come on," she muttered. "Where are you?"

"How about this one?" Pia held up a small book with a photograph of a twisty highway on the cover. The book was called *U.S. Roads and Highways.* Next to the highway was a yellow, triangular YIELD sign.

"Perfect!" Danya exclaimed. She grabbed for the book, but Pia held it out of reach and pointed to the YIELD sign on the cover.

"That's number two on Ferdinand's hero list," she said. *"Receive a sign!"*

Danya shook her head and snatched the book from Pia. According to the table of contents, Southeastern maps were near the end. . . . She flipped frantically through the pages until she found what she was looking for: Southeastern United States Road Map. Grinning, Danya ripped the page from the book and folded it twice before shoving it in her back pocket. She stepped into the hallway, but Pia grabbed her arm and yanked her away, making her stumble a bit on the carpet.

"Wait!" Pia pulled Danya back into the living room just as Danya's dad appeared in the hall. As soon as he went into the bathroom, Danya followed Pia down the hall. The girls snuck into Danya's bedroom, sliding the door shut behind them.

"Okay, you pack some clothes, food, money—whatever you can find," Pia said. "I'm employing covert maneuvers."

Before Danya could ask Pia what "covert maneuvers" were, Pia stuffed two pillows beneath the blankets on Danya's bed, patting them into place until they were roughly the shape of two girls fast asleep beneath the covers. Impressed, Danya went to her closet and pulled out a flashlight, a few sweaters, jeans and T-shirts, and her good luck jar—which was just a mason jar full of a glittery goo her mom helped her make when she was little. It even had an official label on it, the same kind her dad used to label the fancy cheeses he sold, that read GOOD LUCK INSIDE in huge block letters. And under that, in smaller type: *Contained inside this jar is a piece of the sky. Shake it, make a wish, and when the stars settle—your wish will come true.*

Danya knew it was silly, and she didn't *actually* believe it worked, but she still shook it when she needed an A on a math test or when she was a finalist in the spelling bee. Plus she loved the shades of blue, orange, and yellow that swirled together inside to look like the sky. She opened her underwear drawer and grabbed a sandwich bag filled with $46.78, all the money she'd ever saved from allowances and birthday cards. She'd need every penny. All her supplies barely fit into her school backpack.

"How are we going to *get* to Florida?" Pia used one

sharp elbow to give the pillows a final nudge into place and grabbed her overnight bag off the floor. Her things were still packed.

"Sancho," Danya said, like this was obvious. She'd ridden Sancho all around Kentucky—Florida couldn't be much farther than that. "Come on."

Danya pulled her hair into a messy bun on top of her head so it wouldn't get stuck in her backpack's straps, then looped the bag over her shoulders, stumbling a little from its weight. Her dad liked to joke that the backpack was larger than she was.

She motioned for Pia to follow her out the window. As they jumped to the ground, the moon moved behind a cloud, sending dancing silver light over the grass and trees. Somewhere in the night an owl hooted.

Nerves raced through Danya's stomach. In the darkness, the familiar yard seemed spooky and strange, full of long shadows and invisible creatures rustling in the trees. Running away to save Sancho suddenly seemed different— it was grown-up and scary and real in a way that it hadn't been in her brightly lit bedroom.

Then, from somewhere in the gloom, Sancho neighed. Danya swallowed her fear. Sancho was waiting for her. Sancho *needed* her. Danya shivered and ushered her cousin quickly across the backyard.

The orange tent out back was still illuminated by the firefly glow of the Christmas lights in the trees. At the sound of the girls' approach, Sancho lifted his head. Danya stumbled toward him, barely watching where she was going. The sight of Sancho huddled near the entrance to the tent made something in her chest clench. His poor little nostrils were so red. It looked like he'd been crying. No wonder—not only was he going to get sold, but Danya had left him out here all by himself.

"It's okay," Danya whispered into Sancho's neck, burying her face in his mane. Sancho pushed his nose against her cheek. His horsey lips were wet from the dewy grass. It was the closest Sancho could get to giving a hug, and in that moment, Danya knew he was just as devastated as she was.

"We'll fix this," Danya said into Sancho's neck. Sancho pulled back and licked Danya's forehead, slicking her bangs up into strange, swoopy shapes. His way of saying, "I know."

Danya straightened, wiping a teary eye on her sleeve. Out of the corner of her eye she saw Pia tuck *The Adventures of Ferdinand and Dapple, Book One: The Hero's Journey* into her back pocket. Pia caught Danya's eye and gave her a sheepish smile.

"What? You're rescuing someone suffering an injustice.

Get it? Because Sancho's going to be sold to a man who doesn't love him like you do. That's third on the list!"

Danya shook her head, biting back a smile. It was kind of cool that Pia thought she had it in her to be a hero, but they didn't have time to play silly make-believe games right now. At any moment her parents could look out the window and see her, or peek into her bedroom and notice she was missing. They had to move.

She and Pia bridled and saddled Sancho, and then Danya took him by the reins and led him out of the backyard, to the path they took around the pond on their early morning rides. She fished the map out of her back pocket and unfolded it. Sancho's ears perked up, giving Danya the feeling he was as interested in where they were going as she was. She squinted down at the map, following the highway they'd need to take to Florida with her finger.

"Um. Okay . . ." she said. "It looks like Florida is . . . *that* way." Danya pointed south. She climbed on Sancho's back, scooting forward in the saddle so Pia could get on behind her.

"No thanks," Pia said. "*My* legs are longer than Sancho's. I'll walk."

Shrugging, Danya tugged Sancho's ear, and he started forward at a steady clip. Pia jogged along beside them. She was right: with her long, gangly legs she easily matched their speed.

Streetlamps lined the sidewalks in Danya's neighborhood, painting the concrete they traveled white and yellow. They quickly passed neighboring houses and headed down a main street that twisted out of the residential area toward a busy intersection. There, gas stations and fast food restaurants lit up the dark with their orange and blue neon signs. It hardly even felt like nighttime.

"We can follow this street all the way to the highway," Danya said, squinting down at the twisty lines on her map. She held out her finger to judge the distance they had to travel. "It should be pretty close—only half a fingernail away."

It took a little over an hour of walking for Danya to realize that "half a fingernail" of distance on a map was actually quite a *long* distance in real life.

"My legs are getting tired," Pia moaned. During the first half of their walk she bounced along next to them and jogged ahead on the sidewalk. Now she leaned heavily on Sancho, looking like she was about to collapse. Danya gave her hand a squeeze and glanced back down at the map again. Were they even going the right way?

Danya loosened her grip on Sancho's reins so she could

study the map, and Sancho wandered over to the side of the street and started munching on some dandelions.

"Cool pony!" called a teenage boy riding his bike around in lazy circles in the street.

"Thanks," Danya said. Pia plopped down on the sidewalk, staring longingly at the all-night gas station a few yards away. Its fluorescent yellow sign buzzed in the dark.

"Think they have corn dogs?" she asked just as an old Ford flatbed truck rumbled down the street, taking a sharp turn into the gas station parking lot. The teenager on the bike had to swerve out of the way to avoid it. A crate of corn toppled out of the truck, and a few ears tumbled out and rolled into the street. Sancho snorted and took a tentative step forward, snatching an ear of corn with his teeth.

"Not the best time for a snack, buddy," Danya said as the truck engine sputtered off. Sancho kept munching away, and kernels of corn stuck to his lips and nose.

The truck was old and a little rickety, the kind with a big, open flatbed enclosed on three sides by thick wooden planks. It sort of looked like a wooden wagon. Crates of vegetables filled the back, stacked up against the planks in uneven columns. The license plate read SANDY.

The man who climbed out of the truck wore a

knee-length flannel kilt that looked a lot like Danya's favorite plaid skirt. He paired the kilt with leather combat boots, a bright blue baseball cap, and a T-shirt with the words VISUALIZE WHIRLED PEAS written across it. With a grunt, he hoisted the crate of corn onto his shoulder.

"Hey there, little ladies," he said, spotting Danya and Pia. "Y'all know where the highway is?" He heaved the crate of corn into the back of the truck and attempted to slam the gate closed. A rabbit's foot dangled from the key chain on his belt. "I'm heading south and must have got turned around."

South, south, south. The word was like a drumbeat in Danya's ears. They were heading south, too.

"Just go straight along this road, I think," Danya said. The man thanked her.

"Isn't it a little late for youngsters like yourselves?" he said, scratching his chin. "I mean, it's gotta be at least six o'clock!"

Danya didn't know what to say. It was much, much later than six o'clock, but if she told the man that, he'd be even more suspicious. Instead she just shrugged. "You're right, we should probably start home soon."

The man tipped his baseball cap at that and started toward the gas station. Suddenly Pia sat up, a strange spark in her eye.

"I have a plan," she said, pushing herself to her feet. "You wait here."

While the driver was busy inside the gas station, Pia darted across the parking lot to the truck and loaded her arms up with fresh ears of corn. Sancho's ears perked up, and he started trotting toward her.

"Whoa!" Danya wrapped Sancho's reins around her fingers and pulled back while Pia scrambled into the back of the truck, backing up between the crates of vegetables.

"Here, Sancho . . ." she said, waving the corn at him.

"Pia, what are you doing?" Danya hissed. She glanced at the gas station, but the driver was busy paying the cashier and didn't seem to notice them.

"I'm getting us a ride to Florida," Pia said. "You heard what he said. He's going south."

Danya rolled her lower lip between her teeth. This was a bad, bad, bad idea.

"Come on, Pia, let's just walk. The highway can't be much farther."

"Yeah, maybe, and what are we going to do then? You think we can walk all the way to Florida? We nearly collapsed just trying to make it out of Kentucky!"

Danya pressed her lips together. Her cousin had a point there. Sancho tugged on his reins again, letting out an approving "neigh."

"Fine," she hissed. With one more glance at the gas station, she tugged Sancho's ear. Sancho trotted forward and nudged the back of the truck. Danya slid off his back while Pia wiggled the ear of corn in front of his nose. Drooling a little, Sancho scrambled into the flatbed.

He was a teensy bit too short to make it all the way. Danya slid off his back and nudged his bottom with her shoulder.

"Hurry, Pia!" Danya climbed into the flatbed and hid Sancho between two stacks of wooden crates, then coaxed him down so he was lying flat against the truck bed. Then she gathered up husks of corn from the overturned crate and piled them on top of Sancho. "If that driver sees us, we're done for."

Together the girls covered as much of Sancho with husks of corn as they could. The corn was slippery, though, and it shifted and fell into piles around Sancho, not doing much to keep him hidden. Sancho barely noticed. He chomped down on one ear after another, chewing noisily while the girls worked around him.

"*You* could be more helpful," Danya muttered. Sancho gave her a horsey smile. There were corn kernels stuck between all of his teeth.

"Maybe people will think he's a scarecrow," Pia said. Danya squinted at Sancho and tilted her head.

"I don't think so."

"He's back!" Pia whispered. Danya whirled around. The driver sauntered toward them, his attention fixed on a lottery ticket he was holding in one hand and trying to scratch with his thumbnail. He whistled a little while he walked.

"Duck!" Danya hissed as the farmer made his way across the parking lot. Pia and Danya pressed themselves as flat as they could against the truck bed floor. Sancho shook out his mane, causing the corn stacked around him to roll off the sides of his back.

Pia threw an arm around his neck and tried to push him back down. "Come on, horsey," she muttered under her breath.

The whistling came closer. Danya froze as the driver's-side door creaked open, then slammed shut. She eased into a crouch. She had just noticed that the gate at the back of the truck was still unlatched; if they didn't close it, they might simply go tumbling out of the truck, like the crate of corn had. She crawled forward, reaching for the rusty latch.

"Snap, we're going to start moving!" Pia said. Danya chanced a look behind her and saw that her fearless best friend's eyes were wide and nervous. She wrapped one hand around the latch and tried to close it, but it was stuck, rusted into place. The engine started and the truck rumbled beneath them. Giving up, Danya scooted away from the truck's edge. The toe of her sneaker caught against a crate of corn.

"Snap!" Pia called. "Watch out!"

Danya turned and accidentally nudged the crate out of place. It toppled over, causing a corn avalanche. The corn rolled into her backpack, knocking it into the road and dumping clothes, shoes, and the sandwich bag holding all of her money *everywhere*.

"No!" Danya shouted. The truck rumbled away with them, leaving her clothes and money behind. Sancho whinnied and pawed at the floor of the truck bed. Digging was a nervous habit of his.

Pia grabbed hold of Danya's shoulder and pulled her away from the edge of the truck.

"Don't worry. I got this," she said. Before Danya could say a word, Pia jumped out of the back of the truck, tucking into a roll just before she hit the road. Danya's heart leapt into her throat. She clutched the nearest crate of vegetables so tightly her fingers hurt. A teenager riding past on a bike slowed and let out a low whistle.

"Nice!" he called. Pia ignored him. She darted toward the backpack and scooped up all of Danya's things, then sprinted toward the truck. Her fingers brushed the flapping back gate, but then the truck sped up—pulling just out of her reach.

"Be careful!" Danya shouted. She stood and peered over the towering vegetable crates, hoping there'd be a stop sign or a traffic light just ahead—anything to slow them down so Pia could climb back inside. But all she saw was a long, gray stretch of road—they were headed to the highway. An all-too-familiar sense of helplessness filled Danya's chest as she watched Pia run, knowing there was nothing she could do to help her.

Pia seemed to notice she wouldn't make it to the truck in time at the same moment Danya did. But instead of speeding up, she stopped running completely.

The teenager on the bike circled back around. He zoomed past, and Pia's eyes followed him like a cat tracking its prey. She pulled Danya's bag over her shoulder and started to run. As soon as she caught up with the boy on the bicycle, she grabbed his arm and pulled herself onto his handlebars.

"Go!" Pia shouted. The boy looked shocked, but he didn't let that slow him down. He stood on his pedals and sped up until they were directly behind the truck.

"Grab on!" Pia shouted. She tossed the backpack at Danya and it hit her square in the chest, knocking her back into Sancho, who whinnied and kicked at the corn with his hind legs. Pia held tight to the other strap. She and the boy on the bike were pulled forward quickly, causing the bike to swerve beneath them.

"Reel me in, Snap!" Pia yelled. Danya nodded and pulled the backpack to her chest. Even sitting, she was dragged forward by Pia's weight, all the way to the edge of the truck bed. Sancho scooted up and chomped down on the seat of her pants to hold her steady.

"Thanks, buddy," Danya said. She yanked the backpack, pulling Pia all the way up to the edge of the flatbed. The boy on the bike peddled furiously as Pia grabbed onto the gate at the back of the truck, which was flapping back and forth in the wind, and pulled herself inside. For a second she didn't move, clearly exhausted.

"You okay?" Danya asked as Pia sat up. Pia answered with a wide smile that showed off the gap in her teeth.

"Never been better!" She leaned back, easily popping the ear of corn from the door latch so she could pull the back gate shut. "Thanks!" she shouted after the teenager on the bike. Then she laughed and flopped back onto the corn, her eyes wide and glistening with excitement. "That was *awesome*!"

Danya exhaled. Her arms shook from exhaustion and nerves, but she threw them around Pia's neck anyway.

"Don't do that again," she said, giving Pia a tight

squeeze before punching her playfully on the arm. "You could have gotten hurt!"

Pia grinned wickedly. "Got your stuff, didn't I?"

Danya shook her head. The distant glow of the Louisville lights looked like tiny stars pulled down to the horizon. Though she knew it was impossible, Danya imagined she could see her neighborhood. She even picked one of the tiny lights and pretended it was her house. She pictured her mother singing along with the radio in the kitchen and her dad putting away the extra cheese from the market. But as the truck rumbled down the highway, the lights grew dimmer, then disappeared altogether.

They were on their way.

CHAPTER FIVE

Heavy Metal Turtle and the Ghost Hunters

The next morning, sun crept up over the distant hills, casting dusty strips of gold over the pages of Danya's open book. She'd been trying to write a letter to her mom and dad, explaining why she'd run away, but she couldn't get her words down the way she wanted to. She'd picked up the book for a short break, but now she was to the part where Ferdinand and Dapple confronted the cow bandits. The scene was so tense she could hardly tear her eyes away.

The truck was parked in front of an old motel. Turtle, the driver, had checked in the night before to get some sleep.

Danya knew the truck driver's name was Turtle because

he talked to himself—a *lot*. The night before, he'd left the windows of his truck open while he drove, and he blasted heavy metal music and made drumming noises by blowing air through his lips. Most of the time his music was so loud it was impossible to hear anything else, but whenever there was a break, his voice drifted through the cracked back window right above Danya's and Pia's heads.

"The Turtle's burning out," he'd said. "Better find a place to crash . . ."

Even after they'd stopped for the night, Danya hadn't been able to doze off. It was a warm night, and Sancho's body heat made the truck bed cozy for sleeping, but she couldn't lie still. The whole time Pia and Sancho snored under the stars, she kept turning her plan over and over in her head and double-checking the map to make sure they were headed in the right direction. As she watched the sky above grow lighter, she tried to figure out what time it was back home. Had her parents woken up yet? Did they know she was missing?

Danya finally forced herself to put her map aside, lie down, and squeeze her eyes shut, but then she found herself remembering how sometimes her mom slipped into her room before going to bed to plant a kiss on her forehead. If she'd done that last night, both her parents would already know she was gone. They could have called the cops. Or maybe they'd found the missing map book and somehow figured out where Danya was going. They could be on the highway right now, looking for her.

That thought made it completely impossible for Danya to sleep, so she'd pulled the Ferdinand and Dapple book out of her snoring cousin's back pocket and had begun to read. She only glanced up when she heard Turtle throw open the door of his motel room the next morning and stumble to the truck. She crawled over to the side of the flatbed and peered through the wooden slats to watch him. Turtle's long, black hair stuck up from under his ball cap, and Danya was pretty sure his kilt was on backward.

The early summer air was chilly and smelled like dew and fresh-cut grass, and the only sound came when Turtle switched on his radio. The station blared a program called *Ghost Hunters*, about chasing spirits in haunted hotels and old graveyards. It was turned up so loud that, even with the wind rushing past them as they rode down the highway, Danya could hear almost every word, which was annoying when she was trying to pay attention to her book. She burrowed down in a pile of corn to stay warm and tried to tune *Ghost Hunters* out.

After riding all through the night in Turtle's truck, Danya felt like she kind of knew him. For instance, she knew he was a farmer (why else would he have all this corn?), and she imagined the name on his license plate—SANDY—was his wife. They probably even ran the vegetable farm together. Danya pictured Turtle and Sandy walking around in kilts and combat boots, playing heavy metal music for their rows and rows of vegetables. It was probably like a secret ingredient that made the vegetables taste better or something. She pulled out her lucky purple gel pen and wrote in her notebook about magical vegetables fed on heavy metal. Maybe she could write a story about it someday.

Danya also knew Turtle was *really* superstitious—not only had he bought a lottery ticket, but he kept *three* rabbit's feet for good luck. And this morning, after pulling out of the hotel parking lot, a black cat ran out in front of his car, and it made him so nervous he slammed on the brakes, causing a huge pile of corn to topple and roll over Danya's legs.

As the sun rose higher, Danya turned page after page of her book, finding herself so drawn into Ferdinand's adventures that she hardly had time to worry about her parents or the cops or any of the other dozens and dozens of things that could go wrong on this trip. At one point Sancho snuggled up next to her, staring so intently at the words that Danya was sure he was trying to read, too. But then he let out a snore that rustled the pages, and she realized he'd just dozed off again. She scratched him under the chin as she tried to find her place again.

It wasn't until hours later, when an ear of corn flew across the truck bed and knocked the book out of her hand, that Danya looked up again.

"Jeez, Snap, do you go into a coma when you read or something?" Pia yawned and scratched her head with an ear of corn. Her short, wiry curls stuck up all over. Sancho kicked at the air, like he was dreaming of running.

"Sorry," Danya said. "Didn't know you were awake."

"I've been calling your name for like five minutes," Pia muttered. "We aren't on the interstate anymore, you know."

Danya blinked and looked around. Pia was right—they weren't on the interstate anymore. Turtle was driving down an old, dirt road, surrounded by miles and miles of farmland and short, prickly trees with no leaves.

"Uh-oh." All of Danya's worries and anxieties from the night before fluttered back to life in her gut. What was she doing *reading* at a time like this? She should have been paying attention!

Danya pulled herself up to her knees and studied the passing landscape, but the flat, spindly trees and golden fields looked like a thousand other places. She knew they were headed in the right direction, as long as they stayed on the interstate—according to her map you could take Interstate 65 all the way from Kentucky to Florida—but now they could be anywhere. This was a disaster! There was no telling how far off course they'd gone.

"We need to come up with a plan," Danya said, shaking Sancho awake. Sancho grunted, blinking. "Maybe we could sneak out of the truck the next time Turtle stops and hitchhike back to the highway and—"

The staticky sound of her walkie-talkie buzzed from inside Danya's backpack, interrupting her. Sancho nudged her bag with his nose.

"*Danya . . . Da . . . mija, we're . . .*"

"Mom?" Danya grabbed her backpack and dug through her clothes for the walkie-talkie. She'd thought they were too far away to get any reception, but the sound of her mom's voice buzzed in and out, proving her wrong.

"*Danya . . . where are . . . honey? . . .*"

Danya found the walkie-talkie, but before she could hit the talk button, Sancho rested his head on her knee, and a cold, hard knot formed in her gut. Her mom and dad had betrayed her by lying about her grandmother. And now that they knew she was missing, it was going to be that much harder to get to Florida in time to save Sancho before the ownership paperwork transfer went through. Danya stared down at the walkie-talkie defiantly. Why should she answer?

Just as suddenly as it came, the anger dissolved. Danya pictured her mom waking them up for breakfast. Maritza must've found the pillows hidden beneath Danya's blanket and realized she and Pia were missing. Her mom and dad must be so worried about her.

Luckily Danya didn't have to figure out what to say to them right now. The only sound that came from the walkie-talkie was static.

"Do you hear that?" Pia asked, narrowing her eyes.

"What? The static?" Danya lifted the walkie-talkie, but Pia shook her head.

"The radio. Listen."

Pia crawled over the corn-strewn truck bed, accidentally kicking an ear of corn onto Sancho. Sancho caught the corn in his mouth and chomped down, spraying kernels everywhere. Pia leaned in close to the truck's open back window, and Danya followed her. Static punctuated Turtle's *Ghost Hunters* show, as though it was flowing from the walkie-talkie to the radio. Turtle swore and smacked the dashboard with one hand, and when that didn't work, he fiddled with his channels, trying to find a new station.

Danya stared at the walkie-talkie. "You think *I* did that?" Danya asked.

Pia nodded. "You must've tapped into his radio somehow." She bit down on her lower lip, showing off the space where her missing tooth should have been. "What if . . . what if we used the walkie-talkies to *convince* this guy to get back on the interstate?"

"You think we could get him to take us all the way to Florida?"

Pia ran her tongue over the space left by her missing tooth. "I don't think I can stand the smell of corn for that much longer. But I bet he'd take us to the next big city." Pia pulled Danya's bag onto her lap and dug out the atlas. She traced their path across the map with one finger. "Like . . . Nashville, maybe? We can hitch another ride when we get there."

Nashville . . . Danya's parents would never expect her to get all the way to Tennessee in just one night. If she and Pia could convince Turtle to take them there, not only would they be closer to Florida, but they'd have that much more time before her parents caught up with them.

Danya's mind started cycling. "What if we pretend there's been an emergency? We'll say there's this giant earthquake and all the survivors have been transported to Nashville."

"Or!" Pia interrupted. "We could pretend to be a *ghost*."

Danya frowned. "That's lame, Pia," she said. "Remember

when you tried to convince my mom to take us to the movies by telling her aliens crash-landed at the theater? Grown-ups never believe weird stories like that."

"No, it's perfect!" Pia grabbed Danya's hand and squeezed, a big grin on her face. "He's been listening to that stupid *Ghost Hunter* show all morning. We'll pretend to be the ghost of Western Joe!"

"Who's Western Joe?"

"I just made him up," Pia said, shrugging. "But he needs the farmer to go on a secret mission to . . . the Grand Ole Opry House."

Danya inhaled, trying to control her mounting frustration. Pia did this all the time—she always thought things were more exciting when they had some sort of ridiculous plan. Usually Danya thought it was fun, but this was serious. She needed Pia to be more reasonable. "What's the Grand Ole Opry House?"

"It's this place in Nashville. My mom has a postcard of it on the fridge at home. Don't worry. It looks cool. And there were lots of people in the postcard, so it'll be easy to get another ride."

"But . . ." Danya started, but before she could finish her sentence, Pia grabbed the walkie-talkie from her hand and pushed the talk button.

"Helllooooo!" she moaned in a voice so spooky that

even Sancho looked up from his corn. "This is the ghost of Western Joe. . . ."

The sound of her voice echoed inside the truck, shocking the farmer so much that he swerved into the opposite lane and the entire truck jolted. Pia and Danya slid sideways into Sancho.

"Pia," Danya hissed, covering the walkie-talkie with one hand so Turtle wouldn't hear her. "What are you doing?"

"I have a plan!" Pia whispered. Then, into the walkie-talkie, "Right, this is Western Joe. I'm a ghost from the . . . um . . . great beyond and I need you to . . . to run an errand."

Sancho nudged the walkie-talkie with his nose and let out a soft, breathy snort that echoed inside the truck's cabin.

"What the devil . . . ?" Turtle muttered, spinning the radio dial frantically. Danya wrapped an arm around Sancho's neck and pulled him away from the walkie-talkie.

"Or else there will be DIRE CONSEQUENCES!" Pia trumpeted.

Danya's heart pounded in her throat. Pia was going to get them caught. She didn't sound like a ghost *at all*.

"Pia. Give me the walkie-talkie," Danya said, letting go of Sancho and holding out a hand.

Pia frowned. "But I'm just getting started. . . ."

"No, really. Come *on*." Danya tried to remember everything she knew about Turtle. He had a wife named Sandy who he ran a vegetable farm with, and they played heavy metal music for broccoli, and . . .

No, no! Danya forced the image from her mind. She'd just made that up. All she really knew about Turtle was that he liked listening to *Ghost Hunters* and he had a rabbit's foot on his key chain.

Something snapped into place.

Grudgingly, Pia handed over the walkie-talkie. Danya pressed the talk button.

"I am the ghost of luck and fate," she moaned, trying to replicate Pia's spooky ghost voice. "You called me forth with your . . . your rabbit's foot."

The farmer froze. His shoulders went stiff. "How . . . how did you know that?"

"I know *everything*," Danya continued. "Your . . . um . . . lottery ticket shows that you seek treasure. Treasure awaits you! All you have to do is follow these simple instructions."

The farmer fumbled with the rabbit's foot on his key chain. Danya glanced down at her map—according to it, they could take Highway 84 back to the interstate. The exit was just ahead. "Do it for Sandy!"

The farmer was quiet for a long moment. Finally, he

cleared his throat. "What would you need me to do?" he asked.

"To avoid any more black cats, you need to take the next turn . . ." Danya moaned.

For a second, she wasn't sure how the farmer would respond. Danya held her breath, catching Pia's eye. Pia chewed on her lower lip, sneaking a glance at the main cabin. Even Sancho looked nervous. He whickered and shook his mane, trying to hide his nose beneath his front hooves.

"Come on . . ." Pia whispered. She reached for Danya's hand, giving it a squeeze. The exit was just ahead. . . .

In one quick movement, the old truck swerved into the exit lane. Pia let out a silent cheer, and Danya pumped an arm into the air just as they cruised past a sign pointing them to Nashville. Sancho's tail swished and thumped against the truck bed floor.

"Western Joe" directed the farmer all the way to the Grand Ole Opry House using Danya's map as a guide. When the truck rumbled to a stop in front of the large building, the "ghost" told the farmer to close his eyes and count to fifty. When he was done, he had to walk forty paces into the trees and start to dig. He raced for the woods, stumbling over his combat boots as he ran. Pia, Danya, and Sancho snuck out of the truck bed.

Danya hesitated, watching Turtle make his way into the woods. She couldn't help feeling bad for him. She and Pia had led him out into the middle of nowhere with the promise of treasure. How was he going to feel when he realized he'd been fooled?

She opened her bag and looked at its contents, but the only "treasure" she had was her sandwich bag filled with money and the Ferdinand and Dapple book. Sancho came up next to her and stuck his head in the bag.

"Come on, not now," Danya said. Sancho pulled his head out and nudged the bag with his nose, like he was trying to tell her something. Frowning, Danya dug around inside until she found her good luck jar. How could she have forgotten! It was perfect for someone so superstitious!

"Thanks, buddy," she said, ticking Sancho beneath his chin. She tore a piece of her notebook paper out and wrote, *Many thanks, Western Joe*—then slipped both through the open passenger-side window, hoping it would help.

The Grand Ole Opry House was a massive building, with red, white, and blue flags hanging from the windows and a guitar the size of a station wagon sticking out of the grass near the parking lot. Old-fashioned streetlights and little plots of flowers dotted the sidewalk, and strings of lights were hung up above them. It wasn't yet noon, so the lights hadn't been turned on, but Danya imagined they were beautiful.

Out of her backpack, Danya fished the letter she'd started writing yesterday morning. It still wasn't quite finished, but she dropped it into the mailbox on the corner anyway. It made her feel a tiny bit better about sneaking out and running away. Her stomach still knotted together when she thought of how her parents had lied to her, but she couldn't help thinking about the sound of her mother's voice over the walkie-talkie—scared, confused. She had to grit her teeth together and close her eyes to get the voice to go away.

"Okay . . ." Danya said. "Now what?"

Pia wasn't even looking at her. She stared up at the vast building, her brows knitted. She took the Ferdinand and Dapple book from Danya's hands and quickly flipped to the hero's task list in the back. "The next item on our list is to *act in the name of love*. Think someone around here needs our help with their love life?"

Danya stared at her, trying to figure out if she was joking. "Pia, you know we don't have time for that, right?"

"There's always time to be a hero, Danya," Pia said gravely. "Besides, we have tons of time now. How much time did we save by catching a ride instead of walking all this way?"

"But you heard my parents on the walkie-talkie! They know we're missing. They've probably already called the cops and . . . and figured out the location of our walkie-talkie signal." Danya didn't know if that was actually possible, but she'd seen something similar in a movie—and she'd all of a sudden realized how careless they had been acting. She glanced over at the mailbox she'd just slid her letter into, and dread clogged her throat. "My letter! They'll see from the postmark that we're in Nashville!"

Danya tried to stick an arm into the mailbox to dig out her letter, but Pia grabbed her by the shoulders. "Danya, cool it. You're acting crazy. I just want to do this one little thing on the list. . . ."

"*I'm* acting crazy?" Danya pulled away from Pia's hands, shaking her head. "*You're* acting just like that farmer and his stupid rabbit's foot. He thinks he's off to find some great fortune, but he just got tricked."

"How do you know? Maybe you just told him exactly where to find buried treasure."

"Treasure isn't real," Danya muttered.

Pia wrapped her skinny arms around her chest. "What happened to you?"

"What do you mean?" Danya's face heated up.

"I mean," Pia said, scowling, "you used to believe in things, just like me."

Sancho's ear twitched, and Danya reached out to scratch him, avoiding Pia's glare. Without warning, the fire memories filled her head. She could almost taste the smoke at the back of her throat; she could almost hear the sound of Jupiña's whinnies. "I guess I just grew up."

"Maybe you're just not paying attention." Pia turned around and stopped in front of a door marked STAGE CREW ONLY. She wiggled the handle—unlocked.

"What are you doing?" Danya asked.

"Proving a point. I'm going to go through this door and have an adventure, and you're going to come with me."

"Pia, come on. . . ."

"Adventures wait for no man! Or pony!" Pia pushed the door open and ducked inside.

Danya crossed her arms. She wouldn't follow Pia into the building. She wouldn't. Sancho came up behind Danya and nudged her elbow with his big, wet nose.

"I'm not going," Danya said. Sancho grunted, shook his mane, and stomped his feet. He and Danya didn't normally disagree on anything, but when they did, this was *always* how he reacted. Last time was when Danya wanted to buy this cool pink saddle. Sancho *hated* it, and he'd stomped and snorted until Danya finally agreed to get a brown leather one instead.

"So *you* want to go in, too?" Danya asked, exasperated.

She could fight Pia, but she couldn't fight Sancho, too. In response, Sancho stretched his legs out and leaned back, wiggling his rump in the air. Guilt tugged at Danya's heart. He must be stiff from the ride in the truck. . . .

"Fine," she relented. "Five minutes . . ."

Before she could finish her sentence, Sancho snorted and bolted through the door. Danya heard the echoing sound of his hooves beating against the floor.

"Sancho!" Danya called, but the pony had already disappeared into the dark. She raced inside after him.

CHAPTER SIX

The Lovelorn Ghost of Western Joe

It was so dark inside the theater that Danya could barely make out the shape of Sancho's tail as it whipped around the corner. His hooves clip-clopped against the floor as he trotted away.

"Sancho!" she hissed, creeping forward as quickly as she could. "Sancho, get back here!"

The theater smelled like dust and mothballs, just like the coat closet back home. Thick shadows stretched down the hall, penetrated only by the occasional bare, yellow bulb swinging from the ceiling. The floorboards creaked beneath Danya's shoes.

She turned a corner and saw Pia and Sancho standing

on a stage made of shiny wood. Three walls were painted black, and instead of a fourth wall, a thick, velvet curtain hung from the ceiling. Just beyond the curtain Danya heard the echoing sounds of people talking. An audience. The chattering sound reminded Danya a bit of the chickens her dad used to keep in the backyard and she felt a sudden, hard tug of homesickness.

"There must be a show soon," Danya whispered, pushing aside thoughts of home as she came up behind Pia and Sancho. She was suddenly uneasy. If there was a show starting, shouldn't there be actors? Props? Scenery? Instead the stage was bare. Every few seconds, Danya thought she heard someone scurrying here and there in the darkness, but whenever she turned her head, there was no one.

"You know what I think?" Pia whispered. "I think this theater is *haunted*."

She wagged her fingers spookily in Danya's face. Danya batted them away. Sancho whinnied, and Danya patted his neck to calm him.

Just then a low, mournful moan swept over the stage. Sancho snorted and took a few steps backward, his hooves making hollow thumps on the floorboards. Danya grabbed Pia's arm, then dropped it, embarrassed. Pia gave her a crooked smile and raised an eyebrow.

"I'm *not* scared," Danya said firmly. Ghosts were

stupid, she told herself. Just something from fairy tales and stories—not real at all. She pulled her lucky gel pen out of her pocket, trying to think up a story in her head to make her feel better.

But this whole place reminded Danya of the burned-up shed and scorched grass back home. Even though she absolutely did *not* believe in ghosts, she always had a strange feeling like she was being watched whenever she went near that place. She got that same feeling now. Like there was someone waiting in the shadows who she couldn't see . . .

"I don't believe in ghosts," Danya said out loud, more to convince herself than anyone else. Sancho neighed in agreement, his tail twitching nervously. He pawed at the stage floor like he was trying to dig a hole, and when that didn't work, he trotted over to the thick, velvet curtains and hid behind one of the folds.

Pia shrugged. "Sure." She nudged Danya and pointed to the corner on the other side of the stage, where a figure crouched in the shadows. "Look."

The man wore a tweed suit that wasn't quite long enough (there was a good inch of bare skin between the bottom of his suit pants and the tops of his loafers, and his wrists were showing out of the cuffs of his suit jacket). As they got closer, she noted that he also wore a purple plaid shirt with a polka-dot tie. He was very thin, and there was a cowboy hat on his head so large Danya was amazed he was able to sit up straight. He kind of looked like a tweed cowboy-shaped umbrella. He sat on a low stool, his face in his hands. Surrounding him were bits of scenery, boxes of props, and a large, industrial-size fan.

Danya and Pia took a few tentative steps closer. Sancho shook out his mane, and Danya had to grab onto his reins and pull to coax him out of the curtains.

In the dim yellow light backstage the man looked faded and fuzzy, like he wasn't entirely there. In fact, the only parts of him that looked solid were his giant cowboy boots, his giant hat, and the battered old banjo sitting on his lap.

"It's Western Joe," Pia said, gripping Danya's arm. She hopped a little, actually excited by the possibility of a ghost waiting for them across the stage.

"We made up Western Joe," Danya muttered, but she couldn't help the fear that wrapped itself, tentacle-like, around her heart. *Ghosts aren't real*, she told herself. *Ghosts aren't real.* She took another step forward and the stage floor creaked.

The shadowy cowboy suddenly looked up. "Who's there?" he said.

Danya's heart climbed into her throat, and she squeezed her gel pen so tightly the cap fell off. Sancho snorted and pawed at the stage again, yanking back on his reins. Pia grinned, running her tongue through the gap in her teeth.

"My name is Pia," she called out. "And this is Snap and Sancho."

Sancho crept closer to the cowboy and nudged him with his nose. Finally satisfied he wasn't a ghost, Sancho chomped at his hat—like he thought it looked like a tasty treat. Danya pulled back on his reins so he wouldn't try that again.

The cowboy seemed unconcerned by Sancho's attempt to eat his hat. "Would you mind just leaving me alone for a little bit?" he asked, sniffling. Danya and Pia shared a look. Was he *crying*?

"Are you okay, Mr. Joe?" Pia continued. The cowboy wiped his nose with his sleeve.

"Mr. Joe?" The man shook his head. "My name is *Kevin*."

Danya breathed a sigh of relief. Kevin was such a nice, normal, human-sounding name. Not ghostly at all.

"And am I okay?" Kevin hiccupped a little. "Of course I'm not okay! Everything is ruined!"

"Is there something we can do to help?" Pia asked, moving closer to him. Danya shot her a glance. Even though there wasn't a clock backstage, she could almost hear the sound of the second hand ticking and ticking, counting down every minute they wasted and warning her that her parents and maybe even actual policemen were closing in on them. . . .

Kevin's polka-dot bow tie was lopsided, and his nose was raw and red. He laughed, and his laugh turned into a hiccup. "I'm in love, sweetheart. There's no one who can help me now."

"See, he said there's no one who can help him," Danya muttered, grabbing Pia's arm. "So let's just *go*."

But Pia's eyes grew wide. "I *told* you," she whispered to Danya while Kevin blew his nose on his tweed suit jacket's sleeve. "This is our next heroic task. We were meant to be here. Destiny guided us!"

Danya frowned. She didn't see how destiny had anything to do with this—there were probably a lot of lovesick people in Nashville.

Still, she couldn't help but feel sorry for Kevin. His eyes were all red and puffy, and his nose had been rubbed raw, he'd blown it so many times. He looked so downtrodden—like there was nothing in this world that would lift his spirits. Danya thought back to how she felt after her parents told her they were going to sell Sancho and understood what he was going through. Some things were so terrible you just couldn't get over them.

Pia crouched in front of Western Kevin and patted him

on the knee comfortingly. Danya wished she'd done that, but she wasn't bold like Pia was. New people made her nervous.

"It's okay, Kevin," Pia said. "We're going to help you."

He gave another sniffle that was half a laugh. "You can't help me." Hiccup. "Not unless you know how to climb up to the rafters and get my ring."

"What ring?" Danya asked.

Kevin explained that he'd been planning to propose to his girlfriend, Lovelorn Lola, tonight after the show.

"It took me two whole years to save up for that ring!" he admitted. "Lola's performing today—she's a singer." Kevin hiccupped again. "And I had this big plan, see? I'm a stagehand, so I rigged up this device in the rafters. When the performers were doing their curtain call, it was going to send a shower of rose petals over the stage, then I was going to come down from the rafter strapped to a harness and present the ring and ask her to be mine. Well . . ." He motioned to the banjo on his lap. "I mean, I was going to sing it. Had a song and everything."

"What happened?" Pia asked, still crouching next to him. Sancho rested his head on Kevin's knee, like he always did for Danya when she was feeling bad. She heard the ticking clock in her head again—*tick tick tick*—but she tried to ignore it. *Maybe Kevin really did need her help?*

"I set up a ladder on the side of the stage to rig up the petals." Kevin patted Sancho's head absentmindedly and motioned to a bag of rose petals leaning against his stool. "But that ring fell right out of my pocket and onto one of the spotlights overhead. I'm too big to climb out there to get it back—the rafters will snap right in half if I do." Kevin sniffed, then hiccupped again. "It's gone! I'll have to wait two more years to save up for another ring."

Pia stood up. Her neck was craned back, and she stared up into the rafters, her eyes narrowed.

"So the ring fell there, right?" she asked, pointing to a spotlight just below the main catwalk. If Danya squinted, she thought she could make out something sparkling. Kevin nodded, sniffling.

"May as well be outer space," he muttered, leaning against the industrial fan. Pia handed her overnight bag to Danya and wrapped her skinny arms around a rope hanging from the rafters. She pulled herself up with a grunt.

"Pia, what are you doing?" Danya spat out.

"Helping," Pia said with another grunt as she hauled herself up even higher. Kevin stood, accidentally knocking over his stool.

"Is that *safe*?" he asked.

"I'm sure she'll be fine," Danya said nervously, watching Pia climb. Pia wrapped her skinny limbs around the rope and shimmied up, pulling herself onto the catwalk. For the first time, Danya noticed two different socks peeking out of Pia's sneakers—one was green with tiny yellow polka dots on it, and the other was orange-and-blue striped. Pia barely took a second to catch her breath before starting to crawl toward the spotlight.

Kevin was right—the catwalk wasn't very sturdy. It shifted back and forth beneath Pia's weight, creaking and groaning under the strain. Kevin held onto Danya's shoulder and squeezed. He looked so nervous that even his bow tie trembled. Danya wrapped her fingers in Sancho's mane and held her breath as Sancho whinnied nervously.

When Pia was directly over the spotlight, she leaned down and tried to scoop the ring up with her hands, but it was too far away. She frowned, sitting back up.

"I think I have an idea," she called.

"Be careful!" Danya said. Pia twisted around so her legs were anchored over the catwalk, then she leaned backward until she was hanging upside down above the spotlight. She reached out as far as her arms would go. . . .

"Kevin?"

The voice came from the other side of the stage, where a woman had just stepped out from behind the curtains. Her hair was pinned back in cascading blond curls, and she wore a long purple gown.

"What are you doing out here?" she asked, her voice thick with a Southern accent. "The show is about to start!"

"Oh . . . uh . . . hi, Lola." Kevin straightened his bow tie and took off his cowboy hat, giving the girl a sheepish smile. Danya glanced up at the rafters. Pia's fingers were two inches away from the ring. One inch . . .

. . . and suddenly she was falling, cartwheeling through the air like some sort of giant Frisbee. Danya screamed, and Sancho reared back. Pia grabbed onto a rope at the last second—the rope that controlled the curtains, which swept open with a *whoosh*, revealing Danya, Sancho, Western Kevin, and Lovelorn Lola, all standing together onstage. Sancho snorted and trotted in place, suddenly shy. He pawed at the wooden stage, like he was trying to dig a hole to hide in. An audience of several hundred people blinked and stared.

"Kevin," Lovelorn Lola said through a wide, forced smile. "What is going on?"

Kevin was so white he actually did look a little like a ghost. His eyes darted over to the audience below and, for a moment, Danya worried he might faint.

"I . . ." Hiccup, hiccup. "I mean . . ."

"Psst!" Pia hissed from the rafters. Kevin glanced up and she tossed him something, which he caught in one hand. It glittered from his palm, and Danya gasped. *The ring!*

Gripping the ring tightly, Kevin held up the banjo and launched into song. . . .

"Before we grow one moment older . . . I need your hand in marriage, my Lovelorn Lola. . . ."

Danya tried not to cringe. Kevin's voice was *bad*. It cracked a little, sounding off-key. A few members of the audience snickered and giggled. Danya looked over at Lola, wondering whether her reaction would be the same.

For a long moment, Lola stood frozen, staring at Kevin with eyes as wide as two silver dollars.

Someone watching shouted, "Kiss him!" Sancho's ears twitched, and Danya put a hand on his nose. Her heart beat quickly in her chest. Finally, Lola's lips curled into a smile.

"You always were tone deaf, you know that?" she said.

Kevin stood up and held out his hand. "Maybe you could show me how it's done?"

As if on cue, Lola swept out into the center of the stage, facing the audience. She held her head back and took a deep breath . . . then let out the clearest, sweetest, most beautiful note that Danya had ever heard. Lola's voice floated past the catwalk and the rafters, filling the entire space with music. Kevin was so excited he started to dance. Danya's mouth fell open as he moved his skinny limbs across the stage, spinning and twirling around Lola with the grace of a ballerina. He held the banjo close to his chest, like it was part of the dance, too.

Lola's smile held firm as she sang. She spread her arms wide, like she could stretch that note as easily as stretching her back after a nap.

When she'd finished, the note hung in the air all around them. Kevin stopped dancing and dropped down to one knee.

"Can I take that as a yes?" he asked with a crooked smile.

Instead of answering, Lola threw her arms around his neck. He lifted her off her feet and swept her in a wide circle across the stage.

Danya stared, moon-eyed, her heart welling inside her. It was so romantic! Like a fairy tale. She looked up at Pia, and her cousin winked, as if to say, *I told you so . . .*

Danya would never admit it, but maybe Pia was right. Maybe there was always time to be a hero . . . at least in the name of love?

Sancho came up behind her and nudged her elbow with his wet nose. Danya glanced down and saw that he had Kevin's bag of rose petals clenched between his front teeth.

"Sancho, that's sweet, but I don't think I can," she muttered, glancing out at the audience. No way would she go onstage in front of all those people!

Sancho whickered and pushed the rose petals into her hands again. Then Danya's eyes fell on the old, industrial-size fan just behind the main curtain. Maybe she could help the moment feel special without going onstage after all. . . .

Darting behind the fan, she flipped a switch she could only hope would power it up. Sure enough, the fan's blades began to whir.

Grinning, Danya grabbed a handful of flower petals from the bag and tossed them in the path of the spinning blades. The petals whirred and twirled onto the stage around Kevin and Lola like a colorful tornado. Sancho moved his weight from hoof to hoof to hoof, almost like he was dancing. Out on the center of the stage, Kevin lifted Lola off her feet. They kissed long and deep as petals floated around them.

Danya grabbed another handful of petals and leaned forward to toss them into the wind. Then the backstage door slammed open, and she jumped, turning so fast she scattered petals everywhere, coating all the equipment and props stacked behind the stage curtain with a layer of pink.

A police officer with a bushy mustache and a shiny, star-shaped badge affixed to his black uniform walked through the open door. He glared at Danya with beady eyes, and her heart climbed into her throat.

"You!" The cop's mustache twitched as he spoke, and he pointed a thick, calloused finger right at Danya. "I've been looking for you."

CHAPTER SEVEN

The Golden Girls Adventure Club Takes the Mississippi

Danya froze, letting the bag of petals drop to the floor next to her feet. Her parents really did call the cops. Maybe they *could* triangulate her location using the signal from her walkie-talkie! Next to her, Sancho sneezed, sending the petals covering his nose fluttering into the air.

"What's the meaning of this?" Kevin hissed under his breath, quickly leaving the stage. Lola started singing another song to distract the audience from the commotion, but every few seconds her eyes shifted over to where they were arguing.

"We're in the middle of a show!" Kevin said. The man with the mustache and badge puffed up his chest.

"This girl is a trespasser," he said. "The security camera caught her sneaking in through the side door. And she brought a live animal backstage. She needs to be removed from the property immediately!"

The man with the mustache fumbled with his badge, and for the first time Danya read what was written across it: SECURITY GUARD.

Pia scurried down from the catwalk, and her eyes narrowed on him. "Think we should make a run for it?" she whispered to Danya. Danya swallowed, her eyes darting to the hall that led to the exit. Could they make it?

"These girls are here as my special guests," Kevin explained before either girl could move. "I'll take care of them from here."

The security guard bristled and muttered something about checking with his manager before storming out the back door. Shaking his head, Kevin ushered Pia, Danya, and Sancho away, finding them a spot backstage where they could watch the rest of the show. While Danya and Pia perched on a few stools backstage, Sancho plopped onto the concrete floor and immediately began gnawing on a plastic prop apple that had rolled under the edge of the curtain. There were still a few flower petals caught in his mane.

"Are you ladies hungry?" Kevin asked.

"Um, sure," Danya said. She *was* hungry, actually — very hungry — but she couldn't keep her eyes from shifting back to the door where the security guard disappeared and worried about what would happen when he found his manager.

Kevin disappeared and returned a few minutes later with two cheese sandwiches, a real apple, and a couple of grape-flavored juice boxes. He arranged the lunch on a folding table next to the stools, then explained that he needed to start readying the props and costumes for the show and scurried off again.

Danya ate her cheese sandwich quickly, then held out her hand to let Sancho finish her crusts. His furry lips tickled her palm, and when he finished eating, he nuzzled her on the shoulder. Danya patted his head as she slid off her stool.

"Hurry," she whispered, nudging Pia. "Time to go."

Pia twisted around on her stool. "But it's about to be the curtain call!"

"Pia, *come on*," Danya hissed. "If that security guard comes back with his manager, he'll call our parents for sure."

Pia huffed but slid off her stool. Danya scrawled a quick thank-you note for Kevin on a piece of paper from her notebook, and then the girls and Sancho slipped back down the hall and out the side entrance where they'd first snuck in.

The farmer's truck was long gone. Danya hoped he'd found the good luck jar she left him and that maybe one of his wishes came true. She led Pia and Sancho around to the front of the building but far enough from the main doors that the security guard wouldn't see them if he poked his head out. It wasn't quite dark yet, but the sun hung low in the sky, sending shadows over the parking lot. Danya slid the map out of her back pocket as Pia settled herself on the curb, propping her long, skinny legs against the tire of the station wagon parked in front of her. Sancho munched on the grass that had sprouted between the pavement cracks. No one was around except for an old lady in a yellow sweatshirt loitering near the Grand Ole Opry entrance, a stack of glossy brochures clutched in her hands. Danya stared at her from over the top of her map, wondering if she was the kind of person who'd call security on them. But the old lady just waved politely before looking back down at her brochures, so Danya decided she was probably safe.

Turning back to the map, Danya traced a finger along their trail. They were still so far from Florida—in the past day, they'd barely covered any distance at all. It would take hours and hours to ride Sancho all the way to the next big city—maybe even *days*. Danya pulled the sandwich bag of money out of her backpack and counted through the bills, wondering if there was enough for a bus ticket or something. The forty-six dollars felt light in her hands and she frowned, realizing they'd probably need to save the money for food. They'd been lucky so far getting the free sandwiches from Kevin. She folded it up and tucked it into her back pocket.

"Hey, *Snap*!"

Blinking, Danya glanced up from the map. Pia had her head cocked to the side, the Ferdinand and Dapple book in her lap. "I asked if you wanted to know what's next on the list?"

"I'm trying to figure out how we're going to get to Florida, Pia. This is *important*."

"Not more important than this. The next thing on the list is *suffer a great sadness or loss*." Pia looked up from the book, her brown eyes wide with concern.

"It doesn't matter since it's *not real*!" Danya said emphatically, turning back to the map. After that security guard scare she was starting to hear the ticking clock in her head again. *Tick tick tick.* Every second they wasted brought them closer to being caught.

"You aren't even a little bit worried?" Pia wrinkled her nose and closed the book.

Danya didn't know how to answer that. She *was* worried—but she was worried about real things, like the cops and her parents, not predictions from a book. Before she could say a word, though, the Grand Ole Opry doors sprang open, and a steady stream of people filed into the parking lot and began looking for their cars. The lady in the yellow sweatshirt smiled wide and began handing out shiny brochures to everyone who passed. Danya watched as a few people took the brochures, then pulled out keys and headed for their cars.

Not for the first time, it occurred to Danya how much easier this trip would be if only she were old enough to drive. She used to take road trips with her parents all the time. The three of them would pile into her dad's car and drive across Kentucky to visit Thomas Edison's house or the Kentucky Derby Museum. Her dad would scan the radio until he found a station that played Elvis or the Beatles, and then he'd sing along, slightly off tune, while her mom pretended to cover her ears. Her *tío* Beto would come by their farm while her family was away to check in on Sancho, Jupiña, and the rest of their animals. The memory made Danya frown. That was back when they still had the stables. Jupiña always looked so beautiful in their backyard—she had the same chestnut-colored mane as Sancho and huge brown eyes that followed her baby pony everywhere.

Danya shook her head and hugged the atlas to her chest, her heart heavy as she watched people head for their cars.

Her family stopped taking road trips after the fire. Danya lied and said that the trips made her carsick, but really she didn't like leaving Sancho behind. Whenever she was away from him, even for a moment, she'd remember the day of the fire. If Sancho hadn't been with her, wandering around the woods, he might've been in the shed with his mom when it burned down. Danya didn't like to think about that at all. Even though it hadn't happened, the realization that she could've lost Sancho that day was too much to bear.

Danya sighed, pushing the bad memories out of her head. If only this journey could be easy and fun, like the trips her family took before Jupiña died. But maybe Pia was right, if not about the hero's journey, then at least about the suffering part. If suffering was in her future, maybe that was the cost of saving Sancho. She owed him that much.

"Snap? Are you even listening?"

Danya blinked and to her surprise the old lady in the yellow sweatshirt was standing next to Pia. She was small and wrinkled, with wild, wiry gray hair and the kind of wide smile that allowed you to see all of her teeth at the same time. But the thing that really caught Danya's attention was her bright yellow sweatshirt—there was a picture of an old woman skydiving printed on the front. Beneath the sky-diver were the words GOLDEN GIRLS ADVENTURE CLUB.

"This is Karina," Pia said. "She just offered us a ride."

"She *what*?" Danya asked. What kind of person offers two strange girls and a pony a ride?

"Karina is a member of the Golden Girls Adventure Club," Pia explained. "She's here at the Opry House looking for new recruits for their ride down the river."

Danya sat up a little straighter. According to the map, a thin blue thread wound down past Nashville. The Tennessee River, it was called. If they had a boat, they could take the river all the way to Alabama. Even if her parents got the letter with the Tennessee postmark tomorrow, they'd never know to look for her all the way in Alabama! The thought made Danya relax, just a little.

"Anyway, I told Karina all about our situation." Pia stared at Danya pointedly, and when she spoke again, she stretched out her words like she was trying to give her a hint. "You know, how Sancho accidentally wandered onto that barge this morning when he was hunting for fish? And how you and I hitched rides on a steamboat to follow him?"

"Ooooh, right," Danya said, though everyone knew ponies didn't hunt for fish. She was also pretty sure barges didn't cross rivers.

"And now you and I need a ride back down the river so we can get home," Pia finished. Next to her, Karina smiled.

"The other adventurers and I would be just *thrilled* to take you ladies with us," the old woman said. She motioned behind her to a large white bus with the same lady skydiver logo painted on the side.

"Uh . . . that would be great," Danya said. She felt a tiny bit bad about lying to such a sweet old woman, but they could really use the ride. Besides, this exact same thing happened in the third Ferdinand and Dapple book. Ferdinand and Dapple needed to get across the Toa River in Cuba, so they snuck onto a ferry and . . .

Pia cleared her throat and Danya saw that Karina and Pia were staring at her expectantly. She blushed.

"Um . . . did you just say something?"

Karina laughed. "A free spirit! Well, aren't you a girl after my own heart? I'd just said I'm surprised your parents let you come after your pony on your own. Aren't they concerned?"

Danya couldn't help thinking about her *real* parents. She was so worried they'd find her that she hadn't given much thought to how *they* felt. What would they think had happened? They were probably terrified that she was just *gone*!

Guilt crept into Danya's gut. She wrapped her hands around her chest, feeling awful.

"We *are* free spirits," Pia said when Danya didn't answer.

"My parents don't really care what I do. They're too busy fighting. Mostly I look after myself."

Danya glanced over at Pia, surprised. But Pia wasn't looking at her. Was she just pretending again? Danya searched her best friend's face, but she couldn't tell whether or not she was lying.

"Come on, girls," Karina said, gesturing them across the parking lot.

"Pia," Danya said in a low voice, falling into step behind her cousin. "What's up? Is everything okay at home?"

"Everything's great," Pia chirped. "Never been better."

"But what about . . ." *Your parents*, she would have said, but just then she was interrupted by a honk from the white bus that was so loud Sancho flinched and shook out his mane. Danya automatically tickled him under the chin to calm him.

"All aboard," Karina said cheerfully. She ushered them toward the rear of the bus and unlocked the back emergency entrance to let Sancho inside. Pia and Danya rounded the bus and used the normal entrance, taking seats up front. Danya looked back at Sancho, who stretched out in the aisle. There were another dozen or so little old lady adventurers filling the seats behind them, all wearing matching yellow sweatshirts. When they saw Sancho, they cooed and giggled, leaning into the aisle to run their hands over his coarse coat and silky mane. He let out a purr-like snort and pressed his ears flat against his head happily. Danya smiled. His shyness disappeared the moment someone scratched behind his ears.

"This is Simone," Karina said, motioning to the bus driver. Simone looked just as old as Karina, but she was tall, with broad shoulders and a thick, black braid that hung all the way down to her waist. Danya examined the braid in awe. It was as thick as her arm and probably longer than she was.

"Good to meet you girls," Simone said. She stared at them for a beat longer than normal, her eyes narrowing ever so slightly. "You know, you two look familiar."

Instantly Danya's chest clenched. Had Simone seen their photographs on a missing person's poster? Or maybe on the back of a milk carton—she'd read in a book that sometimes there were photographs of missing children on the backs of milk cartons. Did people still do that?

Danya grabbed Pia's hand and squeezed, but Simone just grinned and said, "Maybe it's just because you two are so photogenic. You could be on TV, you know?" Shaking her head, she turned back around and started up the bus.

"She knows," Danya hissed as she and Pia slid into a seat. Pia sighed deeply.

"You are being paranoid," she said. "No one knows anything. She just thought we were pretty. *Chill!*"

Danya tried to chill, like Pia said. She tried to count the trees moving past her window, and when that got boring, she started looking for out-of-state license plates. But the drive to the river took longer than she expected it to. One hour passed, then another. She was just starting to get tired of staring out the window at the blur of buildings and vast, green landscape when she saw something that chilled her right to the bone.

On the highway just ahead stood a huge, electronic billboard. Danya was still too far away to read exactly what the sign said, but she could clearly see the words AMBER ALERT flashing in giant letters across the top. A lump formed in her throat. Danya knew what an Amber Alert was—once her mom explained that when a kid went missing, the cops put out a national alert on every highway and street; that way everyone knew to be on the lookout. Danya pressed her face against the glass, cold dread creeping up her spine as she watched the sign come closer.

Just then the bus seat shifted as Pia stood, propping one foot on the back of her seat. "Hey, adventurers!" she called to the little old ladies through cupped hands. "Let's play a game."

"What are you doing?" Danya hissed beneath her breath. Pia's eyes shifted quickly, toward the Amber Alert sign out the window. *She's distracting them!* Danya realized.

"The game's called adventure bus bingo," Pia explained. "Er . . . it's just like normal bingo, but you have to find things *inside* the bus to win. Got it? Hey, Karina, want to help me make scorecards?"

Karina and Pia quickly whipped up bingo score cards out of a stack of napkins Simone dug out of the glove compartment, and soon the little old ladies were shouting and pointing every time they found a wad of gum beneath their seat or saw a penny sitting heads-side up in the aisle. When they whizzed past the Amber Alert, not one of the old ladies seemed to notice it. Even Simone was too busy watching the rearview mirror to see who was winning to catch sight of the sign.

"That was a close one," Pia said, plopping back down in her seat. Danya nodded. *Too close*, she thought.

Between the game, and Sancho's happy horsey snorts, and the rambling, rocking motion of the bus, the rest of the trip passed quickly, and soon they were driving along the bank of the river, where Danya didn't have to worry about any more electronic signs giving them away.

Sun gleamed over the river, making it shine like glass.

Packed mud spread out along the riverbank. The water wasn't blue like it was on the map—it was green and silver and brown, and there were ripples along its surface that reminded Danya of the wrinkles on Simone's and Karina's arms. It was so wide, Danya had to squint to see the opposite shore. She pressed her face up against the bus window, her breath making little fog clouds on the glass.

The big white bus rumbled to a stop next to a rickety dock. Karina, Simone, and the rest of the adventurers all started to get out of their seats and head for the doors, talking excitedly among themselves. They all headed down to the dock, where a shiny blue-and-white speedboat was parked. At the sight of the speedboat, the adventurers whooped and began stripping down into bathing suits.

Danya froze. There was a green sign sticking out of the ground right next to the water. It read WELCOME TO THE MISSISSIPPI RIVER.

"This is the *Mississippi* River?" Danya could feel her heart racing as she pulled out the atlas and turned to the map in back. "I thought we were headed for the Tennessee River!"

"Heavens no, child! We're an adventuring community," Simone said, stripping down to a blue-and-white polka-dot one-piece bathing suit. "Nothing's as exciting as taking a speedboat down the Mississippi."

"We should know—we've done a bit of everything," Karina added. Underneath her sweat suit she wore a red two-piece with a frilly little skirt. "We've worked at a cannery in Alaska . . ."

"Made tires in New Zealand . . ."

"We were even lumberjacks in Portland for a while," Karina finished. "That was a lot of fun, but you wouldn't *believe* the splinters."

Danya nodded absently, but she was having trouble listening. She stared down at the map, panic rising in her throat. After all this time they were still in Tennessee, miles and miles west of where she thought they were headed.

"Don't worry, Danya. We must be right over here," Pia said, pointing to a spot on the map just north of Memphis. "We made it really far south, see? And we can follow the Mississippi to Louisiana and then cut over to Florida."

Danya nodded woodenly, even though she really didn't think it'd be quite as easy as "cutting over to Florida" like Pia said. *Tick tick tick*, she thought, her anxiety growing.

Still, they *had* gotten farther south—and they'd traveled much more quickly than they would have if they were walking. If she went down the river with the old lady adventurers, they'd get farther still, and they'd avoid any more Amber Alert signs, at least for a little while. Sighing, Danya stuck the atlas in her backpack and tried to stay positive.

"We're adventurers, too," Pia said to Karina and Simone, motioning to herself and Danya. "We traveled all the way from Kentucky. On horseback!"

Simone and Karina shared a confused look. "I thought you came from Mississippi? You know, from up the river?" Karina said.

"Pia meant we *want* to be adventurers. You know, someday . . ." Danya said quickly. Then she lowered her voice, whispering to Pia, "Don't say Kentucky! It'll just make them remember that there are girls missing from Kentucky, and then they'll think of the posters and realize those girls are us!"

"Snap, you made those posters up. You don't even know if they're *real*."

Danya swallowed, hoping Pia was right. Karina grabbed two orange life jackets and tossed them over to Pia and Danya. Pia stared down at the jacket like it was the ugly sweater she got for Christmas last year. It'd been covered in green sequins—Pia said it made her feel like a can of Sprite.

"Why do we need these on a boat?" she asked.

"Safety first." Simone zipped a life jacket over her swimsuit. "You wouldn't want to get hurt, would you?"

Pia muttered that she didn't think she needed her jacket because she was on the swim team at school. Danya, on the other hand, pulled her life jacket on immediately. She swam okay in the shallow end of the community pool, where she could stretch until her toes skimmed the slick floor, but she was certain her stubby arms and legs were no match for the wild river waves. She'd sink like a rock.

"*You* said we were going to suffer a great loss," Danya pointed out, zipping up her jacket. Danya didn't believe that, but she figured it'd be a good way to convince Pia to be safe. "You think we can fit one on Sancho?"

"We have plenty—maybe you could tie a few of them together?" Simone was still unloading the bus, removing towels and coolers and more life jackets. Danya turned to Sancho. She hadn't exactly thought about how tricky it might be to get him on the boat. The pony shook his heavy mane and snorted, then pawed at the dusty ground. He looked at the little speedboat, and his eyes grew wide and frightened beneath his mane.

"Come on, buddy, it'll be okay." Danya leaned forward and pressed her forehead against Sancho's. His ears flicked back and forth and he let out a low, mournful whinny. "You know I would never let anything bad happen to you," Danya whispered. And she meant it. After the fire, after losing Jupiña, Sancho was her responsibility now. For a moment, he was silent. Then Sancho licked the side of Danya's face and flicked his ears forward, his nostrils flared. He looked resigned. Brave, even.

"Sancho's in," Danya said.

Carefully, she and Pia and Simone and Karina strapped Sancho into four different life jackets—one for each leg.

"There, there, Sancho," Danya whispered. Sancho nudged Danya's shoulder and gave an encouraging snort. She realized then that she was even more nervous than Sancho. Smiling, she rubbed him behind one ear to thank him for trying to make her feel better. She checked her pockets, pushing the sandwich bag of money to the very bottom so there was no chance it would fall out.

With Sancho all ready to go, Pia and Danya followed the little old ladies onto the speedboat. It rocked beneath their feet as they climbed aboard, and Danya grabbed onto the guardrails, holding so tightly that her knuckles turned white. She'd never been on a boat before, and she hadn't thought it would be like this.

Sancho came over to her and licked the side of her face. Danya felt a surge of pride. If Sancho was going to be brave, she could be, too.

"Don't be nervous," Pia whispered to Danya. "It's a speedboat, not a canoe." Danya nodded and tried to relax as the speedboat began to move, cutting through the waves and sending up a fine spray of water.

Despite her nerves, it was the perfect time to ride down the river. The sun was low in the sky, but the air was warm, with just a hint of a breeze. The tall, brown grass to either side of the river swayed easily in the wind, which blew over the water and created little ripples in the waves. After a while, one of the Golden Girls Adventurers cracked open a cooler and started passing around bottles of fizzy organic pear cider and peach juice. Danya and Pia helped themselves. They even clanked the bottles together in a toast before taking a swig.

"To the adventure!" Pia said. "To becoming heroes!"

"To saving Sancho!" Danya added. She lifted her bottle to take a drink, but just then the boat hit a wave and the juice ended up all over her face. She sneezed and wiped the sticky liquid off her cheeks.

The waves were getting choppier. There were rocks and logs sticking out of the water around them. The Golden Girls Adventurers were all alert. Karina steered the boat through the water, her eyes narrowed in concentration. When she saw Danya watching her, she winked.

"Don't worry," she called out over the noise of the engine. "This is the fun part."

Danya nodded, but she wasn't sure she agreed. Her stomach lurched like she was on a roller coaster. Rapids shook the boat—it bounced high on the waves, then dropped back down. Water churned every which way, and it made Danya feel like she was in a blender. With one hand she held tightly to the guardrails, and with the other she held onto Sancho. Her pony's mane stuck to his neck and hung over his eyes in thick, wet clumps. He let out a reassuring whinny to let Danya know he was all right.

Then Danya saw the large rock jutting out of the water ahead.

"Watch out!" she shouted.

"Batten down the hatches," Karina called back. The old lady jerked around the rock at the last second, and the boat teetered to the side. Danya was sure it would flip over, but it righted itself at the last second.

Shaken, Sancho snorted and reared back. Danya grabbed for his reins, but they were slick from the river water, and they slipped from her fingers. Sancho's eyes grew wide. He tried to come back down to all fours, but he lost his balance, and toppled overboard into the river.

"No!" Danya screamed. "Sancho!" She crawled to the back of the boat and watched Sancho bob in the water. She was about to dive into the waves after him, but someone grabbed her and pulled her back.

"Those waves are too dangerous!" Simone said, shouting because the roar of the water all around them was too loud. "He'll be fine as long as he has those life jackets—we'll just have to go downstream, where the waves are calmer, and wait for him there."

"We can't just leave him." Danya blinked back tears. "He needs me."

"Don't worry, Danya! I've got this!" Pia charged for the side of the boat, but Danya grabbed her sleeve before she could leap into the river. She tried to wrestle Pia away from the boat's edge, but Pia was too strong and wiry.

"What are you doing?" Danya yelled, yanking on Pia's arm. "I can't lose you, too."

"You gotta trust me, Snap," Pia said. She easily twisted her arm out of Danya's grip and performed a perfect swan dive into the river. A second later she bobbed back to the surface, though Danya could only make out the orange of her life jacket in the treacherous gray waves.

Danya pulled away from Karina and leaned over the side of the boat. Pia was a strong swimmer, but Karina was right—the waves were just too powerful. Pia kicked and kicked, but a wave swept over her, forcing her beneath the water. Her life jacket kept her afloat, and she popped back up a second later, spitting out a stream of river water. Then another wave crashed over her. This time she didn't come up again.

"PIA!" Danya shouted, louder than she ever thought she could. Something ripped through her—some strange mixture of anger and adrenaline and fear. Without thinking, she leapt into the waves. She was going to save her friend! She was going to save Sancho! She wasn't ready to suffer a loss, no matter what Pia's hero's journey list said.

The water hit her face like a slap and suddenly everything around her was cold and wet and heavy. Her hair came loose from its bun and was quickly weighted down with water, until it was like an anchor strapped to her neck. Working her arms and legs through the treacherous river was like trying to fight a wall. It zapped her of her strength within seconds. Still, Danya pushed onward. The water clouded her vision until she couldn't see a thing and it plugged her ears, making everything around her sound much too close, and so far away.

All at once the river grew calmer, and there were fewer rocks and sticks poking up from its depths. Danya blinked and the water in her eyes cleared. She worked her arms through the river and soared forward, almost like she had a motor fixed to the seat of her pants. Quickly, she swam over to Pia, wrapped her arms around her, and lifted her from the waves.

Pia's blue lips trembled, and she blinked, her eyes unfocused. When she was finally able to see, she looked not at Danya, but at the sky beyond her head.

"Thanks, Sancho," Pia muttered.

Danya frowned, confused. Had Pia inhaled so much water she'd gotten Danya and her pony confused? Then, suddenly, it dawned on her. Holding tight to Pia, Danya looked over her shoulder.

Sancho was just behind her, his tiny legs kicking wildly through the water, the life jackets buoying him up in the waves. He held the collar of Danya's sweater firmly between his teeth. He was the reason it was suddenly easier to swim. He was the reason Danya could soar through the waves with ease.

Danya reached up and wiped Sancho's sopping-wet mane out of his eyes. She felt a rush of emotion toward him—gratitude, love, relief that she hadn't lost him. Together the three adventurers swam to the other shore and climbed onto dry land, coughing up river water and gasping for breath. Danya collapsed onto the beach and spread her arms and legs, almost like she was making a snow angel.

When she could finally breathe, she sat up and wrapped her arms around Sancho's neck, her small fingers getting caught in the pony's wet mane.

"You saved my life!" she shouted. Sancho licked her head—she could feel his scratchy tongue all the way through her wet curls. She hugged him tight, and tears pricked at the corners of her eyes. There was only one other time Danya had come so close to losing Sancho—on the day of the fire, the day the ground in her backyard burned black. Danya squeezed her eyes shut and tried to force the memory out of her head, but instead it just became more vivid, almost like she was reliving it all over again. She remembered seeing the flames lick at the sky as she and Sancho raced for the stable. The fire had scared him and he'd reared—just like he had on the boat. But Danya could hear Jupiña whinnying. She'd slid off Sancho's back and raced across the yard, but before she could reach the stable, she'd stumbled and fallen, scraping her knee on a root poking up from the yard. . . .

Sancho licked Danya on the side of her face, drawing her out of the memory. Behind them, Pia had made a full recovery. She jumped to her feet and began bouncing in place.

"Man, what a rush!" she shouted. "We should do that every week!"

Danya didn't exactly agree, but she was still so thrilled to be alive that she didn't argue. She only knew that she was done with tiny speedboats and whitewater rapids, at least for now. Danya stood, and her hands went immediately to her back pocket to feel for the sandwich bag.

The pocket was empty. Their money was gone!

A sharp, raw pain cut through Danya like a knife. But even as the tears pricked at her eyes, she couldn't help thinking . . .

Suffer a great loss.

Danya shook her head, wondering for the first time if Pia was right. Without the money, they certainly were lost.

CHAPTER EIGHT

Elvis Goes to White Castle

Danya and Pia stood at the bank as Simone, Karina, and the rest of the Golden Girls Adventurers cut the engine of the boat.

"Thank goodness! Are you little ladies okay?" Karina flitted around the front of the boat and steered it toward them with the intention of docking. During the last portion of the trip, the river had grown considerably calmer, and the old ladies bobbed along in their speedboat, the light breeze tugging at the ruffles on their swimsuits. Danya felt like the breeze tugged at her heart, too. They looked so worried for her and Pia! Karina's face was white as a sheet, and Simone looked like she was about to faint. Danya waved at them sadly.

"We're fine! Go on without us!" she called back.

"Nonsense! We couldn't leave you behind . . ." Simone yelled, fussing about with the ropes at the front of the boat. "Once you three get back on, it'll be smooth sailing from here!"

"What do you two think?" Danya asked, turning to Sancho and Pia. The river had slicked Sancho's mane against his head so only his two little golden brown ears were sticking up. They shivered when the wind blew, and he whinnied softly.

"Your call, Snap," Pia said. "It's an adventure either way. But there *is* undiscovered territory to be explored. . . ." She motioned behind them to the dirt path alongside the river. A sign sticking out of the dirt read MEMPHIS CITY LIMITS. "Besides, we're already in Memphis—if we keep going, we could grab another ride in the city."

Danya considered the sign. Pia was probably right—it made more sense to head for the city than to risk their lives continuing downstream.

"No, really," Danya called back to Karina, "we're close to home now! But thank you for the adventure! Thank you for *everything*!"

Karina waved back. "If you're sure," she shouted, "then you're welcome, little free spirit!"

"Good luck!" Simone called. At least Danya *thought*

that's what she said. The wind snatched at Simone's voice, and all Danya heard was the word *luck* echoing over the roar of the water.

Danya was so happy to be on dry land, she didn't even mind the dirt and sticks still clinging to her wet hair and clothes. Sancho nudged her arm. He, too, looked wet and tired.

"Oh, buddy! Are you cold?" Danya stood and wrapped her arms around Sancho's neck, rubbing her hands up and down his sides to warm him. He nuzzled into her shoulder, shivering.

Unlike Danya, Pia seemed energized by their brush with death. She hopped up and down, unable to keep still. Danya pulled the waterlogged map out of her back pocket, and Pia peered over her shoulder.

"Come on! Race you to the path."

Danya raised an eyebrow. She only now realized how exhausted she was, and after that swim she wasn't even sure she could stand. She knew they had to keep going—she could still hear that insistent *tick tick tick* in the back of her head—but she was having a hard time making her arms and legs move.

"You can have the first turn riding Sancho," Pia offered.

"Riding Sancho sounds good," Danya said. The girls loaded him up with their sopping wet bags, then they took turns ducking behind a tree to change. The clothes in Danya's backpack were damp with river water, but they were clean and dryer than the ones she was already wearing, so she pulled them on. At least it was warm out. She'd be dry again in no time.

Danya climbed onto Sancho's back, and Pia took the reins and led Sancho toward a beaten dirt road that cut through the waist-high grass lining the river. Hills rose in the distance, covered with fuzzy green trees that reminded Danya of the piles of broccoli at her father's friend Mr. Martinez's vegetable stand. She wrestled her curls into a ponytail as she rode. The river water and wind had frizzed her hair, and fuzzy tendrils kept blowing into her eyes and tickling the back of her neck.

As the sun fell lower in the sky, a silvery fog settled over the river and trees. Before long it started to get dark, and Danya began to think about her parents. She'd been away from them for almost a full day now. What were they doing? Were they sitting at home, waiting for her to call? Or were they actually on the road plastering missing persons posters all over the highway, maybe helping the police in their search? The thought made Danya feel terrible.

Then, not far off in the distance, Danya saw a faint line of light. They drew closer, and she realized the light was coming from a city—Memphis! Skyscrapers jutted toward the clouds like steel mountains, and Danya could see the lit-up arches of a massive bridge stretching across the river. Just ahead was a huge, pyramid-shaped building. In the dusky early evening, the entire city looked bathed in gold.

Pia spun in place giddily, and even Sancho seemed to stand a little straighter. His hair had dried during the walk and it puffed up around his head, made bigger by the humidity in the air. He kept shaking his head to get the strands out of his eyes, and Danya wished she had an extra ponytail holder to give him. She giggled out loud at that: *Pony*tail holder.

"What's so funny?" Pia asked. Danya explained her joke, and Pia actually groaned out loud, punching her playfully on the arm. Even Sancho whickered, and Danya thought it sounded like he was laughing.

"Now I'm going to think of that every time I put my hair in a ponytail," Pia said. Danya giggled again and ran a hand over Pia's short, wiry curls.

"When do you ever put your hair in a ponytail?" she asked.

"Good point. Look, we're almost there!" Pia said, smiling her wide, missing-tooth smile. Eventually the little dirt road merged with a busy, paved street, and the dried grass and trees became buildings and fast food places and streetlights. The smell of fried food drifted out of the

113

restaurants and made Danya's mouth water. She swallowed her hunger, thinking of all the money they—no, *she*—had lost. Along the way she and Pia counted up what change they had left. It came to just seventy-three cents, and that was including a Canadian quarter and a button that kind of looked like a penny.

"Snap? Hey, Snap? Are you in there? Can you hear me?" Pia snapped her fingers just inches from Danya's face.

Danya shook her head. "Sorry. What did you say?"

"What do you think this means?" Pia held up the Ferdinand and Dapple book and pointed to the next item on the hero's task list: *6. Offer your service on a royal mission.* "It can't mean real royalty, right?" Pia wrinkled her nose. "There isn't any real royalty in Memphis."

"Pia . . ." Danya pressed her lips together, trying not to let her frustration creep into her voice. "I think it's more important that we find something to eat, don't you?"

She was sure Pia was going to argue, but instead Pia sighed and nodded. "You're right. I'm starving."

Danya pulled Sancho's reins, and the three of them started down the street, peeking into the windows of every fast food place they walked past. Danya's stomach rumbled every time she caught the smell of french fries or fried chicken, and several times she ducked inside to see whether she and Pia could afford to buy anything. But even the cheapest items at the cheapest places cost at least a dollar.

The good news was that no one in Memphis had recognized them, and Danya didn't see any Amber Alerts anywhere. Maybe news of their disappearance hadn't reached Memphis yet. Or maybe Pia was right—maybe Simone thinking she recognized them was a fluke and Danya really was being paranoid.

"Maybe we can search the street for quarters?" Danya suggested after peering through another three restaurant windows.

Pia shook her head. "Snap, *look*!" She pointed to the fluorescent white sign glowing next door, the words WHITE CASTLE written in blue across it.

"What, the sign?"

"The *sign*—exactly!" Pia said. "The next item on the list is about royalty, and that place is called White *Castle*. It's a sign!"

"That's a fast food restaurant, Pia," Danya said. The building was squat and grayish, surrounded by trim, rounded shrubberies. Cheesy turrets were carved into the low roof. It didn't look very royal to her.

"It's better than nothing," Pia said, dragging her toward the entrance.

A man pushed open the door to the castle, and the heavy, greasy smell of hamburgers and french fries wafted out. Danya closed her eyes and breathed in the scent. Her stomach rumbled painfully.

"Fine," Danya said. "You never know, right? Maybe we can split a small fries."

They tied Sancho up just outside, and he immediately plopped down and started munching on one of the shrubberies. The girls walked into the castle. It was empty, except for a table of Japanese tourists just next to the door. Or at least Danya assumed they were tourists because of their cameras and maps. They all looked like they were sixteen or seventeen, with multicolored hair gelled and sprayed into the strangest shapes. They wore platform shoes and shiny black pants. Their table was covered with hamburger wrappers and little, colored scraps of paper that they were folding into interesting shapes.

One of the tourists looked up and made a tiny paper frog wave. Danya smiled, then looked quickly away, feeling shy. She walked up to the counter and waited as a large man wearing a grease-stained apron walked over to her.

"Welcome to White Castle," he said, scratching his wobbly belly. "Would you like to try our ten-stack combo meal?"

"No . . . um . . ." Danya's stomach gave a rumble that

nearly shook the counter. She gripped her coins so tightly, she could feel them leaving marks in her skin. "Do you have anything we could buy for seventy-five cents?"

The man with the greasy apron frowned. "Cheapest item is the small fries and that's a dollar."

Danya felt like crying, but she forced a smile. "Thanks anyway," she said. She tucked a frizzy curl back behind one ear and turned to Pia. "No luck."

Pia frowned. "What about the royal mission?"

"Pia . . ." This time, Danya didn't bother to keep the irritation from her voice.

"Five minutes," Pia said, making a cross over her chest. "Just to scope the place out."

While Pia circled the restaurant, as if intending to find a king hiding under a table, Danya walked over to the table behind the Japanese teenagers. She tried to ignore the delicious smell of frying potatoes and meat. When her hunger grew too strong, she lowered her head to her hands and clenched her eyes shut.

"Are you okay?" A girl from the other table swiveled around and leaned over the back of her booth. Though her English was perfect, her voice held the hint of an accent— she spoke the words just a little too carefully. Danya lifted her head.

"I'm fine," she said, smiling weakly.

The girl had shiny black hair and straight bangs. She wore a short black dress with a floppy bow tied at the collar. Maybe this will make you feel better," she said, picking up a piece of yellow paper and quickly folding it into a little frog, which she set in front of Danya. *"Ribbit ribbit . . ."* she croaked, making the frog hop across the table.

Danya couldn't help but laugh. She temporarily forgot about the hunger pains shooting through her stomach. "Can you show me how to do that?"

The girl—whose name was Eiko—invited Danya over to her table, and she and her friends showed Danya how to fold the multicolored scraps of paper into all different shapes: hearts and swans and cranes and frogs. When Eiko saw Danya eyeing their tray of hamburgers, fries, and milk shakes, she pushed it toward her.

"You are hungry? You should eat," she said.

Danya didn't need to be told twice. She grabbed a hamburger from the tray and shoved it into her mouth. She caught Pia's eye across the restaurant, and Pia bolted over. The girls ate happily while the tourists told them all about their trip.

"We are break-dancers," Eiko explained. There were two other girls at the table with her—Chi and Kyo. Chi had pink-and-red-tipped black hair that she'd gelled up into swooping spikes so it looked like flames. Kyo's hair, on the other hand, was shaggy and short and bright blue. She also had a nose ring and wore a strange, black mesh tank top over a blue sports bra the same color as her hair.

"Our crew, it is very big in Japan," Kyo explained. She spoke haltingly, her English not quite as good as Eiko's. "But we want to be American stars."

Chi giggled and folded a swan, which she tucked into Pia's hair. "You look so pretty. I love your hair," she said, poking at Pia's short, spiky curls. Pia smiled and slurped her milk shake while Danya picked apart her hamburgers, saving the lettuce and tomatoes for Sancho.

Pia and Danya were just finishing up their french fries when the doors to White Castle swung open and a man walked in.

He wore sunglasses even though it was dark outside. His white suit was covered in rhinestones, and a white-and-gold cape was draped around his shoulders. Danya had never seen anyone dressed like that; he looked important. There was a gold belt hanging low over his ample belly, and he had thick, wavy black hair and long sideburns.

"I wonder who that is," she said under her breath.

Chi looked up. She and Kyo spoke quickly in Japanese before Chi finally said, "He is called . . . how do you say . . . the King?"

"The *King*?" Pia nearly choked on her french fry.

Without another word, she pushed away the tray of food and slid out of the booth. She grabbed Danya's shirt and hauled her to her feet.

The King was just finishing up his order when Pia and Danya reached him.

"Whoa!" he said. Pia stood so close to him that he nearly tripped over her when he turned around. "Well, hello there, little lady. You gotta watch where you're going."

The King's voice was deep and slow, like all the hope had drained out of it, and up close Danya saw that there were dark circles under his eyes and faint frown lines crisscrossing his face. He tried to move past Pia, but Danya shifted into his path, stopping him. Maybe Pia *was* right— maybe they were supposed to help him.

"Mr. King," Pia said. She dropped into a low bow, her nose almost touching the white, tile floor. "My cousin and I are on a hero's journey, and now that we've found you, we are at your service. Ask anything of us. It would be our pleasure to serve you."

The King cleared his throat. There was a long stretch of silence. Danya swallowed awkwardly—was it possible the book really was guiding them?—and tugged at Pia's elbow. "Pia . . . get up," she muttered. Glaring at her, Pia stood.

"That's very kind of you, little ladies. But I don't think you can help me," the man said.

"Really?" Pia didn't bother concealing her disappointment.

"Are you sure?" Danya piped up, surprising herself. "You don't need help with *anything*?"

The King frowned. "Some help would be nice, lil' ladies, but unless you got two tap dancers hidden in your jean pockets, there's nothing you can do for me. Tonight was supposed to be my comeback show. I've got a sold-out nightclub across the street, and my dancers all up and quit." The King shook his head, and the frown lines next to his mouth deepened. "What am I supposed to tell all those people who paid to see me? You just can't trust Broadway types, you know?" He huffed and shook his head.

Danya considered this. She definitely didn't know any tap dancers. But she looked back at her new friends, still happily folding origami shapes on the table, and an idea struck her.

"I don't know any tap dancers," she said. "But I *do* know three Japanese break-dancers."

Thirty minutes later, Danya, Sancho, Pia, Eiko, Chi, and Kyo were across the street at the King's nightclub, a low, brick building called the Boogie Woogie Café. They all huddled together in a backstage dressing room filled with glittery, sparkling costumes.

Eiko and Chi were combing Kyo's hair into the same

swoopy style as the King's. Their hair had already been gelled and set in place, and they'd all found their own white jumpsuits covered in rhinestones.

"Would you like me to do your hair?" Chi asked once the other girls were finished with her. Before Danya and Pia could answer, Eiko and Kyo were combing their hair back and spraying hair spray over it to get it to stay in place.

"No, really, we need to go ..." Danya started to say, but just then Chi attacked her curls with a thick, sticky cloud of hair spray. Danya squeezed her eyes shut, and the rest of her sentence dissolved in a fit of coughing. She could feel her thick curls stiffen on top of her head.

"Don't worry, Danya," Pia reassured her as Eiko pulled tubes of makeup out of her bag and started painting her face. "It's already dark. How much farther could we get tonight, anyway?"

While Eiko smeared glittery powder on her cheeks, Danya pulled her lucky gel pen out of her pocket and nervously wove it between her fingers. *Tick tick tick*, she thought. It *was* late, and there was still such a long journey ahead of them. But Pia was sort of right. They didn't have a place to stay, and Danya didn't know how safe it was to travel in the dark.

"Besides," Pia pointed out, "the King said he would

pay us. And we need the money if we're going to get to Florida."

Danya tapped the pen against her leg, not noticing the purple smears it left behind on her jeans. The King *had* said he was going to pay them twenty dollars each. Not to mention the extra crate of apples he'd promised for Sancho. (In his spare time, the King was an award-winning baker. His specialty was apple pie with cheddar cheese baked into the crust.)

"Fine," Danya agreed. "We can stay." It was only Monday still, and the bald man was planning to come back for Sancho in four days. There was still time. She could get her parents the money to pay back their loan before then *and* keep Sancho.

Chi sat on the floor next to Sancho, braiding his mane. When Chi was done, he rolled onto his back so she could outline the heart on his belly with glitter. The glitter tickled his belly, and he wiggled around, kicking his hooves in the air.

"Now go find your seats," Kyo said, finishing Danya's face with a dab of lip gloss. "The show is about to start!"

Danya hesitated as Pia led Sancho out into the audience. "Maybe we can find the King now? Then we can get our money and apples and head out?"

"What are you talking about? We *have* to stay and watch the show!" Pia's face was covered in glitter, and her usually short, spiky hair looked full and swoopy. "We just completed number six! Don't you see? Everything is working out."

"Maybe just *one* song," Danya said doubtfully. But once again, she wondered if Pia was maybe a little bit right. They had found a king, and he had needed their service. Could the hero's journey be working?

There were two velvet seats reserved just for them right in the front row, and someone had even blocked off part of the aisle so Sancho had a place to sit. Pia grabbed Danya's arm and pulled her into a reserved seat.

Just then the house lights went out, replaced by blue and green and red spotlights. Smoke filled the stage. The King walked out and grabbed the microphone.

"I'd like to dedicate this song to my most faithful servants," he said. The people in the audience around them leapt to their feet and screamed and clapped. The King searched the audience until he found Danya and Pia in the seats up front. "Without these two little ladies, there wouldn't be a show tonight, folks. Put your hands together for the littlest Elvises!"

The crowd went wild, and Danya felt all of her nerves disappear. She turned to Pia, and they wove their hands together, bouncing up and down as the people around them cheered. A sparkling disco ball spun high above them, making the glitter on Pia's cheeks and Sancho's belly shine and dance in the darkness. Smoke filled the room while the King crooned.

"Love me tender . . . love me sweet . . ." he sang. He came up to the edge of the stage and knelt, winking down at Danya and Pia.

"Thanks, ladies!" the King called as Kyo, Chi, and Eiko danced behind him. "You really saved me, you know?"

"Anytime, Mr. King!" Danya shouted.

The crowd around Danya and Pia roared with applause and catcalls as the King's song drew to a close. Danya was swept up in the excitement, but as the noise died down, she couldn't ignore the nerves clawing at her stomach. Even though she'd told Pia they could stay, she still felt like something was a little *off*, though she couldn't put her finger on what. She glanced over at Sancho, and he lifted his head from the floor, pricking up his furry pony ears. It was almost like he knew something was wrong, too. Stumbling to his feet, he nudged Danya with his nose. His way of saying, "Time to go . . ."

"Pia," Danya said, giving her friend's shoulder a shake. "We really should leave."

"Oh, come on, one more song!" Pia said. "He's just getting warmed up!"

"But . . ." Before Danya could argue, a skinny, pimply boy with wiry black curls and a long, hooked nose stumbled down the aisle, flashlight in hand. The bright white beam swept over the seats as the boy moved, stopping every few feet to unstick his sneakers from the floor. He stopped right next to Sancho.

"This club's eighteen and older," he said, shining the white beam of the flashlight into Danya's face. "You two look like *minors*. I'm going to need to see some ID."

As Danya tried to think of an explanation, the pimply boy's eyes narrowed.

"Wait a minute . . ." A grin crept over his face. "I recognize you! You're the missing girls!"

CHAPTER NINE

Giving Chase in Graceland

"Run!" Danya yelled, and she, Pia, and Sancho leapt from their seats and raced for the side entrance.

"Wait!" the boy called. The red velvet chairs were bolted to the ground, and the girls had to crawl over people's knees and dodge toes and soda cups in their effort to escape.

"Watch it!" someone called at the same moment a woman yelled, "Hey! That was my foot!"

Danya muttered an apology, but the music drowned out her voice. At least the lights in the club were low enough that no one else could make out their faces. The pimply boy tried to shine his flashlight at them, but he was having a hard time holding it steady as he pushed his way down the aisle.

Pia leapt over an empty seat and played limbo with a man's outstretched legs. Danya was not nearly so coordinated. She knocked over drinks and stepped on toes. Sancho, however, had the hardest time of all. He tried to barrel down the aisle after Pia and Danya, but he was just too large, and his pony bottom got stuck in a seat as he tried to crawl beneath a man's legs. He let out a terrified whinny, and Danya froze, whirling around so quickly she almost fell onto an old lady's lap.

"Sancho!" she called. Sancho wiggled and wriggled until he pulled his rump free. Just as he started to trot forward, a skinny hand shot out of nowhere and grabbed his tail.

"Got you," the pimply-faced boy yelled, yanking on Sancho's tail. "I have your pony, runaway girls. Now give yourselves up before someone gets hurt."

"Take that!" Pia grabbed a to-go soda cup off the ground, pulled herself onto the back of a man's seat, and launched it, grenade style, at the boy. It exploded over his wiry curls, dripping sticky root beer all over his face. Sancho shot forward like a bullet. People in the aisle leapt to the sides and crawled onto their seats to get out of his way. Tripping and stumbling, the boy followed them.

Once Danya and Sancho made it to the door, Pia

grabbed another soda from someone's hand and dumped it onto the floor.

"Hey!" the boy shouted as his sneaker pulled right off his foot, sticking to the soda-covered floor. He stopped to yank it back on, and Danya, Pia, and Sancho hurried out the side door and into the dark alley right behind the nightclub.

"Keep running," Danya said to Pia. Sancho agreed, pushing them forward with his nose. Before the door swung shut behind them, a group of boys wearing polo shirts and backward baseball caps stumbled down the alley, something thick and foul-smelling sloshing out of the plastic cups they carried.

"Hey, look!" one of them called. "It's a pony!" He snickered and lurched forward, pawing at Sancho. When he dropped his cup, sticky, clear liquid spilled everywhere, spraying Danya's and Pia's legs. Danya grabbed Sancho's reins, and they raced out of the alley toward the main strip. It was completely dark now. Streetlamps and nightclub signs glowed from the sides of tall buildings, turning the concrete shades of red and orange and blue.

"What are you girls doing out so late?" asked a lady wearing a tinfoil hat, pushing a shopping cart full of cans and bottles.

"We're on an adventure!" Pia yelled as Danya pulled

Pia and Sancho toward a well-lit road in the opposite direction. Danya had taken one step into the street when a taxi whizzed past, startling her so much that she fell back into Pia, and they both tumbled onto the sidewalk in a heap. Sancho whinnied and reared back, his eyes wide and wild. As soon as he dropped back down to all fours, he started to run.

"Sancho, wait!" Danya leapt to her feet, brushing an old banana peel off her shoulder.

She and Pia ran, chasing Sancho past stoplights and telephone poles and down a highway that twisted away from downtown Memphis until it felt like they'd left the city lights far behind them. Streetlights flickered around them now, lighting their way as they ran past diners and gas stations, cars and trucks rumbling down the street next to them.

Finally, panting, Sancho skidded to a stop. Just in front of him stood a white, iron fence covered in black musical notes.

Danya grabbed Sancho's reins, thoroughly shaken. "Don't you *ever* do that again!" she yelled, her heart thudding painfully in her chest. Sancho lowered his head, pawing at the sidewalk sheepishly. When Danya's breathing returned to normal, she sighed and scratched him under his chin.

"You scared me," she said, giving him a hug.

"Danya, look!" Pia said, pointing down the road ahead of them. Danya followed her gaze to a blue-and-white sign standing near the street. "Graceland," Pia read out loud. "Wow, that sounds pretty. What do you think it is?"

Graceland. Danya turned the word over in her head. It *was* a pretty name. It sounded like something out of a Ferdinand and Dapple book. Maybe it was a place for wayward travelers with nowhere to stay? The thought filled her with so much longing that she dropped Sancho's reins and took a step closer to the fence. Sancho leaned his head against her arm, and Danya patted him absently. Her arms and legs and everything hurt.

Pia snapped her fingers in front of Danya's face. "Danya. Danya. Danya. Snap! Come on, stop doing that!"

"Sorry," Danya muttered. She rubbed her eyes with the palm of her hand. She was a minute away from falling asleep standing up, like a cow.

"Look, I know you're not going to believe me," Pia said. "But I think we should check out this Graceland place. It's a sign, Danya. We've been wandering the streets all alone and suddenly—"

Before Pia could finish her sentence, Graceland's iron gates began to open with a creak. Pia turned to Danya, wide-eyed.

"*See!*" she hissed.

"See what? That we got here late enough to sneak in after the cleaners?" Danya said, pointing. A tiny pink car with the words SPEEDY FAST CLEANING CREW written across the side in loopy letters pulled down the street, stopping for a beat to wait for Graceland's gates to open. Then, tires screeching, it sped around the corner and down the street.

"It's still a sign," Pia muttered. The girls and Sancho ducked through the gates before they could swing shut again.

Together the girls headed down a twisting driveway lined with towering trees. There, at the end of the driveway, was a *palace*. Or at least it looked like Danya had always imagined a palace would look when she read about them in stories. Columns stood like sentinels to either side of the two French doors. Spotlights shone from somewhere, making the white walls of the mansion glow pink and gold. Two stone lions guarded the entrance. Sancho clomped up next to one of them and nudged its mane with his nose.

"You like the lions, buddy?" Danya asked. In response, Sancho curled up at the base of the statue and started to snore.

"No, Sancho, come inside with us." Danya tried to wake her pony up, but he snorted in his sleep, shaking his mane.

"Danya, leave him, he's happy here," Pia said.

Danya frowned, then leaned over to give Sancho another shake. Grumpily, he eased his eyes open and pushed himself back to his feet, following slowly behind them.

"I just don't think it's safe to leave him out here by himself," Danya explained.

The front door was heavy. Pia and Danya pushed it open together and walked into the main room of the palace in awe, Sancho clomping along at their heels.

Everything was white and blue and gold. Heavy blue curtains hung from the windows, and a thick, white shag carpet covered the floor. Spiky gold mirrors hung from all the walls. Danya turned in place, taking it all in. She'd felt tired before, when they were wandering the streets looking for a place to sleep, but now she was wide awake and ready to explore. Even Sancho seemed to have a little more energy. He sniffed at the white shag carpet and tried to take a bite out of one of the curtains. Danya attempted to wrestle the fabric out of his mouth, but he only let go after getting distracted by one of the mirrors, then trotting to the other side of the room to examine his reflection.

He trailed along as Danya and Pia went from room to room, examining the strange, vintage furniture, switching on the old-fashioned radios and televisions, giggling at the huge, golden mirrors. Danya kept worrying that they'd run into a security guard or someone. But then Pia cartwheeled down the length of a room filled with sparkly suits, and Danya started to relax a little. Next, they linked hands and spun in the middle of a room that looked like a jungle, with Astroturf floors, lamps made out of bamboo and grass, and driftwood coffee tables. There was a long hallway filled with golden and silver records. Out back was a lit-up pool with a little waterfall and a beautiful, bright pink car. Pia wanted to take a swim, but Danya reminded her that they needed to catch some sleep before morning. Sancho sniffed at the pool curiously and tried to take a drink, but the chlorine made him scrunch up his face and spit the water back out.

They all finally ended up in a bedroom, where they changed into clean T-shirts and curled up amid the blankets and pillows on the giant, king-size bed. For a moment Danya felt a tug at her heart. She missed her parents. She used to crawl into bed with them at home, and sometimes they'd even have an impromptu pillow fight before tucking her in for the night.

Then Pia pulled out the Ferdinand and Dapple book, opening it to the hero's list. This time Danya didn't groan or roll her eyes. It was comforting to see the familiar book. And after their encounter with the King, she was going to have to rethink this whole *Hero's Journey* business. Sancho crawled onto the bed with them and pushed his nose into

Danya's lap as Pia examined the list. The next hero's task was *7: Give chase to the enemy*.

Pia bounced up and down on the bed, giggling. "Cool!" she said. "A chase!"

Danya lifted an eyebrow. She was not entirely sure a chase sounded like fun. She glanced down at Sancho, but he was asleep in her lap, snoring softly. Next to her Pia bounced higher and higher, then flopped down on her back, making the pillows around her fly into the air. Now *that* looked fun. Danya leapt to her feet, and the girls tried to see who could bounce higher, while Sancho snorted in his sleep, kicking his little legs like he was dreaming of chasing a rabbit. They tossed pillows into the air and jumped until they were too tired to stand.

Then they flopped back into the pillows. Danya yawned and, before she knew it, she was drifting off to sleep.

While Danya slept, she dreamed.

She wandered the halls of Graceland, following a bright, golden spot of light. Danya didn't know why, but she had to reach that light. Fear crawled over her skin, but she forced herself forward to be brave. The light seemed so close, just around the corner. But when Danya turned the corner, she'd find an empty hall and the light would appear to the left, across the room, and bob away.

Graceland was spooky at night. Mirrors hung on

every wall, reflecting Danya's frightened face back at her. Sparkly, rhinestone-covered suits were on display in glass cases, and at night they looked like people waiting for her in the shadows. It wasn't until Danya crept close enough to touch the glass that she realized the suits were empty. No one was there.

Fear grew in her chest. The light appeared again, and Danya followed it outside. But as soon as the doors swung shut behind her, Danya realized she wasn't at Graceland at all. She was home, in her backyard. Suddenly everything felt familiar, almost like déjà vu. This had happened before.

Danya was playing in the grass with her magnifying glass, Sancho crouched down beside her. Her mom had just brought home *Gulliver's Travels* from the school library, and Danya had read the entire thing in one night. There was this part where Gulliver found an entire civilization of miniature people, so Danya was searching the yard for tiny villages and houses. If there were tiny people out here, she and Sancho would have to make sure not to step on them.

The day was hot and dry, though, and as Danya held her magnifying glass over the grass, the ground began to burn. Tiny curls of smoke drifted toward the sky. Danya patted it out with her hand.

The dream changed. Suddenly it was hours later, and Danya was wandering through the woods alone. Just ahead of her, a fire crackled and grew, eating at the night like a living thing. Angry flames leapt across the dry grass. Something deep and painful flickered to life in Danya's chest. She needed to run, to find her parents or Pia or . . .

That's when she realized—Sancho! He was in the fire, hurt, and she had to save him. Despite her fear, Danya raced forward, toward the flames. But the closer she got to the fire, the farther away it seemed. She thought she heard someone shouting, *"Help! Help!"* and she tried to run faster, but no matter what she did, Danya couldn't reach the flames

"Help!" she heard again. Then the sound changed. "Hey!" someone said.

"Hey, you, girl! What are you doing here?"

Danya blinked her eyes open groggily as a bright circle of light bobbed across the room. She rubbed the sleep from her eyes and stared into the light, the nightmare still fresh in her head.

The light bobbed closer. As Danya's eyes adjusted, she saw that it illuminated a tall, skinny man wearing a security guard uniform. He stood in the hallway just outside the bedroom.

"Hey!" he said. "You girls aren't supposed to be here."

A guard! Danya grabbed Pia's arm and shook. Still confused, the guard stepped into the bedroom.

"Mom . . ." Pia mumbled in her sleep. "Daddy . . ."

"Pia, I think it's time for the chase!" Danya whispered. The guard came closer.

It was like Danya flipped a light switch. Pia's eyes shot open, and she leapt to her feet as the guard approached the edge of the bed. The mattress wobbled beneath them.

"Take that!" Pia yelled, kicking a pillow at the guard. The pillow flew at his face, and he dropped his flashlight, which rolled under the bed. Danya looked around for Sancho but didn't see him curled up in bed next to her. Fear crawled up Danya's throat.

"Let's *go*!" Pia shouted.

"We can't leave without Sancho," Danya said. Just then, the guard lurched toward the bed. The girls stumbled out of the bed and bolted from the room.

Just outside the door was a bathroom, its door ajar. Water dribbled into the hallway from beneath the frame, making the floor all slick and slippery.

"Wait." Danya clutched at the wall for balance as she slid over the wet floor. She pushed the door open and there was Sancho. He'd nudged the bathtub faucet on with his nose and was eagerly slurping up water with his long, pink tongue. The tub had overflowed and there was water *everywhere*.

"Come on, Sancho!" Danya yelled.

Sancho's ears pricked up, and he bolted forward, his hooves slipping and sliding over the slick tile. The bedroom door flew open, and the guard stumbled out at the exact same moment that Sancho lost his footing and slid, nose first, into the hallway, knocking the guard to the ground.

"Way to go, Sancho!" Pia yelled, pumping a fist into the air. Sancho quickly regained his footing, and they raced around the corner—immediately finding two much larger guards at the end of the hallway. Danya yelped. The guards pointed at her, Pia, and Sancho and started racing down the hallway toward them.

"This way!" Pia led Danya and Sancho down one hallway, then another, the guards at their heels. They were fast, and Danya was pretty sure she wouldn't be able to outrun them. She looked over her shoulder as they sped around another corner, into the hallway filled with golden records. They needed a plan!

"They're gaining on us!" she shouted, and Sancho grunted, whipping his tail back and forth nervously. Pia looked over her shoulder and nodded.

"Okay," she said. "You run ahead. I'll stall them!"

"Pia, no! I'm not leaving you!" Danya said. They *had* to stay together! If they got split up, how would they ever find each other again?

But Pia just shook her head, waving Danya forward.

"Danya, get on Sancho and make a break for it!" she shouted, peeling the golden records off the wall and flinging them at the guards like they were Frisbees.

The first guard took a record right in the face and fell to the ground with a thump, groaning as he rubbed the red mark appearing on his forehead.

But the second dodged the first record Pia sent flying and lurched toward Danya and Sancho. Sancho reared, kicking at the air with his front hooves. Terrified, he circled behind Danya and swept between her legs, forcing her onto his back. Wobbling in her saddle, Danya grabbed for Sancho's reins to steady herself, and he shot down the hallway.

Behind them, Pia pulled down two more records and threw them forward at the same time. They curved around each other midair, clocking the second guard on either temple. The first guard was standing again, though, and heading toward her. . . .

"Pia!" Danya yelled.

"GO!" Pia insisted. "I'll meet you at that big white gate covered in musical notes in five minutes. *Promise.*"

Danya tugged on Sancho's ear, urging him faster. The rest of the hallways were empty, and Danya and Sancho made it to the front door easily. Sancho pushed the door open with his nose and ran across the grounds.

The Graceland grounds were empty. Golden light shone from the horizon—the sun would be rising soon—and it sent strange shadows across the rolling, green lawn. Danya held tight to Sancho as they tore across the grass, afraid to look behind her in case another guard was on her tail. But when she reached the gates to Graceland, Danya pulled on Sancho's reins to get him to stop. The gates were wide open. They'd closed behind Danya and Pia on the way inside, so why would they be open now?

"Hey, you there!" someone yelled. Danya spun around in her saddle and saw a police cruiser parked just inside the gates. The security guard had called the cops!

The cruiser door swung open, and a police officer stepped out. He started walking toward them, reminding Danya of a character out of a Ferdinand and Dapple book. Moonlight bounced off his bald head, and his dark eyes had a sinister look to them. Sancho shook his head and took a few worried steps back. Danya's chest clenched. This whole night was surreal. Danya suddenly had a flash of Ferdinand sitting atop Dapple, dressed as a knight about to battle a foe. Ferdinand had been an ace jouster. Back before the fire, Danya and Sancho used to practice in her backyard, using a tennis racket instead of a lance.

Suddenly Danya knew exactly what to do. Holding Sancho's reins tight, she imagined that she was actually a knight about to enter into a jousting tournament. She straightened her leg—she didn't have a weapon, so it would have to do as her lance.

"Hi-yah!" she shouted into the morning. She gave Sancho's reins a mighty shake, and the two of them tore down the sidewalk at a speed that Danya could only assume had not been known by man or beast before. The cop took a step backward.

"Wait! What are you doing?"

She aimed her leg at the cop and kicked the flashlight out of his hands. It arced high in the air, and Danya caught it in one hand. Sancho raced toward the horizon, where a bright orange ball of sun crept over the distant hills.

As they rode past the big white gate covered in musical notes, Danya twisted in her saddle, certain Pia would emerge from the shadows to vault the fence and chase her and Sancho down. But the street behind them was empty.

CHAPTER TEN

Goats, Windmills, and Straying from the Path of Righteousness

Danya and Sancho rode away from Graceland at a breakneck speed. Behind them, the cop fumbled with his car keys, which rolled under the back tire of his cruiser. He mumbled something under his breath and dropped to his knees to try and find them. Only when she was sure they'd left him behind did Danya pat Sancho's neck to get him to slow.

"Whoa, buddy!" Sancho slid to a stop, and Danya led him around in a circle, taking in their surroundings. They'd somehow wandered far from Graceland, and Danya wasn't entirely sure where they were. The buildings here were farther apart, separated by long stretches of trees and grass. Danya slid off Sancho's back, and together they tried to retrace their steps to Graceland, but no matter where they turned, they couldn't find the white gates covered with musical instruments again. Instead they wandered aimlessly down crowded sidewalks and past towering buildings.

Even worse, there seemed to be police officers and security guards *everywhere*. Twice Danya saw the flashing blue and red lights of a police cruiser and had to stumble down a narrow alley to hide.

"What are we going to do?" Danya whispered to Sancho after ducking behind a row of dumpsters when a man in a blue suit and hat walked past. He'd turned out to be a mailman, not a police officer, but that didn't stop Danya from feeling like the cops were closing in on them. She crawled out from behind the dumpsters, pulling a soggy piece of lettuce from Sancho's hair. The lettuce was wilted and brown, but it made Danya's stomach rumble just the same. They'd wasted so much time wandering around the city, and now the sun hung high overhead, telling Danya it was well into the afternoon. Sancho grunted and shook out his mane. Danya sighed, patting his neck.

"You're right," she muttered. "Pia *would* know what to do."

Thinking about Pia made Danya's heart sink all the way down to the soles of her sneakers, and she had to bite down on her lower lip to keep herself from crying.

How could she have let this happen? Pia had been so brave staying behind to fight that security guard, and what had Danya done? She'd left her there alone while she and Sancho ran to safety. What kind of a hero did that? Pia could be lost, or scared, or worse—captured. And it would be all Danya's fault.

"No." Danya shook her head defiantly. She refused to believe her cousin had been taken by the security guards—Pia was too fast, too smart. She was out here somewhere, and Danya just had to find her. "Come on, Sancho, we can't give up. Pia would never give up on us."

Tugging Sancho's reins, Danya looked around for a direction that seemed familiar. She thought she recognized a funky-looking fountain at the end of the street, so she steered Sancho toward it, hoping she was finally on the right track. As they got closer, Danya's heart lifted. The old, twisty tree hanging over the sidewalk looked familiar, too. And there was a crooked sign pointing to Hal's Pancake Palace that she *knew* she recognized. . . .

Then, from somewhere in the distance, drifted the sound of music.

"You think you're slick, but I know your tricks. . . ."

Despite her frustration, a smile unfolded on Danya's face. She recognized that song! It was a country song, a favorite of hers and Pia's. They played it on the radio all the time. Sancho pushed her forward with his nose, so excited he shifted his weight from hoof to hoof to hoof, like he was dancing.

"*And I'll get there first 'cause I'm quicker!*"

"Come on, buddy," Danya said, walking toward the music. "Let's see where it's coming from."

Together they headed down an alley Danya had missed when they'd come this way before. The music grew louder. Heart thumping, Danya and Sancho followed the alley to a wide, open square surrounded by tall buildings. It was like the music was a sign. Danya couldn't explain it, but she just had this feeling they were headed in the right direction. If Pia was around here and she heard that song, Danya knew she'd head for the music, too.

A crowd filled the square around them, all watching something Danya was too short to see. She stood on tiptoe but had her view blocked by a man's hairy arm. Blowing a frizzy curl out of her eyes, Danya tried hopping up and down—and almost got hit in the face with a woman's handbag.

Sancho grunted and nudged her arm. Danya turned to tell him to quiet down—she was trying to *think*, after all—but he dropped to his front knees, motioning for her to climb onto his back.

"Good thinking!" Danya said. Carefully, she crawled

on and rose to her feet, wedging the toes of her sneakers beneath the saddle. She tightened her grip on Sancho's reins, swaying back and forth as he stood. Together they were nearly seven feet tall and towered over everyone around them. Nervous for a moment, Danya glanced around for the Graceland guards or police officers. They were nowhere to be seen. Sighing in relief, she started searching the crowd for Pia.

Speakers lined the square, blasting Athena music as a group of people in black leotards leapt and twirled in the middle of the crowd. Danya's heart thumped faster. A flash mob! She'd seen videos of flash mobs on YouTube before—normal people would randomly burst into a choreographed dance routine in a public place, just for the fun of it. For the briefest moment Danya was so enchanted by the dancers she stopped searching for Pia. They were so graceful, with their arms and legs swaying and turning as one.

All except for the dancer on the end. She leapt through the air when the dancers around her interlocked arms, spinning together in a circle. And when the other dancers came together to form a human pyramid, the dancer at the end tried to break dance.

Danya narrowed her eyes to watch the strange dancer better. She wore a pair of oversize novelty sunglasses and a fake nose, and her clothes weren't even black. And there was something about her long, gangly limbs and crazy curls that seemed familiar. . . .

"Pia!" Danya shouted. Sancho was so excited to see Pia again that he shot forward, his hooves beating against the pavement. The crowd parted to get out of his way, and Danya locked her knees and tightened her grip on the reins, somehow managing to stay upright even as they tore through the thick mob of people. She and Sancho raced past the black-leotard dancers (now performing pirouettes in perfect unison) and would have collided with Pia if Sancho hadn't screeched to a halt inches from her sneakers. Danya lost her balance and fell forward, tumbling onto Sancho's neck.

"We thought we'd lost you!" Danya gasped. There was hair covering her forehead and all inside her mouth. Regaining her balance, Danya scrambled down and threw her arms around Pia, nearly knocking her to the ground.

"Once I heard the Athena song, I came straight here," Pia explained. "I figured you'd know to come. Then there was that flash mob and, well, I guess I kind of got carried away."

Danya grabbed her cousin's hand and led them away from the crowd. Sancho followed.

"We gotta keep a low profile," Pia said. "I think we should try to find a ride a little outside the city. . . ."

After hours of walking south down a small highway, the farmhouses became fewer and farther between. Danya began to lose hope they'd ever hitch a ride. Sancho yanked on his reins, practically pulling Danya down the narrow driveway of the nearest house. "Buddy, what's going on?" she asked, tugging back on the reins.

Apparently he was hungry; a basket of peaches sat in the bed of a pickup truck parked in the driveway.

"We gotta keep moving," she said. "We're still so far." With her free hand she pulled the map out, as if to show Sancho, but just at that moment the wind snatched it from Danya's hands. For a moment it hovered in the air just in front of her, but when Danya reached out to grab it, the map danced forward, disappearing behind the truck.

"No!" Danya raced after the map, following as it ducked beneath the old red pickup truck, blew past the little house, and disappeared into the backyard.

Danya flew around the corner—then skidded to a stop, her mouth dropping open. The yard behind the little house was absolutely filled with goats. They covered every single blade of grass, turning all that Danya could see white, black, brown, and *furry*. Tall fences surrounded the goats, and thick trees lined the yard. Though Danya heard the rumble of cars driving past, she couldn't see the street at all. A windmill stood at the far corner of the lawn, its blades whirring in the wind.

The goats bleated, and one clomped forward to chew on the sleeve of Danya's sweater. Danya swatted him away, searching the sea of white and black fur for her map. But every time she thought she saw a flutter of paper it turned out to be a tuft of fur or the sun glinting off a wet, black nose.

"Whoa," Pia said, coming up beside her. Sancho grunted and nudged her arm. Even he sounded distressed.

"How am I supposed to find the map now?" Danya said, nudging aside another goat—this one was trying to eat her shoelaces. Sancho snorted, then pushed the goat away with his nose. He didn't like sharing Danya.

"I've got an idea," Pia said. She grabbed Sancho's reins and pulled herself onto his back.

"Wait, what are you—" Danya started, but before she could say a word, Pia yelled, "Heeyaw!" She tugged on Sancho's reins, and the two of them charged forward.

For a split second Danya felt a stab of jealousy (she didn't like sharing Sancho, either). But then the goats scattered, spooked by the crazy girl on the horse racing around them in circles, shouting at the top of her lungs. They darted to the sides of the yard, bleating and snorting. Danya searched the now-empty yard until she saw it—the map!

Grinning in relief, Danya raced forward as the wind blew the map over the grass and into the windmill. It caught the bottommost propeller, hovering for a moment just out of Danya's reach. Then the wind blew harder and the propellers started to turn.

Danya stood at the base of the windmill, dumbfounded. She watched the map cling to the propeller as it spun around and around. She couldn't just walk away—she *needed* that map! How else was she going to find her way to her grandmother?

But it was so high up! And the propellers were spinning faster and faster . . . Danya swallowed, trying to think of a plan. Pia would crawl right up the side of the windmill without a second thought and get the map herself—but she was busy. Danya could still hear her racing across the yard and yelling at the goats to move as she tried to gather them together. Taking a deep breath, Danya wrapped her arms around the base of the windmill and began to climb.

Bricks stuck out at strange angles, creating hand- and footholds that made it easy to climb up. But once Danya reached the propellers, she hesitated, nervous. The map was all the way at the very tip of one of the propellers—which meant Danya would have to crawl out after it.

"Pia could do this," Danya told herself. It made her feel braver. She waited for the wind to slow, then took a deep breath and grabbed onto the propeller.

Whoosh! The propeller whipped away so quickly that the world around Danya blurred. She clutched onto it for dear life as it spun and spun and spun, gathering speed every time it whipped around. It took Danya a full three spins before she found the courage to open her eyes.

The map was still clinging to the very edge of the propeller, glued down by the force of the wind. Danya scooted forward, but the propeller was spinning so quickly. She could feel her grip growing slack. She wouldn't be able to hold on much longer. And the map was still so far out of reach.

"Help . . . !" she yelled. But the wind snatched away her voice before anyone could hear her.

The windmill whipped Danya around and around, so fast the world blurred together. She clenched her eyes shut, holding to the propeller for dear life.

"Danya!"

Danya's eyes flew open, and she craned her neck around, barely able to make out Pia and Sancho racing across the yard.

"Pia!" Danya yelled. "Pia, help!"

Pia reached the windmill quickly, slid from Sancho's back, and climbed up the base until she was just a few feet from the propellers. Danya whipped past her once. Then twice.

"Pia, I can't get down," she said. Pia nodded, then scurried back down. She searched the ground, finally grabbing a bit of fence that looked like one of the goats had been gnawing on it. She aimed . . . and threw. . . .

The fence post whizzed through the air like a spear, wedging itself between two of the giant propellers. The one Danya clung to jerked, then came to a stop.

Danya let out a sigh of relief. Carefully, she slid to the edge of the propeller, grabbed the map, and crawled back down.

"What on earth were you doing?" Pia asked.

Danya quickly explained about the map. "I thought it's what you would do," she added. Pia shook her head.

"Are you kidding? I'd never be brave enough to do that! What if you'd fallen off one of those propellers?"

"I don't even want to think about that," Danya said, shuddering. But she couldn't help grinning—she'd done something even Pia was too scared to do. That had to be worth something, right?

"Hey! You girls!" called a voice from the direction

of the house. The grin dropped off Danya's lips, and she whirled around, nearly tripping over a goat nibbling at the hem of her jean shorts.

A girl crossed the yard toward them. She couldn't have been more than a few years older than Danya and Pia, and she had short, wispy red hair pulled back in pigtails that stuck out from her head like antennae. She wore an over-size muumuu that dragged on the ground behind her.

"What are you doing in my backyard?" she demanded, propping her hands on her hips. A goat started sniffing at her muumuu, but the girl gave him a sharp look, and he backed away with an indignant bleat.

"I . . . uh . . . you see, my map . . ." Danya muttered, but one of the goats was licking at her socks, and she was so distracted she couldn't seem to force the words from her mouth.

"It was just a misunderstanding," Pia explained as Danya gently shoved the goat away with her sneaker. "We'll leave."

The girl stared Danya down, her brown eyes narrowing into teeny, tiny slits. Then she turned to Sancho, and her eyes grew even narrower—until Danya couldn't be certain they were still open at all.

"I suppose you're hoping I won't notice y'all are run-aways, right?"

Danya and Pia shared a look, and Danya felt the hair on the back of her neck stand on end. *Runaways?*

"What makes you think we're runaways?" Danya asked, trying to keep her voice even.

"There are posters with your faces on them plastered all over the city," the girl said, moving closer. "Plus I've heard the news report about the missing girls and their pet pony at least three different times today. And, oh yeah, there's an Amber Alert on every major highway in the United States. I even know your names—Danya, Pia, and . . . Sanchez, right?"

"Sancho," Danya said numbly. Every muscle in her body clenched. There were *posters* everywhere? And radio programs and Amber Alerts all across the country? Everything Danya had suspected was true—her parents were worried, and everyone was looking for them. This was a disaster. The girl stood face-to-face with them, now just inches away. Danya adjusted the fake nose that Pia had let her borrow to disguise her identity. Pia grabbed her hand and squeezed. Even she knew they were done for—*doomed*.

"Don't look so devastated," the girl said, clapping Danya on the back. "Even though you were trespassing, and damaging my property, and probably plotting to steal my goats, I might be convinced to make you a deal. See, my horse, Boxer, has a bad leg and isn't able to run today. Which is a problem, because I got a yard full of goats that need to be rounded up before tomorrow morning so I can drive them off to the Louisiana. You let me borrow your little pony for an afternoon of work, and I won't tell the cops where you are. How's that sound?"

"Why do you have a yard full of goats?" Pia asked at the same time Danya excitedly spit out, "How are you getting to Louisiana?"

The girl looked back and forth between the two girls. "What do you mean how am I getting there? I've been driving since I was nine years old, and I have a truck with a trailer attached for the goats," she explained to Danya. Then, turning to Pia, "The goats are part of my business. So what do you two say? We have ourselves a deal?"

Before answering, Danya glanced down at the map still clenched in her hands.

"If you let us hitch a ride south with you, we do," she said, shoving the map back into her pocket. "We're trying to get to Florida."

"Florida, huh?" The girl screwed up her lips, thinking. "Well, I supposed I could be convinced to take you as far as . . . New Orleans?"

Danya and Pia shared an excited look. New Orleans!

Getting a ride that far south would *more* than make up for the morning they'd wasted wandering around Memphis!

"Deal!" Danya said, sticking out her hand to shake. The girl shook, a smile splitting her face.

"The name's Circe," she said, pronouncing it *Sir-see*. "Of Circe's Goats and Cleanup Crew. Good to meet you."

CHAPTER ELEVEN

The Forbidden Fruit of Juggs Casino

Sancho thundered around the goats in Circe's backyard, hooves kicking up clouds of dirt as he ran. Danya clung to his neck, and behind her stood Pia, her sneakers shoved beneath Sancho's saddle for balance.

"*Heel!*" she shouted at the top of her lungs. She gripped Danya's shoulder with one hand and waved at the stampeding goats with her other. "Heel, goats, heel!"

"You keep saying that!" Danya yelled up at her friend. "I don't think you know what it means."

"It's working, isn't it?" Pia called back down.

Meanwhile, Circe sat comfortably on an old lawn chair, her feet propped on an overturned bucket. While the girls worked, she ate a sandwich, lazily turning the pages of a paperback novel. It wasn't until they'd gathered the goats around her truck that Circe put her book down and sauntered over to the trailer to unlock the latch.

"Good work," she said to Danya and Pia as the goats tromped up the gate to the trailer and huddled together inside. "Now, if you want a ride, you better hurry." She tapped her bare wrist like she was wearing a watch. "We're on a schedule."

Circe helped Danya load Sancho into the trailer with the goats. Then, after giving him a quick kiss on the forehead to say goodbye, the girls crowded into the truck's main cabin. To their surprise, Circe pulled two more sandwiches out of her glove compartment.

"Better eat these," she said, tossing a sandwich to each of the girls. "You look like you're about to drop dead from hunger."

Danya tore into the sandwich, unable to believe just how good plain old peanut butter and jelly could taste on an empty stomach. Next to her, Pia downed her entire sandwich in a single bite.

"Dees er so gud," she said through a crumb-filled mouth.

While they drove, Pia peppered Circe with questions about her life: How was it that she got to live on her own when she was so young? How'd she make any money? In exchange, Circe told the girls all about her goat business.

"People from neighboring cities hire me and my goats to come in and clean up the litter from their parks and schools and highways," she explained, though Danya was so nervous she could barely focus on what she was saying—Circe was a *terrible* driver. She was too short to reach the pedals, so she kept a brick on the gas. She steered with one hand, tapping a beat out on the side of the truck with the other. It made Danya so uneasy that every few minutes she tested her seat belt to make sure it still worked.

"Goats are great animals for a farm, you know?" Circe continued, whistling a completely different tune from whatever she was tapping on the roof of her truck. "*Much* better than pigs. And my goats will eat anything, so business is booming."

"Pigs?" Pia asked. Unlike Danya, Pia seemed to love Circe's driving style. She sat sideways in her seat so she could stick her legs out the passenger-side window, and whenever she wasn't asking questions, she yodeled along with Circe's strange, off-key whistling.

After a few hours of tapping and whistling and yodeling it was enough to give Danya a headache. And then there was the snorting from Sancho and bleating from the goats out back—Danya couldn't help wondering if they were trying to sing along, too.

"Yeah, I used to sell pigs," Circe explained. "And peaches, but, uh, that didn't turn out so well. Don't ask. Anyway, the goats are new. I've been wanting to make a fresh start."

At a sign pointing the way to New Orleans, Circe took a sharp turn, causing the entire truck to rock. Danya slid over her vinyl seat, nearly hurtling into Pia's lap. Hair hanging over her eyes, she pushed herself back up, blowing the thick curls away with a puff of air.

That's when she saw it: red and blue police lights flashing in the rearview mirror. For a moment she was so shocked that all she could do was open and close her mouth wordlessly.

"Cops!" she finally croaked, at the exact same moment a robotic voice issued from the police car's speakers:

"We know Danya and Pia Ruiz are with you," the voice said. "Pull to the side of the road immediately!"

Eyes narrowing into thin slits, Pia whipped around to face Circe.

"You!" she yelled. "You traitor! You called the cops on us!"

"I . . . I didn't." Circe's face was pale as she watched the police cruiser approach. "I . . ."

"You're the only one who knew where we were," Danya said. "It *had* to be you."

"Pull to the side of the road!" came the voice from the cruiser. Circe's eyes flitted to the rearview mirror. A resigned look passed over her face, and she pulled up on the emergency brake. The truck skidded to a stop, and Danya shot forward, her seat belt cutting into her neck as it stopped her short.

"Look," Circe said, glancing again at the rearview mirror. "I didn't call the cops—I swear it. There was a time when I would have done that sort of thing, but I'm trying to start fresh. Turn over a new leaf, you know?"

"Why should we believe you?" Pia shot back. Circe closed her eyes, then shook her head.

"I had a friend in a similar situation once. Or she would have been a friend, but I messed everything up. I'm not going to make that mistake again.

"Besides," she added after a short pause. "I'm going to get in a lot of trouble when they find out I'm driving. I don't *exactly* have a license, being only thirteen and all."

Danya studied Circe's face—she looked sincere. "I believe you," she said finally.

"Guys, this is a nice moment and all, but we're about to be captured by the cops!" Pia said.

"Don't worry about it." Circe pushed open the

driver's-side door, a determined look on her face. "I'll take care of it, okay? Just ahead is an old dirt road most people don't know about. Follow it south and you'll get to New Orleans, no problem."

"What are you going to do?" Danya asked. Circe took a deep breath.

"Release the goats!" she yodeled. Then she hopped out of the car and raced for the trailer.

"What does *that* mean?" Danya asked, but Pia didn't stop to answer her. Grabbing her arm, she kicked her own door open and pulled Danya out.

"I think it means she's going to *release the goats*," Pia whispered, motioning for Danya to duck as the two of them crept around the back of the truck.

Circe snuck toward the police cruiser, bending low so the officer couldn't see her. When he leaned over to grab his radio, she raced toward the back of the trailer and quickly pulled out the latch.

"Hey!" the officer called, fumbling with the radio as he pushed open his car door. "You're supposed to stay in your vehicle."

But he was too late. The goats tumbled out of the back of the trailer in an avalanche of fur. Bleating and snorting, they raced for the officer in a terrifying stampede. His eyes grew wide. He stumbled back a few steps.

"Wait . . . no!"

And then they were upon him, chewing at his shoes and pants and the sleeves of his shirt. He tried grabbing for his nightstick, but a brown-and-black-spotted goat got to it first.

"*Meh eh eh!*" it cried, chomping down on the stick with its front teeth. The police officer pulled the nightstick away, then lost his balance in the struggle. Hair flew in all directions as he went down and the goats moved in on him, licking his cheeks and forehead with tiny pink tongues.

Just then Sancho crept out of the back of the trailer, his tail tucked between his legs.

"Sancho!" Danya hissed, her heart aching. He looked so confused! At the sound of her voice, he trotted over to the side of the truck, relieved to be away from the goat mob.

"Go!" Circe peeked around the side of the trailer, waving at Pia and Danya to run.

"We can't leave you!" Danya insisted. "How will you get the goats back in the trailer? You need our help!"

Circe just scoffed, shaking her head.

"I'll get them into the trailer one goat at a time, just like I always did before you two troublemakers came along." She smiled then, waving them on. "I can take care of myself. *Now, go!*"

"Thank you!" Danya mouthed wordlessly. Then she, Sancho, and Pia raced for the windy dirt road that would lead them to New Orleans.

The girls took turns riding Sancho down the road, the air around them so hot and humid it felt like they were inside a mouth. As they got closer to the city, Danya could feel her nerves whirring to life inside her. The more people around, the more chances someone would figure out who they were. Eventually they made their way to a street filled with yellow, pink, and green houses. Lush vines and flowers dripped from overhanging balconies, and old-fashioned lamps dotted the sidewalk. Danya froze, watching the people stroll down the streets.

"Maybe we should go around New Orleans," she whispered to Pia. She adjusted the fake nose propped on her face. "This is bad news—someone here will recognize us for sure."

"If we go around the city, there's no chance we'll find a ride," Pia pointed out. "Just act like you belong, and no one will notice you."

The girls and Sancho started to cross the narrow street, then leapt back onto the sidewalk as a carriage driven by a man in a velvet cape and top hat rolled past them, nearly taking off their toes. It wasn't until the carriage disappeared in a cloud of dirt that they felt safe enough to try again.

"Maybe we can get Sancho a job pulling one of those things?" Pia said. She coughed and waved a hand in front of her face to clear the remaining dust from the air.

"You know we're supposed to stay *under* the radar." Danya tugged on Sancho's ear to get him to move a little faster—she didn't want to get trampled by another carriage.

"Snap, I was joking. And besides, in case you didn't notice—we're broke."

Danya pursed her lips. She couldn't exactly argue with that.

"Ooh! Your pony is *so* cute!" someone said from across the street, interrupting Danya's thoughts. Sancho seemed to enjoy their attention. He shook his mane out, trotting in place while Danya swiveled around in her saddle. To her horror, two women teetered toward them on dangerously tall stiletto heels. They were beautiful, with intricately curled hair, heavy eye makeup, and layers of multicolored beads glittering from their necks. Danya gaped as they approached. Now that the women had seen them, they couldn't hide or run away, so Danya crossed all her fingers and toes for luck, hoping they wouldn't recognize them.

As the women came closer, Danya realized they both

looked *exactly* like a character from the fourth Ferdinand and Dapple book—Dulce, the tavern girl Ferdinand was helplessly in love with. Danya had always loved how her grandmother described Dulce's cascading, raven-colored curls and glittering beaded necklaces. For a second she forgot her nerves, admiring the women's hair and jewelry.

The women stopped in front of Sancho and patted him on the nose. "Aren't you a purty pony? Oh, you're such a purty pony!" one of them cooed. Sancho snorted, and Danya thought she detected a blush creeping over his fur. He stood up a little taller, tossing back his mane.

"What are y'all doing out here?" the second woman asked. A plastic name tag attached to her tank top said her name was Tina. "You're too little to take this town on your own! Where are your parents?"

Danya felt some of her nerves ease up a little. At least the women didn't seem to know who they were—that was a good sign. She tried to think of an explanation fast, but it was Pia who answered.

"See, we were on this tour group that was just here, but a carriage whizzed past and kicked up all this dust, and when the air cleared, the rest of the group was gone."

The two women shared a look. "How about you come along with us," Tina said. "You got a number you can call, don't you? We'll let you borrow a phone so you can find the rest of your group. Maybe grab you a soda while you wait?"

"No thank you," Danya said at the same time Pia said, "That sounds great!" Danya tried to shoot her cousin a "we're not supposed to draw attention to ourselves!" look, but Pia carefully avoided her eyes.

"We work across the street at Juggs," the other woman said. "We're waitresses. My name is Molly."

"I'm P . . . rissy," Pia said, changing her name at the last second. She winked at Danya. "And this is Dakota. My sister."

They all shook hands, and Molly and Tina ushered them across the street, not listening to their protests.

"What are we doing," Danya said under her breath. "We don't have anyone to call, and the longer we hang out with them, the more likely they are to recognize us!" Pia waved her worries away.

"They're going to give us a *soda*," she said. "And I'm thirsty."

Juggs, it turned out, was a bar and casino that had been built in a renovated church. Danya hesitated near the door as Pia bounded up the steps. Then, with a sigh, she tied Sancho up outside and, with a kiss on his forehead, hurried after Pia, Tina, and Molly.

The church still had stained glass windows and pews,

but now there were slot machines lining the aisles. Little blue-haired old ladies sat in front of the machines, diligently slipping in quarter after quarter. A huge, fluorescent green angel hung from the rafters above them, and a stone bust of Abraham Lincoln stood next to the door, a curly blond wig perched on his head.

"I'll grab the cell from my purse," Molly said, handing Pia a soda before tying an apron over her short skirt. "Y'all wait right here, okay? Children aren't supposed to be back here."

Danya and Pia nodded. Tina patted them on their heads and grabbed a tray of drinks, then she and Molly teetered across the bar on their sky-high heels.

"What are we doing here? Why are we waiting?" Danya hissed as soon as the women were out of sight.

"We're not actually waiting for them," Pia explained, finishing half the soda in one gulp before handing the rest to Danya.

"Then what are we doing here?" Danya said, taking a drink of soda. The bubbles tickled the back of her throat, making her cough. Her parents didn't usually let her drink soda. "We should *go*."

"Go? Are you *kidding*? This place is amazing. I just meant we needed to do a little exploring."

"But Pia, we . . ."

"I know, I know, we're on a schedule and someone might recognize us. Just hold on one minute, okay? I have an idea."

Before Danya could argue, Pia darted across the casino. She snatched the blond wig off the Abraham Lincoln bust, grabbed a handful of sparkly beads from a basket near one of the slot machines, and pulled an abandoned shawl off the back of an empty chair.

"What are you doing?" Danya demanded as Pia raced back over to her. "That's *stealing*."

"I'll give it all back, promise. Now climb on my shoulders. If kids aren't allowed in here, we need to become a grown-up, fast."

In response, Danya crossed her arms over her chest, shaking her head. If Pia thought there was any way she was climbing onto her shoulders and wearing a wig when they should be finding a ride to Florida, she must've bumped her head on Circe's windmill.

"Come on, Snap," Pia pleaded, shaking the beads in her hand. When Danya still wouldn't budge, Pia stomped her foot, much like Sancho sometimes did when he was annoyed about something. "Look, I have a plan to get us some money. Doesn't that sound nice? Money could buy bus tickets, you know. And maybe even some real food.

Besides, everyone's on the lookout for two kids and a pony, not a grown-up blond woman."

Slowly, Danya lowered her arms. Pia *did* have a point there. "Fine," she muttered. Then, with a smile, "You know, this is your worst plan yet. No one's going to believe we're a grown-up."

Pia took this as agreement. In a flash, she hoisted Danya onto her shoulders and tossed up the wig. Danya flapped her arms around to steady herself, a little surprised when the curly hair landed on her outstretched fingers. She pulled the wig over her own dark hair, then wrapped the shawl Pia handed up to her over her shoulders. It was so long it covered Danya's legs and Pia's head and shoulders.

"Don't forget your beads," Pia whispered, passing her the brightly colored necklaces. Danya strung them around her neck, swaying back and forth as Pia walked over to a mirrored wall.

Looking at her reflection, Danya had to smile. Almost all of her hair was hidden beneath the curly wig (though one long, frizzy strand of brown twisted down around her shoulders). Plus the beads gave her a little added something that made her feel beautiful, like Molly and Tina. As long as no one saw her stubby little arms, she and Pia would definitely pass as a grown-up.

"We look good," Pia said from beneath the shawl, letting out a low whistle.

"Hey, torsos don't talk," Danya whispered, adjusting her wig. "How, exactly, is this going to make us any money?"

Pia dug into her pocket for their last quarter. She blew on it for good luck. "According to the hero's list, we need to taste the forbidden fruit," she said, sliding into a seat in front of a slot machine. Danya wobbled on her shoulders and Pia grabbed her legs to hold her steady. "Gambling is forbidden, and look—this slot machine has little pictures of fruit on it."

"Wait, you want to *gamble* our last quarter away? Pia, no!" Danya tried to grab the quarter from Pia's hand but started losing her balance again and had to steady herself by holding onto the back of their chair.

"According to the list, after doing the fruit thing we, apparently, *receive supernatural aid.* So maybe an angel will help us win some money. Here goes nothing!" Pia slid the quarter into the slot machine and pulled the lever. Three pictures popped up: one strawberry and two cherries.

Danya watched, amazed, as the machine pinged and five quarters dropped into a tray just below it, clinking against the metal. That was . . . surprisingly easy.

Pia whooped. "How much do you think we need for lunch?" she asked, digging the coins out of the tray. "Now what were you saying about gambling away our last quarter?" she asked, holding up the coins.

"Fine," Danya said. "Let's keep going."

Pia slid coins into the slots again and again. Every few minutes, more quarters spilled into the tray, clinking happily. Pia handed them up to Danya, who collected them in her shawl and counted. They had three dollars . . . then four.

"Maybe we should stop now," she whispered to Pia. They had enough to get some hot dogs for dinner from a street cart, and she didn't want to press her luck. Danya tugged her wig farther down over her forehead and glanced around. Luckily no one seemed to be paying them any attention.

"Just one more," Pia said, sliding a coin into the slot. Then she slid another coin in and another . . .

"Pia!" Danya warned, just as her friend was sticking another quarter into the machine. A light went off at the top of the slot machine, and three strawberries lined up in a row: *Jackpot!* Coins poured out into the tray, faster than Danya could count them. Pia began stuffing them into their pockets.

"I *told* you this would be the forbidden fruit!" Pia hollered.

"Pia, hold still," Danya muttered. She tried to grab onto Pia's shoulder, but at that second, Pia jerked forward to catch a quarter spilling from the tray, and Danya lost her balance, toppling backward. She fell to the floor with a grunt, scattering her curly blond wig, sparkly beads, and stolen shawl across the floor.

"Danya, I'm so sorry!" Pia said, her arms filled with quarters.

"Hey—what's going on here?" someone shouted. Danya and Pia glanced up. A security guard was standing at the end of the pew. He looked . . . well, not so happy.

"Time to go!" Pia said. Shoving the coins in her pockets, she grabbed Danya's arm and the two scrambled over the pews, dodging little old ladies with blue hair as they ran.

The guard tried to follow them, but he was too tall, and he knocked his head on the fluorescent angel hanging from the ceiling. The angel wobbled, then came crashing down, blocking his way to the door.

"And that's receiving supernatural aid!" Pia yelled. Groaning, Danya pulled her toward the door.

Sancho was rolling around on his back in the grass, his belly facing the sun when Danya and Pia raced outside, dropping quarters they had no time to pick up. When he saw them, Sancho rolled back over and stumbled to his feet, looking a little sheepish.

"Sancho, there's no time for this!" Pia shouted.

"You're as bad as me," Danya muttered, climbing onto the pony's back. Sancho snorted at her and pawed at the dirt with his hoof.

Together the three of them raced around the corner until they were certain the guard was no longer chasing them.

"That was awesome!" Pia exclaimed. She pumped the air with her fist. "How much did we get?"

Danya slowed Sancho to a stop and counted their winnings on his back. Pia handed over the extra quarters from her pockets. All together, they had nearly fifty dollars!

"Woo-hoo!" Danya said. "Florida, here we come!"

"This is the life!" Pia ran up and down the street and jumped in the air. "I don't ever want to leave. I don't ever want to go home!"

Danya watched her cousin whoop and run. She tried to feel as excited as Pia looked, but she felt bad about running away from Dulce and so much more anxious than she had a few minutes ago—they'd almost been caught again!

But then Sancho nudged her on the shoulder and

horrible sparks of anxiety went off in her gut. This was exciting, sure. But it didn't make any sense at all if they didn't get to their destination, if they didn't find her grandmother and get enough money to keep Sancho from being sold.

She slid off Sancho's back and put her forehead to his nose, closing her eyes.

Sancho *was* her home. She couldn't lose him.

CHAPTER TWELVE

The Pirate's Booty and the Dark Mermaid

The girls traveled over the bumpy road and through the trees, and before long they were heading up the wharf toward a restaurant called the Pirate's Booty. As she bounced along on Sancho's back, the scent of onion rings drifted toward them, and Danya's stomach rumbled. Pia had been holding Sancho's reins and jogging along next to them, but at the sound of Danya's grumbling belly, she pulled Sancho to a stop.

"You hungry?" she asked.

Danya shrugged. She was hungry, but they'd been making such good time and she didn't want to take a break while they were ahead. "I'll be fine," she said, forcing a smile. "I can go for another hour or . . ." Just then her stomach grumbled again.

Pia giggled and Sancho shook his head, whickering.

Danya slapped his neck playfully. "It's not funny," she muttered.

"Look, Snap, if we don't eat, we'll just move slower," Pia pointed out. "Let's get some lunch, then I promise it's back on the road. Deal?"

"Fine, deal," Danya agreed. Pia was right—if they didn't take care of themselves, they wouldn't move as quickly as they could. She steered Sancho over to the Pirate's Booty, closing her eyes to breathe in the smell of greasy onion rings and hamburgers.

The wooden building was shaped like the front of a ship. A mermaid held out an apple at the stern, and a black skull-and-crossbones flag hung from the roof. Now the smell of french fries wafted heavily through the air.

"Look—it's close to the marina. I bet they have really good . . . arrrtichoke dip!" Pia scrunched up her face like a pirate when she said "arrr," and Danya giggled. Sancho snorted behind them, then trotted up to the mermaid and started gnawing on her apple.

"He looks hungry," Pia said. Danya nodded.

"Okay. Let's get him a real apple."

They tied Sancho up next to the mermaid and headed

toward the front door. Without Sancho by their side, Danya was a little less nervous that someone would recognize her and Pia—everyone was on the lookout for two girls and a pony, after all. But she still hunched her shoulders, trying not to meet anyone's eyes as they made their way to a table.

Inside, the restaurant looked even more like a pirate ship, with drawbridges leading to different levels and tables shaped like ship's wheels. Photographs of customers papered the walls, and Danya couldn't help studying them as she walked past, wondering about the stories behind the pictures. Once they were seated, they ordered a burger apiece (along with a couple of tomatoes for Sancho). While they waited for their food, Pia told joke after joke:

What kind of socks does a pirate wear? *Arrrgyle.*

What are pirates afraid of? The *darrrrrk*!

How much does it cost a pirate to get his ears pierced? A buccaneer!

"Get it?" Pia asked after the last joke. "A buck an ear? It's funny!"

Danya laughed so hard soda shot out of her nose, soaking her skirt and spraying down half the table. Pia was so good at distracting her from her worries.

"Gross," she said, trying to wipe it up with her napkins. "I'm going to find some paper towels in the bathroom."

Danya skipped down the steps and headed to the

bathroom, feeling giddy and light after all the pirate jokes. She was glad they'd decided to stop and take a break—she and Pia had needed some time to rest. Her dad always used to say, "You cut more trees with a sharper ax," whenever Danya got too singularly focused on completing a goal. Danya had never really gotten what that old saying meant, but now she thought she had an idea. Still, she made herself a promise that as soon as she cleaned up the soda at the table, she'd pull out the map and sketch out a plan with Pia—then hit the road again.

A waiter pushed open the double kitchen doors at the end of the hall, carrying a tray of fajitas. Chicken and peppers crackled in a cast-iron skillet next to a plate piled high with fresh veggies and tortillas. Danya watched the waiter rush past, and suddenly, without any warning, she was overcome by how much she missed her parents. She counted back the days in her head, realizing it was already Tuesday—fajita day! Every Tuesday her mom made tortillas from scratch and her dad cooked up peppers and onions and chicken on the grill outside. Even Sancho helped by nibbling up all the food that fell on the ground.

Danya's throat felt dry, and tears pricked the corners of her eyes. She wanted to go home, she realized. But not without Sancho. She reached forward to pull open the door to the ladies' room, then hesitated. There was an ancient-looking pay phone next to the door, and she had a pocket full of quarters. Maybe she could give her parents a call . . . just to hear the sounds of their voices?

Sliding a quarter into the pay phone, she dialed her phone number and waited while it rang.

Her mom answered. "Hello?"

Danya inhaled sharply. Her mom sounded tired and . . . sad. Was that because of her? Danya opened her mouth, but a noise on the other end of the line cut her off—shuffling and banging of some sort and unfamiliar voices shouting instruction. The words got stuck in Danya's throat.

"Danya?" her mom said into the phone. In the background another phone started ringing. Someone barked an order to pick it up. Another voice cut in, this one louder.

"Keep her talking," the voice commanded. Danya gripped the phone tightly. The cops!

"Danya," her mother said in a shaky voice. "Baby, is that you?"

There was more arguing and shouting behind her. It sounded like someone said, "We're zeroing in on her location!" Danya heard her father's voice rising above the commotion.

"Maritza, is that her? Give me the phone." Then,

"Danya, sweetie, where are you? Danya?" Her father's voice was scratchy and weak—like he'd been crying. "*Mija,* tell us where you are. . . ."

There were more voices now—loud shouting voices Danya didn't recognize. She hung up the phone and pressed the palms of her hands to her eyes to keep from crying. Her parents sounded so stressed! So scared! What was she doing?

"Sancho," she said out loud, her voice a croak. "I'm doing this to save Sancho. . . ."

Even though she knew it was the right thing to do, Danya couldn't help the pang of guilt deep in her chest. *She* did this. She was the one who'd made her parents stressed and sad.

By the time she made it back to the table, a teenage girl Danya didn't recognize was sitting with Pia. Danya stared at her, wishing she'd found Pia on her own. Hearing that her parents were so worried, so upset—it really got to her. She needed her best friend right now.

Pia giggled at something the teenage girl said, and Danya cleared her throat.

"Sorry," she said. "I guess I forgot the paper towels."

"No worries . . ." the girl said, dabbing at Danya's spilled soda with her sleeve. She was short, with broad shoulders and black hair tied back in a ribbon. She wore thick-rimmed red glasses, and Danya could see a tattoo of a mermaid just above her wrist as the pulled back her damp sleeve.

When the girl saw Danya eyeing the tattoo, she stopped cleaning. "I got it because I write the weekly newsletter for the cruise ship outside. Well, it's my parents' ship—or they manage it, I mean. They let me do a newsletter as long as I help them out with some of the cleaning stuff. Anyway, I have all sorts of nautical tattoos—there's an anchor on my ankle and a couple of fish swimming across my back."

She flexed her arm, making the mermaid wiggle, like she was swimming. Pia giggled, and Danya even managed a smile. The girl seemed pretty nice, but Danya still searched her face to see if there was any sign she recognized them. It didn't seem like she knew who they were. Besides, if she'd been living on a cruise ship for a while, maybe she hadn't heard about the Amber Alert or seen any of the missing kids posters that Circe had mentioned.

"My name's Violet," the girl said, pulling up a chair. "And that's the *Sailing Swan Cruise Ship*. You can see it through the window."

Danya leaned toward the window and pushed aside the curtain. Sure enough, there was a huge, white ship docked in the water just outside. It even looked like a swan. The sides stretched out into huge wings, and the top floor was shaped like a swan's curved neck and head, ending in a black balcony that looked just like a beak.

"Wow . . ." she breathed. "That's so cool. Do you get to travel everywhere?"

"It *is* pretty cool," Violet agreed. "I travel to a ton of different places, but I *really* want to be a reporter and write about all the big news events. I have a blog and everything— it's called the *Mermag Rag*. You should check it out!"

Pia stuck another onion ring into her mouth. "Where are you going next?" she asked.

"Our final destination is Puerto Rico," Violet said. "But we're docking in Pensacola first. It's been an easy trip, too. The entire East Wing is closed because some lady accidentally flushed her swimsuit bottom down the toilet, and it stopped up all the plumbing, so there are all these empty rooms on one end of the ship." She grinned, and the smile took up her entire face. "All the mini-fridges are still fully stocked and everything. Some days I just hang out back there watching TV and working on my blog. It's great as long as you remember not to flush the toilets."

Danya's chest seized up when Violet mentioned she'd been watching TV, and she tried to catch Pia's eye. But then Violet pushed her chair back and stood up.

"Anyway, I should get back. We're disembarking as soon as all the luggage is loaded up."

Pia and Danya shared a look as Violet headed to the *Sailing Swan. Close one*, Danya thought.

"You're thinking the same thing I am, right?" Pia said, shoving the last onion ring in her mouth. "We *have* to get onto that ship."

"Wait, what?" Danya said. She hadn't been thinking about that at all—she'd been too worried that Violet would guess who they were. But now that Pia mentioned it, she couldn't help turning the idea over in her head. *Pensacola* . . . that's in *Florida*. And Violet said there was an entire empty wing no one was using.

"I don't know." Danya pushed back the curtain again, staring out at the *Sailing Swan*. It looked safe enough floating there at the dock. But how were they supposed to get on board?

With a shiver Danya leaned back in her seat. The curtain still hung back from the window, and now she had a good view of the stacks and stacks of luggage piled by the dock. No one seemed to be watching it. Frowning, Danya pressed her face up against the glass. There, at the very edge of the luggage pile, were two huge trunks. An idea began to form in Danya's head. A very Pia-like idea.

"Pia," Danya said, smiling. "I might have a plan."

A few minutes later the girls and Sancho crept up to the luggage. The men who were supposed to be loading were crowded at the end of the dock eating their dinner. Danya crouched on the dock and peered over one of the oversized trunks, watching them carefully. Sancho crawled forward on his front hooves, his tail trailing behind him.

"We have to be cautious," Danya whispered to Pia. "If those men see us . . ."

"Those men aren't paying any attention," Pia said, pushing open a trunk. "Now get in."

The first trunk was filled with clothes and makeup. Sancho crawled inside easily and curled up on a silk robe.

"Are you sure you'll be okay, buddy?" Danya asked. In response Sancho licked her upside the face.

"I think that's a yes," Pia said, closing the trunk on his head. "Now come *on*."

Danya reluctantly patted the trunk, sending happy thoughts to Sancho through the lid. She and Pia hurried over to the other trunk, which was so large they were both able to squeeze inside.

"Just don't poke me in the eye with your big ole feet," Danya joked as Pia pulled the lid closed. Everything around them got dark, with only a few pinpricks of light streaming in from the cracks.

"You're worried about me?" Pia shifted around on her side of the trunk, accidentally elbowing Danya in the leg. "That hair of yours is already going up my nose."

"Shh!" Danya hissed. "I think someone's coming."

Footsteps headed down the dock, stopping just outside the trunk. Someone grunted, and suddenly the trunk lurched into the air. Danya covered her mouth with her hand to keep from crying out. The trunk wobbled and swayed and shook. By the time the men lowered them back to the ground, Danya felt seasick. Across the trunk, Pia shuffled around. Danya groped through the darkness until her hand enclosed Pia's foot.

"Wait," she hissed. They couldn't climb out of the trunk yet—not until they were sure the men weren't coming back. Pia groaned but kept still. Time ticked slowly by. Danya didn't get bothered by small spaces, but with Pia tapping her foot anxiously against Danya's palm, she was losing her patience. She was also beginning to realize that they hadn't showered in a few days. . . .

"Someone will hear you!" Danya whispered to her. "Hold still."

"Can't help it," Pia mumbled back. "I feel like I'm in a jail cell."

Danya waited until they hadn't heard the men's groans or footsteps for five whole minutes before she released Pia's foot.

"Finally," Pia grumbled. She threw open the lid and crawled out. "I thought we were going to be in there forever."

"We need to find Sancho," Danya said, crawling out herself. She wasn't as tall or bony as Pia, so it hadn't been so uncomfortable for her to curl up inside the trunk, but her neck was still a little sore. She stretched as she wandered around the dark luggage area, looking for Sancho. Pia stood on her tiptoes to peer through a circular window.

"Hey—we're moving!" she said.

Danya's chest clenched, but then she saw Sancho's trunk sitting beneath a pile of duffel bags and relaxed. She hurried over to the trunk and pushed it open. Sancho's head popped up, a pair of men's flannel boxers sitting over one ear.

"How you doing, buddy?" Danya asked, tickling him beneath his chin. He shook his head, sending the boxers flying.

"Come on," Pia said, crouching next to her. "We need to get to the East Wing so we're out of sight of the other passengers."

The girls helped Sancho out of the suitcase, then hurried to the exit. There were two staircases—one twisting off to the left and the other going right. The right-handed staircase had a thick rope strung across it, holding a sign reading EAST WING: CLOSED FOR RENOVATION. Pia ducked beneath the rope, leading the way.

Violet was right—the East Wing was abandoned.

Long, empty hallways stretched out before Danya and Pia and Sancho, carpeted in swirly red and gold patterns. Elaborate glass sconces lined the walls. They couldn't see the Gulf of Mexico from here, but Danya could feel the water moving beneath them, causing the ship to lurch and sway. Without thinking, she wrapped a protective arm around Sancho's neck.

"We should find a room," Danya pointed out. "It's nearly dark."

"Good thinking," Pia said. The girls crept all the way down to the end of the hallway and pulled the door open. The room was huge—a suite. Circular windows overlooked the inky black sea, and at the foot of the queen-size bed was a towel folded up like a stingray, a pair of sunglasses perched where his eyes should be. Danya grinned at her reflection in the sunglasses, wondering how long the stingray had been sitting here.

"Cool!" Pia said, pulling open the mini-fridge. It was filled with jars of nuts, fruit, and sodas.

Sancho curled on the foot of the bed next to the stingray. Before drifting to sleep, he nudged the towel animal with his nose, like he wasn't sure if it was actually real.

While Sancho slept, Danya and Pia went out on the balcony. From there, they watched the cruise ship pull away from the dock in New Orleans.

"Here we go!" Pia shouted. She waved at the city lights as they grew smaller and smaller. Even Danya couldn't help feeling happier. They were finally really headed to Florida. This was actually going to work. They were going to make it to her grandmother's!

But just as quickly as the rush of happiness hit her, it ebbed away. Sure, it looked like they were going to make it to her grandmother's house—and now that they were on the abandoned wing of a cruise ship, no one would recognize them. But what did that mean? What if her grandmother decided not to help her after all? What if all of this had been for nothing?

Danya's fear stayed with her long after Pia pulled her back into the room, the shores of New Orleans far behind them.

The girls took turns showering. As Danya pulled on her very last clean T-shirt, she realized she'd need to be more careful in the coming days. She wouldn't want to meet her *abuelita* for the first time covered in mud from the river or in a goat-gnawed sweater. This T-shirt would have to last all the way to Florida.

The room had cable, so Pia insisted they stay up late watching television—but then promptly fell asleep on the bed, cuddled up next to Sancho and snoring softly. Flipping the television off, Danya grabbed a blanket and pillow and tried to make Pia comfortable. But Danya just wasn't tired. She couldn't stop the worries from circling her head. What if her grandmother didn't recognize her when she showed up on her doorstep? Or what if she recognized her but didn't care what happened to Sancho? What if she didn't even *live* there anymore?

As she stood, she noticed the Ferdinand and Dapple book lying open on the nightstand. Danya picked it up. It was open to the list of hero's tasks. The next item read: *Experience a profound shock.*

Sancho snorted and nudged Danya with his nose.

"Oh, hey buddy," Danya said, rubbing him under his chin. "Didn't realize you were still awake."

Sancho grunted and pawed at the bed with his hooves. Danya knew what that meant. He was getting cabin fever. Usually when he felt like this, Danya took him on a ride around the neighborhood. That didn't quite work on a boat.

"Come on," Danya said. "I have an idea."

Sancho leapt down from the bed, and Danya grabbed the Ferdinand and Dapple book and then, at the last minute, pulled a notebook and her lucky purple gel pen out of her backpack as well. She led Sancho out of the room and up to the top floor deck. The cool wind brushed against her cheek like a kiss. All around her was water—deep black nothingness stretching forever. The sky above her was dark and velvety and speckled with stars.

Danya let out a breath, feeling overwhelmed. She'd never imagined the world could be like this—magical and exhilarating, but also heartbreaking and scary. Just like something from a story.

Sancho came up next to her, nudging his head into the crook of her elbow. She looked down into his dark eyes and couldn't help chuckling a little.

"Do you need some attention?" she asked, scratching behind his ears. Sancho purred like a cat. "Oh, buddy, I didn't mean to ignore you. I've just been thinking."

Sancho shook out his mane, and Danya took that as a cue to continue.

"I've always thought adventures were only for stories, you know? But this . . . this is starting to feel like an adventure. Life is starting to feel more and more like a story every day."

Danya hesitated, trying to make sense of her complicated feelings. "The only problem is I don't know what kind of a story we're in yet. Amazing things have happened . . . but there have been a lot of scary things, too. Things I wish hadn't happened at all." Danya sighed, thinking back to that afternoon and how scared her parents had sounded on the phone. "I'm hurting people I love, Sancho. I don't know what any of it means."

For a long moment, Sancho was quiet. Then he chomped down on Danya's book with his front teeth.

"Hey, what are you doing?" Danya said as he pulled the book from her grip. She yanked it back out of Sancho's teeth, rubbing the drool from the pages.

And that's when she noticed it—the page Sancho had turned to was one of her favorite parts of the story. Ferdinand and Dapple has just defeated the evil bandit who'd stolen Ferdinand's aunt's cattle, and now they were lying together in a field, staring up at the stars, wondering how their lives were going to turn out. They were nervous about their future and frightened that the bandit would come back and seek revenge, but they were still able to enjoy the beauty of the stars.

Danya looked over at Sancho, surprised to find there were tears stinging in her eyes. This moment with Sancho was just like that. Ferdinand and Dapple's journey hadn't been easy, either. They'd faced evil, and they'd been scared, but they'd stayed together. Maybe, if she kept trying, Danya really could become a hero someday, too.

Swallowing hard, she closed the book and set it on the

deck next to her feet, sliding her notebook and lucky pen out of her back pocket. Propping the notebook open, she wrapped an arm around Sancho's neck and looked back up at the stars, enjoying the wind on her face.

Maybe, just this once, real life could be better than some story, she thought. Maybe that was her profound shock. Then she uncapped her pen and began to write for the first time since Jupiña died.

CHAPTER THIRTEEN

Fear and Personal Demons in Gatorville

The next morning, Danya and Pia woke to find half-eaten candy wrappers and empty peanut canisters strewn around the floor. Across the room the mini-fridge door hung open, with Sancho's wiggly bottom sticking out of it.

"Sancho!" Danya sat up in bed. Sancho froze, then slowly eased out of the fridge. There was a candy bar wrapper stuck to his cheek and chocolate smeared across his long nose.

Pia leapt out of bed and checked inside the fridge. "Ugh, he ate *everything*," she said.

Danya rubbed the sleep from her eyes. The first thing she saw was her writing notebook. It was on the floor, hidden beneath a pile of candy wrappers. She jumped out of bed and grabbed it, flipping open to the last page. Three or four pages had been ripped from the notebook, leaving behind only a smudge of chocolate on the last cover.

Last night, while looking out over the sea with Sancho, Danya wrote down all her strange thoughts, questions, and fears. She'd written about life and stories and what she thought it meant to be a hero. She even thought it was pretty good—probably one of the best things she'd ever written. And Sancho had *eaten* it.

Sancho crept across the room, his tail between his legs. Chocolate covered his hair, and he had a guilty look on his horsey face. Danya groaned, licked a finger, and wiped the chocolate from his fur. Sancho tried to nuzzle her hand, but Danya frowned and pulled away. She'd *liked* that story.

"What are we going to do for breakfast?" she said to Pia, tossing her ruined notebook in the garbage can next to the bed. Sancho harrumphed and plopped onto the floor, pouting.

Pia pulled on her sneakers without bothering to untie them, then opened their room door, peeking into the hall. "It's cool, Snap. Cruises like this always have huge buffets. I'll just sneak downstairs and grab us some pastries."

"Someone might see you!" Danya said. Pia shrugged.

"And what are they going to do? Call the cops? We're

in the middle of the Gulf of Mexico." Without another word, Pia slid out the door and padded down the hall.

While she waited for Pia to return with their food, Danya switched on the television and flicked through the channels. Her mattress wobbled as Sancho climbed onto the bed and curled up next to her. He put his pony head on her knee and snorted, but Danya slid off the bed and sat down in the nearest chair.

"I'm not ready to forgive you yet," she grumbled. Sancho shook out his mane and swatted the bed with his tail. There wasn't much on TV, and Danya was just about to turn it off when she saw something that made her mouth drop open.

It was a photograph of her and Pia! Danya turned the volume up as loud as it would go, her fingers shaking.

"It's now day three of *Runaway Watch* here on channel three, and there's still no sign of Danya and Pia, the two wily eleven-year-old girls who've stolen the country's hearts since their disappearance last Sunday. . . ."

Before the newscaster could finish, the hotel door swung open. Danya leapt to her feet, the mattress wobbling beneath her legs. Someone must've seen the broadcast! Someone knew they were hiding on the boat! She grabbed the first thing she found as a weapon—the stingray-shaped towel—and held it over her head.

Pia stumbled into the room, Violet right behind her, holding her by the arm.

"I knew it!" she said. "I knew you'd take the hint and sneak onto the boat." Violet pushed the door shut behind her, and her eyes went to the television across the room, which was still blasting the news report on Danya and Pia's disappearance.

"Shoot, I was hoping you wouldn't see that." Violet dropped Pia's arm and plopped down on the edge of the bed.

"You knew we were the missing girls?" Danya asked.

Violet switched off the television. "Of course! This report is running on nearly every television on the boat. I've seen it like six times. I'm just glad you guys decided to sneak on board. I was worried you'd be too nervous to hide in the luggage."

"You wanted us to sneak on? *Cool*," Pia said, putting the pastries, a few juice boxes, some silverware, and plates of fruit down onto the breakfast table.

"Pia, this is not cool," Danya interrupted, slowly lowering the stingray-shaped towel. "She knows about us. She could tell someone."

"I'm not telling anyone anything," Violet said. "Look, when I saw you guys in that restaurant, I just thought this was a good chance to get the scoop on the biggest story of the year. If you let me hang out with you for a while and answer a few of my questions, you can stay here as long as you like. Okay?"

Sancho nudged her with his nose, and finally, grudgingly, Danya scratched him behind the ears to show she'd forgiven him. "I don't know. If you post that stuff on the Internet, won't people come looking for us?"

"Yeah, you'd have to agree not to write anything until we got to her grandmother's house," Pia said.

Violet pursed her lips, considering this.

"Deal," she agreed, and she and Pia shook. Danya hopped off the bed and crossed over to the table of pastries, pulling the map out of her back pocket. She unfolded it and spread it over her lap. Violet came up behind and looked over her shoulder.

"The ship is docking in Florida, right . . . there," Violet said, pointing to a spot on the map.

Danya was so excited that for a moment she forgot Violet was there.

"We're close, Pia! If we walk all day today and all day tomorrow and only stop to sleep for like an hour, we might be able to make it to my grandmother's house by . . ."

Violet pulled a notebook and pen from her back pocket. "That's twice you've mentioned your grandmother now. Is that where you're going, to visit her?"

Danya turned bright red. She'd have to be more careful

about what she said! "Maybe," she mumbled, taking a bite of a croissant to cover up her fumble.

"Don't forget, we have to face a personal demon," Pia interrupted, picking at a bagel. "That's next on the list."

Violet pushed her glasses up the bridge of her nose. "Wait, I don't understand. Why do you guys have to face something? And what list are you talking about?"

Pia tried to explain the hero's list while Danya pulled her orange juice box across the table and took a big gulp, turning this all over in her head.

"We should probably skip the personal demon thing," she said when Pia was done. She counted the days back in her head and swallowed. "It's already Wednesday, and we're still so far away. . . ."

"No way!" Pia waved Danya's suggestion away. "You can't tell me you don't believe in this, Danya. Not after everything that's happened. All we have to do is battle one little demon." Pia speared a piece of pineapple with her fork.

Danya folded the map up and stuck it in her back pocket. It sure did seem like things were happening out there that she couldn't quite explain. But they had a goal, and now that everyone was watching *Runaway Watch*, it was even more important that they stay under the radar. How did Pia not see that?

After another hour or so, Violet left, explaining that they'd be docking soon.

"We have to go, too," Danya said as soon as Violet slipped out the door. Sancho nudged Danya's elbow in agreement.

The girls gathered their things and what was left of the pastries from breakfast. The bagels and croissants had all gotten hard and gross, but Danya was already hungry for lunch and didn't know when they'd be able to find food again, so she insisted they stuff them in their backpacks. Together they snuck down the hallway to the steps leading outside. There was a little alcove at the end of the corridor. On one wall was a door marked OFFICE and just past that was a long hallway, at the end of which a long line of people stood waiting to be let off the boat.

"We'll just hang back till they're all gone," Pia said. She stopped by the office door, where there was a cardboard box labeled LOST AND FOUND. "Ooh, sparkly," she said, pulling out a pink jump rope and a skateboard covered in band stickers. "Hey, Sancho, want a ride?"

Danya shushed her, frowning. Voices sounded on the other side of the office door.

"Violet!" Danya hissed to Pia, pointing to the door. She lifted a finger to her mouth, motioning to keep quiet.

"Mom, you don't understand," Violet said behind the closed door. "I've already betrayed them."

"*I* don't understand?" another older voice said angrily. "Violet, it sounds like you're telling me that those two missing girls are hiding on this ship!"

"Well, yeah, but look at this! Look at all this money."

"She sold us out," Pia hissed. Danya nodded, a lump rising in her throat. She couldn't believe Violet would do that. She'd thought she was trying to help them. "What money do you think she's talking about?"

"Our parents must be giving a reward to whoever turns us in," Danya said, her voice cracking. Was this the *profound shock*? Her parents couldn't afford a reward. That was almost worse than Violet's betrayal.

"We've got to go. Now," Danya said. But before the girls and Sancho could sneak into the hallway, the door shot open. Violet stood in the office holding a laptop, a tall woman with the same short-cropped black hair and glasses right behind her.

When she saw Danya and Pia, Violet's eyes became two wide circles. "No! You can't leave!"

"Violet, please calm down and call the police," said her mother. "Girls, I'm going to need you to come with me."

"Wanna bet?" Pia said. As Violet's mother headed toward them, Pia belly-flopped onto the skateboard and launched forward. Violet and her mother leapt out of the way as Pia went barreling down the hall past them. "Danya, Sancho, come on!"

Danya quickly climbed onto Sancho's back and pulled his ear. He tore down the hall after Pia, Violet and her mother stumbling after them.

"Danya, Pia, wait!" Violet called. But Danya and Pia were going too fast to slow down. Pia's skateboard shot toward the line of people, who, screaming, pushed to the sides of the hall to let her past. Pia leapt from the skateboard before it rolled off the ship and grabbed for Sancho's reins, tugging Danya and her pony off the ship and down the dock toward land.

Danya brought Sancho into a trot, Pia running beside them. The dock led from the *Sailing Swan* down to a half-empty parking lot. They turned a corner at the end of the lot, and walls loomed ahead of them. A green-and-white sign announced that they'd reached Gatorville.

"Let's go inside," Pia yelled to Danya and Sancho. "It's our only choice!"

Danya glanced back over her shoulder at the ship. She didn't see Violet and her mother yet, but she knew they had to be just behind them. "Fine," she told Pia. "Let's go."

The entrance was shaped like the long, scaly mouth of an alligator, complete with jagged teeth and bloodred eyes.

Just beyond the alligator head looped a huge roller coaster. Danya could hear the distant sound of children laughing and screaming. Sancho stopped walking and shook his head, taking several steps back.

"Come *on*," Danya said, grabbing hold of Sancho's reins. She managed to pull the pony forward another few feet, but then Sancho dug his back hooves into the dirt and snorted, absolutely refusing to take another step forward.

"It's okay," Danya said, sliding off his back. "He'll have to hide out here. We probably can't bring ponies inside anyway."

The girls tied Sancho up near a small clearing of grass and dandelions, hidden from view by a thicket of trees. Sancho immediately started munching on the weeds, and when he turned his face up to watch Danya walk away, his whole muzzle was already yellow from the flowers.

The girls peeked out from behind the trees, but there was still no sign of Violet.

"Maybe we should just keep moving," Danya whispered. "If they haven't caught up to us yet . . ."

"You think it's going to be hard for them to catch up to us on the road?" Pia said. "They'll expect us to keep moving. If we hide out here until they give up, we'll have a better chance. Come on." Pia quickly paid their entrance fee, and together the girls crept beneath the rows of gator teeth.

Just inside Gatorville was a souvenir shop. Posters of alligators in swamps papered the walls. Danya ducked behind a stand of ceramic alligators and baseball caps designed to look like alligator heads.

"Maybe we should hide," she said. Pia bounced down the aisle behind her.

"Nonsense! Let's start looking for actual alligators." She stood on her tiptoes to see over the cases of souvenirs. "I wonder if there's a place where they let guests wrestle them. Do you think it costs any money?"

"Did someone say alligators?"

Pia and Danya both looked up to see a man standing at the end of the aisle. He was short and old, with fuzzy gray hair and an actual eye patch over one eye. Danya's own eyes widened at the sight of the patch, and she looked him over, taking in his black vest, striped shirt, and bright red scarf. She looked down at his legs and actually gasped—his pant legs were rolled up, revealing two wooden peg legs. He looked like he walked out of the Pirate's Booty restaurant. Danya turned to Pia, almost expecting her to ask the pirate if her was afraid of the darrrrrk.

"Wow," Pia said. "You're a real pirate, aren't you?"

The pirate looked over at Pia and winked with his good eye, holding out a hand for her to shake.

"The name's Petey," he said "Been working with the gators here for nearly twenty years."

Petey narrowed his eye, considering the girls carefully. "Say, you two look mighty familiar. You come here often?"

Danya's stomach dropped.

"We're reality television stars," Pia broke in before Danya could figure out what to say. "We're on that show *Square Dance Idol*. You've heard of it, right?"

"You know, I sold my TV awhile back. Must've seen y'all on a billboard or something. Now is my hearin' goin' or did one a' you gals say you wanted to meet a real live gator?"

"Ooh! I did," Pia said. Petey winked again (or maybe it was a tic? Danya couldn't be sure; he seemed to wink every few minutes). He spun in place and hobbled down the aisle.

"Reality television stars?" Danya hissed at Pia.

Pia smiled wide, showing off the missing space in her teeth. "Cool, right? I've been wanting to use that one for a while now. Come on."

Danya opened her mouth to mention her hiding idea again, but Pia grabbed her arm and pulled her along after him before she could say a word.

Petey led the two girls through the rest of Gatorville, past a merry-go-round filled with alligators and crocodiles wearing funny hats and around Gator Splash!—a ride consisting of dozens of twisty waterslides that let out into a huge pool. The girls dodged crowds of people holding alligator-shaped souvenir cups and had to hurry to keep up with Petey as a parade of actors dressed in reptile costumes marched behind them.

"This place *rules*!" Pia exclaimed, turning in place as she tried to take it all in. "When I grow up, I want to live here."

Danya shrugged. She could see what Pia meant—the place was pretty cool—but she couldn't keep herself from glancing over her shoulder every other minute, certain Violet and her mother had found them after all. Sweat gathered at her hairline, and she wiped it away with the back of her hand. Had it been this hot the entire time they'd been traveling? For some reason it seemed worse now. . . .

"You ain't seen nothing yet," Petey exclaimed. "This is my favorite part!" He led them into a building and showed them the alligators' cages and where they got fed, explaining how the specifically designed lights lining their tanks kept them warm and cool at all the right times.

Finally, he took them out back, to a giant arena lined by rows and rows of cracked, plastic seats. The arena had a four-foot fence surrounding it. Danya felt her heart give a little leap, and for a split second she stopped worrying about how much time they were losing or whether Violet and her mother had caught up to them. This place was so cool! She walked over to the fence and wrapped her hands around the chain links, searching the arena for something exciting. Were they going to see a real alligator perform?

"Whoa there, little lady. Might want to take a step away from that fence. The show'll be startin' soon. . . ."

Danya nodded, but before she could step away, she caught sight of something in the middle of the arena, glinting. Something gold.

"Do you see that?" Pia said in a whisper, coming up behind Danya. Danya swallowed, studying her cousin nervously. Pia had that look in her eye. It was the same look she got right before she decided to climb up to the roof to test out her theory that a vacuum would work as a hovercraft.

"Pia," Danya said carefully, "I don't think—"

"I think that's gold . . ." Pia interrupted her. Her eyes lit up like two matches. "And we need gold. For Sancho."

Before Danya could say another word, Pia scrambled up the side of the fence and dropped into the arena. Her long legs were a blur as she raced toward the sparkling object in the center of the arena.

She dropped to her knees in the middle of the arena and began to dig. Swallowing, Danya glanced at the audience gathered around them. People in the stands leapt to their feet, yelling and shouting for Pia to get out. What had Pia been *thinking*? Someone was sure to recognize her crazy hair and long, gangly limbs now! Besides, the show was going to start soon, and if Pia didn't get back here, they'd be caught or worse—Pia would be trapped in the arena with a bunch of alligators.

A security guard made his way over, and, unsure of what else to do, Danya pulled herself over the side of the fence and started to run. Maybe she could get to Pia and they could outrace the guard before one of the audience members told him who they were—that is, if the guard didn't know already.

Pia enclosed her fingers around something and pulled it from the dirt just as Danya reached her and yanked her to her feet. Danya glanced back over her shoulder, but the security guard froze at the side of the arena. Danya swallowed. That couldn't be a good sign.

"Pia, *hurry*, we need to—"

"Look at this!" Pia said, holding something up. "Isn't it just—oh."

Danya looked down at the object in her cousin's hands: a chocolate sheriff's badge covered in shiny golden tinfoil.

"I thought it was real gold," Pia mumbled just as a space in the dirt slid open, revealing a secret trapdoor on the other side of the arena. Danya's heart thudded in her chest, and for a moment she forgot about Violet and the security guard and the crowd of people who surely recognized them from *Runaway Watch*. Through her fear she could only think one thing: *What's in* there?

For a long moment nothing happened. Then an alligator crawled out of the hole, whipping its long, rough tail. The green scales were dull, and the sound of its snapping jaws echoed over the arena. Danya's heart dropped as the gator wriggled across the dirt, moving faster than she thought possible on those stubby legs. The crowd in the stands let out a collective gasp.

"We . . . we've got to go," Pia said, huddling close to Danya. The sound of Pia's voice made goose bumps crawl up Danya's arms. Pia sounded scared. Danya didn't think she'd ever heard her cousin sound that way before.

"Maybe it won't . . ." Danya started to say, but before she could finish her sentence, the alligator whipped around and its beady, black eyes found the two girls.

"See us," Danya finished. Fear flooded her chest as the alligator started toward them.

CHAPTER FOURTEEN

The Alligators, the Fight, and the Escape

The alligator sped toward Danya and Pia, its tail cracking behind it like a great, scaly whip. Its clawed feet kicked up dirt in the arena, filling the air around Danya and Pia with thick clouds of dust. It chomped as it moved, its jaws making wet clomping sounds that left Danya feeling ill. She stumbled backward, knocking into Pia. To her surprise, her fearless cousin was trembling.

"What do we do?" Pia hissed. Before Danya could answer, Petey leapt over the side of the four-foot fence and raced between the girls and the alligator, his peg legs leaving pockmarks in the dirt. He plopped down on the head of the gator, forcing its teeth shut with a snap.

"You little ladies should get out of here," he shouted as the gator wriggled beneath him.

Just then, the gator pulled one of Petey's peg legs off and crushed it to splinters between its teeth.

"I think he needs our help!" Danya said, unable to pull her eyes away from Petey. He laughed at the alligator, but she could see the fear in his eyes.

"How's that taste?!" Petey said as the gator chomped his peg leg to pieces. "There's more where that came from—got a whole closet full of peg legs at home."

"You need to grab its jaw and clamp it shut," Pia yelled at Petey as they backed away toward the fence. She fumbled around inside her bag and pulled out a banana.

"Use your arms," Danya added, trying to be helpful. Pia hurled the banana with a grunt. The alligator wriggling beneath Petey caught the fruit in midair and swallowed it with a chomp. "I saw on Animal Planet that the muscles to open their jaws are really weak and—"

"You girls need to get out of here!" Petey called again. "It isn't safe."

The alligator was starting to pull free. Petey grabbed one of its stubby legs and flipped it onto its back.

"Take that!" Pia yelled. She pulled a croissant out of her bag and hurled it at the alligator's head.

"You can't fight an alligator with pastries!" Danya shouted.

Pia just shrugged. "Why not? They're hard as rocks." She fumbled through her backpack and finally held up the glittery pink jump rope from the boat's lost and found. "Petey, use this!" she yelled, tossing the jump rope over to him.

"Tie its mouth," Danya yelled. Petey fumbled one-handed for the rope and wrapped it around the gator's jaws. "Its mouth is the worst part."

"I think he's good." Petey stood, hobbling around on one leg as he wiped his hands on his jeans. The alligator tried to open its mouth, but the jump rope held tied. The moment he straightened, a sound like the roar of an ocean wave washed over all three of them. . . .

It was the audience. They were going wild! They were on their feet, shouting and hooting, clapping so enthusiastically Danya actually took a step backward, like she was worried the force of their applause would knock her down.

"Wow," she said.

"Impressive, ladies." Petey hopped over to the girls on the single peg leg still attached to his body. "I should be offering you my job."

"Wouldn't say no to that," Pia said, grinning. "And

that's number eleven on the list—face a personal demon. . . . Snap? Hey, Snap, are you listening to me?"

Danya wasn't listening. Cold dread clogged her throat as she watched the audience leap to their feet, clapping and cheering. With all of those people watching them, someone was sure to recognize her and Pia from *Runaway Watch*! In fact, she suspected someone had already called the cops and told them where to find them. This was a disaster.

Almost as soon as that thought entered her head, Danya spotted someone in the audience—Violet! There was no sign of her mother, but Violet was shoving past cheering audience members as she tried to make her way to the arena, her red-framed glasses glinting in the sun. Danya grabbed Pia's arm.

"Pia . . ." Danya said. "Violet's here! We have to go. Like, now!"

"We can't go," Pia insisted. "Petey just offered us a job."

Danya blinked. "Wait, what? You can't take a job!"

"Why wouldn't I? It could be fun!"

From the corner of her eye, Danya saw Violet moving closer. "Come on!" she hissed, and yanked Pia toward the edge of the arena.

"Hey, watch it," Pia muttered. "I'm coming, I'm coming."

The two girls scrambled back over the side of the arena

as the audience rushed in around them, snapping photographs and shoving scraps of paper into their faces for autographs.

"*Runaways!*" Danya thought she heard someone say. Then, "Call the police. . . ."

"Pia," Danya hissed. "Let's go!"

Pia was busy smiling at her fans, signing autographs, and posing for photos, but when Danya grabbed her arm, she rolled her eyes.

"All right! I said I was coming."

"Where y'all going!" Petey called, hopping after them. "I'll be in my office if you change your mind! It's just down by . . ." The crowd's cheers grew louder, drowning out the sound of his voice.

"Wait!" another voice yelled. Danya glanced up in time to see the very tip of Violet's floppy sun hat shoving its way through the crowd toward them.

Ducking away from the crowd, Danya pulled Pia beneath the bleachers, where the two of them could catch their breath. It was dark under there, and the ground was covered in discarded soda cups, sticky wads of watermelon-flavored gum, and a thick film of gooey *something* Danya couldn't identify.

Danya nudged a discarded fish-shaped mask with the

toe of her sneaker. "Maybe we should grab the mask? We could, like, use it to hide our identities. . . ."

Pia wrinkled her nose, and Danya thought her skin actually turned a little green. "You aren't seriously thinking of putting that on your face, are you?"

Danya swallowed, staring down at the mask. There was something brown crusted over the side, and the other half of the fish had been eaten off by mice. Pia was right—there was no way that was touching her face.

The two girls crept forward, bent low so they wouldn't knock their heads against the bottoms of the bleachers. Danya didn't think Violet had seen them hide, but she had no way to be sure. When she and Pia reached the end of the bleachers, she hesitated.

"Why did you stop?" Pia asked. "I thought we had to keep moving."

"We do, but . . ." Danya swallowed. Just across the walkway leading to the arena was the ticket booth, with a rickety sign out front reading GATORVILLE! $8 SHOW TICKETS! $10 FOR REAL BITE! It looked deserted enough, but Danya had no way of knowing whether someone from the audience would wander around to this side of the bleachers and spot them. She didn't know if they could chance it.

Behind the booth was a tiny wooden shed—the perfect

hiding place. But Danya and Pia had to make it across the walkway without Violet or anyone else seeing them first.

"Okay," Danya said, letting out a whoosh of breath. "We run for the shed on three. One . . ."

"Three!" Pia squealed. Then she grabbed Danya's arm and yanked her out from under the bleachers.

CHAPTER FIFTEEN

Death, Fortune, and the Circus

Danya's heart beat wildly in her chest. As she and Pia raced across the walkway, she whirled around to see if anyone was watching them. But the wind blew her hair over her eyes, and the next thing she knew she and Pia were stumbling into the shed, slamming the door behind them.

"Whoo!" Pia said with a sigh, slumping against the door. "That was close."

"Close?" Danya said between gasps for breath. "Pia, we're still on the run, we're wasting time, and we have to find a way back to Sancho. We just traded one bad hiding place for another!"

"I'm working on that." Pia's eyes were already narrowed,

scanning the contents of the dimly lit shed. "Hey, aren't those from the parade?" she said, pointing to a pile of scaly fabric on a shelf over her head. Danya shrugged, and Pia quickly climbed on top of a wooden sign of an alligator wearing sunglasses and pulled the fabric off the shelf. It fell to the floor in a heap.

"What are we going to do with those?" Danya said, nudging the fabric with her foot.

"I have a plan," Pia announced, wobbling a bit on the alligator sign as she jumped back to the ground. She snatched a hat shaped like an alligator's long, tooth-filled mouth. "We're going incognito."

A few short minutes later the girls crept across the parking lot, dressed in oversize reptilian costumes. Pia was covered head to toe in green scales, an alligator nose poking out from her head like a visor, while long, pointy teeth hung down over her face. Her tail swept behind her lethally—it'd almost knocked Danya over twice.

Danya was less excited about her own snake costume, which was little more than an oversize, scaly silver tube sock. Her legs were bound together awkwardly, which meant she had to kind of hop along instead of walking like a normal person. At least there were two armholes, so she could use her hands.

"Sancho!" Danya called when they reached the clearing

where they'd hidden him. She wasn't quite used to her snake costume, and as she tried to rush forward, she stumbled over her own tail and ended up crashing, face-first, into the half-eaten dandelion patch near Sancho's feet.

"Ugh," she muttered, spitting out a mouthful of weeds. She couldn't see Sancho, but she felt a tug on the top of her snake costume and suddenly she was being lifted to her feet. As soon as she was standing, Sancho started licking her face with his scratchy tongue. Horsey kisses.

"Ew," Danya said, giggling as she swatted Sancho away. "I missed you, too, buddy. Can't believe you recognized me in my costume!"

"What's next on the map?" Pia asked. Danya pulled the map out of her back pocket. She squinted down at it, studying the trail that stretched across the page.

"It looks like we need to get to Orlando," Danya said, following their trail across the map with one finger. "It's probably too far for us to ride Sancho. Maybe we should find some sort of—"

"What about that?" Pia interrupted, pointing past the tree grove where they were still hiding and across the parking lot. Danya squinted through the tree branches, seeing a large, charter bus parked near the entrance. Curly red words on its side read TALLAHASSEE SCHOOL FOR THE CIRCUS ARTS.

"You want to join the circus?" Danya asked.

"No." Pia shook her head. "Well, I mean, not today. But it looks like they have a bus big enough to fit Sancho."

"Tallahassee *is* closer to Lake Buena Vista. . . ." Danya chewed on her lower lip, studying her map. "But what if they aren't headed back tonight?"

"They have to go back *sometime*."

Danya supposed that was true, though there was still the question of how they were going to sneak on board a circus bus with a pet pony without being recognized as nationally famous runaways.

A trio of performers stood not far from the bus's back tires. One of them juggled seven different multicolored bottles, while another walked in circles around him on her hands. The third—dressed like a clown—was hunched over, trying to pin a plastic flower to his shirt. Before he could get it right, the flower squirted a stream of water directly into his face.

Danya giggled. Pia pulled her alligator mask back down over her face. "Come on," she said, and started across the parking lot. "Let's go talk to them."

"Why would we talk to them? Wait, do you think we can convince them we're part of the circus, too?" Danya trailed after Pia, giving Sancho's reins a tug to get him to follow them through the trees and across the parking lot. He snorted, and when Danya looked down to see what was wrong, he licked her upside the face, pushing her curls back beneath the snake mask.

"Oh, thanks, buddy!" Danya said, making sure the rest of her hair was carefully tucked beneath her mask. Sancho was right. If they ran into Violet again, she might recognize them.

"Hi," Pia said, approaching the performers. The juggler looked up, startled, and dropped one of his bottles. The acrobatic girl who'd been walking around on her hands caught it with her foot seconds before it hit the ground. As she wrapped her toes around the glass, Danya saw that her toenails were painted sparkly orange.

"Hi," the upside-down girl said, tossing the bottle back to the juggler. She turned on her hands so she could face Danya and Pia, and her thick, brown curls trailed on the ground behind her. "You guys need help or something?"

"Are you really in the circus?" Pia took off her alligator head and turned awkwardly in her suit. Her long, scaly tail trailed behind her, and static electricity made her already spiky hair stand straight up.

"Pia!" Danya hissed. "Your *mask*."

Sancho whinnied and kicked at the concrete, causing the clown to look up from his plastic squirting flower, but Pia just waved their concerns away.

"We're studying to be performers with the Tallahassee

School of the Circus Arts," the clown explained. He flicked the flower, and a sad stream of water dribbled onto his shirt. "You two look like performers. Are you with Gatorville?"

"Not *exactly* . . ." Danya explained. "We're actually looking for a ride to—"

"We're both really curious about circus school," Pia interrupted. "Like, did you guys have to go to high school first? And do you get to pick your specialty right away? I think I'd be a wicked lion tamer."

"Pia, come on." Danya shook her head. "We actually need to get to Lake Buena Vista. Could we ride with you?"

"Oh, you're with Disney, then?" The upside-down girl flipped back onto her feet and shook out her bushy brown curls. "We could probably fit you in back. We're leaving in . . ."

"Half an hour, I think," the juggler said.

"That's right—in half an hour. Do you need help loading up your pony?"

"That would be great," Danya said. She smiled at Pia before realizing her friend couldn't see her beneath the giant snake head. Too bad. If Pia hadn't noticed the circus bus, they'd have been stranded for sure.

The formerly upside-down girl led Sancho up the steps to the bus while Danya and Pia struggled to get their costumes through the door. They followed Sancho all the way to the very back. Danya got stuck between the seats a few times; snake costumes were not designed to easily slip down bus aisles—even Sancho didn't have as much trouble as she did. They angled their tails beneath the seat so they could sit down. Sancho plopped down in the middle of the aisle, letting out a huff of air that made the hair hanging over his eyes flutter.

"I feel sorry for you, buddy," Danya said once she was in her seat. "Tails are really difficult."

Sancho's head popped up, and he blew air out from between his lips indignantly. He swished his long tail back and forth.

"Right, right," Danya said, giggling. "I forgot, *your* tail isn't difficult at all."

Sweaty after her climb up the steps, Danya pulled her snake head off and set it down on the seat next to her. She glanced out the window, still nervous that Violet or someone from the Gatorville audience would manage to track them down. But the parking lot was empty.

"I'm Da . . . Dakota," she lied to the acrobat girl, using the same fake name Pia had given her before, even if they hadn't been recognized yet. "And this is, er . . . Polly."

She motioned to Pia, who grimaced. *"Polly?"* she whispered to Danya when the other girl had her head turned. "My fake name was *Prissy!*"

"And that's better?" Danya hissed back. "Anyway, thanks so much for all your help," Danya added loud enough for the acrobat girl to hear.

"Don't mention it." The girl shook her head. Her hair seemed to get bigger and curlier every time she moved. "My name is Penn. Make yourselves comfortable. The other performers will start boarding soon."

Pia and Danya sat at the back of the bus, huddled in their alligator costumes, watching as the performers filed up the stairs. First were the tightrope walkers in their skin-tight, sparkly spandex uniforms. They took the seats near the door, and instead of sitting down like normal people, they balanced on the backs of the seats, rising to their tip-toes and doing back bends. They looked graceful, Danya thought. Like ballerinas.

"Show-offs," Pia muttered, and Danya laughed.

Next, a group of clowns crowded onto the bus. Danya tried to count them, but there were just too many—fat clowns and skinny clowns, sad clowns and happy clowns, clowns so tall that they had to crouch down to get into the bus and clowns short enough to walk beneath the bus seats without crouching at all. All of the clowns—every last one—piled onto the same seat near the window.

Danya watched as they fit together like a jigsaw. Two tall, skinny clowns sat down first, and three short, fat clowns climbed onto their laps. A sixth clown stretched out on the back of the seat. Two tiny clowns huddled on the floor, and another tall, lanky clown slid below the seat, with only his head still in the bus aisle. He placed his head on his folded arms and immediately fell asleep.

"Wow . . ." Danya said, not turning away until they were all seated. "Do you think they're practicing?"

"Why else would they sit like that?" Pia added, wrinkling her nose. "It looks really uncomfortable."

After the clowns, were more performers in bright, sparkling outfits—lion tamers and jugglers and a group of trapeze artists who Penn sat next to and started talking with animatedly.

"You know," Danya said, "no one else is dressed like an alligator."

"It got us onto the bus, didn't it?" Pia said. Before Danya could comment, one last performer climbed on.

This performer didn't look like the others. She wore a flowy dress with long sleeves, and she was very small and very old. Her arms and legs were so thin that Danya imagined her bones must be the size of pencils, and she walked with a cane, hobbling a little as she made her way down the aisle. Despite her size, she didn't seem frail—her energy seemed to fill the entire bus. Rings glittered from each of her fingers, and gold and pearl necklaces were strung around her neck.

The old performer grinned at the others as she made her way to the back of the bus. She settled into the seat right in front of Danya and Pia.

Danya nervously clutched her snake head in her lap, trying to decide whether she should wear it for the entire trip. Someone could still recognize them after all—you could never be too careful. Before she could decide, the woman turned in her seat and smiled at Danya. Her eyes were huge and rimmed in thick, long eyelashes.

"Hello there," she said. "My, what beautiful reptile costumes."

"Thank you," Danya and Pia said together. When the old woman didn't turn back around, Pia cleared her throat.

"What do you do in the circus?" she asked.

"Oh, I'm retired," the old woman explained. "But I used to do a bit of everything. I started on the tightrope, and when my bones got too old for that, I did a little clowning and lion-taming. Now I teach at the school."

The woman's thin, brightly painted lips twisted into a smile. She slipped a deck of cards out of one of her sleeves so gracefully they seemed to appear out of thin air.

"I also do this," she said, spreading the cards out

across the back of the seat. Danya and Pia leaned forward in awe.

The cards didn't look like the normal red and blue playing cards Danya had at home. These were larger, for one thing, and they weren't covered in numbers and symbols. Instead they displayed beautiful, elaborate pictures. One showed a blindfolded woman in a white dress holding two crossed swords. Another showed a single golden cup balanced on a man's palm.

The bus started to move, and the old woman swept the cards back up into one wrinkled hand.

"I am Madame Angelica," she explained, shuffling the deck. The bus rocked back and forth a little as it pulled out of the parking lot, but Madame Angelica held fast to the cards, shuffling them easily. "I read the tarot. Tell people's futures."

"Like a prophet?" Pia asked, pulling the Ferdinand and Dapple book out of her bag. Danya knew from reading the book so many times that hero's task number twelve was *Speak to a prophet*. When she'd first read the book, she'd had to ask her mom what that word meant because she'd never heard it before.

"Ah . . ." Madame Angelica said, batting her long, dark eyelashes. "It seems you've been expecting me. Well, then, I suppose I could reveal a little of your futures. Just a taste, okay?"

"Really?" Pia shot Danya an eager look, and even Danya couldn't help feeling a tiny thrill of excitement. She knew tarot cards were fake, but she'd never had her future read by a professional fortune-teller before.

"Sure," Madame Angelica said. She fanned the cards out so the beautiful pictures were facedown and all Danya could see was the scrolling black-and-gold design on the back. "Pick a card—just one!—and I'll tell you what it means."

Up to the challenge, Sancho sat straight up and began nibbling at a card on the end.

"Sancho!" Danya warned, but Madame Angelica just laughed and flipped the card over.

"Don't worry," she said, showing the card to Danya. A huge, golden cup covered the card, filled with silver water. "This is the ace of cups, a wonderful card. It means he is loved."

Sancho grinned, swishing his tail, and Danya tickled him beneath the chin. Next, Pia inched up in her seat, pulling off one of her alligator gloves. Madame Angelica told her to think of a question, and Pia nodded. She wiggled her fingers over the cards—then snatched one half-hidden by the fortune-teller's thumb. Smiling, she flipped it over.

The card depicted a knight sitting atop a white horse. The knight wore a golden mask that looked like a skull, and he carried a black flag. There was a single word written below him: DEATH.

Pia's face went pale, and the smile slipped from her lips. "I'm going to die?" she asked in a quiet voice.

"Pia, no," Danya insisted, even as nerves pricked at the back of her neck. She forced herself to look away from the creepy death card. "This isn't real—it's just a game!"

Madame Angelica laughed and took the card from Pia's frozen hands. "Oh, the death card." She shook her head. "This might be the most misunderstood card in my entire deck. No one's going to die, child. The death card indicates a passing, yes, but not necessarily of a life. Think of it as a passing of an event."

Madame Angelica blinked and studied Pia's face for a long moment. Finally, she nodded.

"Something has happened to you, my dear," she said. "Something huge. It feels like everything has changed."

"Wait, what? Nothing in Pi—I mean Priss—I mean *Polly's* life is changing," Danya said, hoping Madame Angelica didn't notice how badly she'd stumbled over the name. But even as the words were leaving her lips, she felt a tug in the back of her head. That wasn't entirely true, was it? Danya had noticed the signs, even if she hadn't wanted to believe them. Pia had been secretive lately. For the first time in their lives, there'd been things Pia kept from her, things Danya didn't know. Pia shot a guilty look at Danya, then looked back to the fortune-teller — nodding silently.

Madame Angelica smiled and reached forward, giving Pia's hand a squeeze.

"Have hope, my child! The passing of one thing does not mean the passing of all things. Give this time, and things will get better. You will see."

Danya shifted in her seat, not quite sure what to say. She thought of how odd Pia had been acting during this trip, how she'd been weirdly happy some moments and strangely sad at others. Something was going on with her best friend, and she didn't know what it was.

Danya pulled at a loose thread in her snake costume. There'd been a time when she'd wondered if she and Pia were really just two halves of the same girl: Pia was the adventurous, athletic, and loud side, and Danya the cautious, smart, and thoughtful one. But now Danya looked at her best friend and saw an entirely different person. Someone she wasn't even sure if she really knew.

As Madame Angelica began shuffling her deck again, Danya tried to catch her cousin's eye. But Pia kept her head bowed, staring at her own hands, which were clenched in her lap.

"And now you, my dear," Madame Angelica said.

Danya held her breath and pulled off one snake glove, letting her fingers hover above the cards. She still didn't believe in this stuff, she told herself. But now she wasn't so sure. Pia's reading had seemed pretty accurate.

"Before you choose," Madame Angelica said, "I want you to think, *hard*, about the question for which you seek an answer."

Danya nodded. She closed her eyes and thought about Sancho, about her grandmother, about her parents' money troubles and her hero's quest to save the day. As she lowered her hand to the deck of cards, she let one question fill her head.

Will I get what I came for? Will I find a way to save Sancho?

Her fingers settled onto a card. Opening her eyes, she slid the card out of the deck and flipped it over.

It was a picture of a young boy wearing a red tunic and a green, feathered cap. The boy held a golden circle with a picture of a star inside it. The card was upside down and Danya started to turn it over, but Madame Angelica stopped her, placing one wrinkled hand over her own.

"Oh no, you must leave it as it is," the fortune-teller said. "The position of the card is almost as important as the card itself. It all tells me something about how your future will unfold."

She took the card from Danya and stared down at it with narrowed eyes. For a moment the old woman was quiet.

"I see," she said finally. "This is the page of pentacles. You are seeking fortune, no? You are on a long journey?"

Danya's heart leapt into her chest. She nodded.

"This card tells me you feel guilt. Blame. It's standing in the way of your success, preventing you from seeing the fortunes you already have."

Fear and nerves pierced Danya's chest like a hot knife. She swallowed hard as the image of fire in the sky and air thick with smoke filled her memory. She heard Jupiña's scared whinnies, felt Sancho's neck grow cold with fear beneath her hands as they raced toward the stables.

"What are you talking about?" she asked in a small voice.

Madame Angelica smiled, shaking her head. Her frizzy blond hair puffed up around her face. "You are blaming yourself for something. But the fates say you must let this go. Whatever it was, it was not your fault. In order to get the fortune you seek, you must forgive yourself."

Danya's eyes burned, and she had to look quickly away.

Forgive herself? For what she did? The fortune-teller was wrong. That would be impossible.

"Child," Madame Angelica continued. She leaned forward, taking Danya's hand. "We all think we know what we need from this life, but only time can show us whether or not we are correct. This is a good card—it tells me you are brave and pure of heart. You will be successful, ultimately. But you must look to yourself. Find your inner strength to deal with the hand you've been dealt."

Madame Angelica smiled and slipped the card back into the deck." Good luck to you both, you great adventurers. The road ahead will be dangerous, treacherous, and very possibly terrifying." She winked. "But a true hero's path is never easy."

CHAPTER SIXTEEN

Mud, Rain, and Tears

As the bus bumped along, the sky outside Danya's window grew darker. Madame Angelica was taking a nap now, and most of the other performers on the bus were sleeping as well. Danya wished she could sleep, but her mind was moving too fast. Finally, she pulled out her notebook and her lucky purple gel pen. On the very last page, she jotted down a line for each day she'd been away from home. There was one for the night they crept onto Turtle's truck, one more for the night they spent at Graceland, and a third on the cruise ship. . . .

Three whole days away from home. Danya felt suddenly light-headed as she looked down at her wobbly pen marks. That meant today was Wednesday. She had one more day to reach her grandmother and get the money for Sancho. She capped her pen and tapped it against her leg, thinking. What would happen if the bald man showed up at her house and Sancho wasn't there? Would her dad get in trouble? They had a contract, Danya knew, and her dad had already spent the money the man gave him paying for the mortgage. Could her dad go to jail if she didn't get home in time?

Danya shook her head, trying to force that horrible thought away. Sighing, she reached down to scratch Sancho's head, worried he might be uncomfortable, but he was fast asleep, too. The hair hanging over his nose fluttered as he snored.

Outside, thunder rumbled and the clouds broke open. Rain poured down. It slapped against the ground and the side of the bus and tapped on Danya's window like an old friend. She sighed and leaned against the window, watching the lines of water trail down the glass. Pia wasn't sleeping, either, but they hadn't spoken since they'd gotten their fortunes told. Danya hadn't been able to think of a thing to say. Every time she opened her mouth, the only thing that came to her mind was . . .

In order to get the fortune you seek, you must forgive yourself.

She clenched her eyes shut and pressed her forehead against the rain-cooled glass, trying not to think about it.

Before long, the bus pulled off of the well-lit highway and traveled down a dark, muddy road. For the first time since picking a card from Madame Angelica's deck, Pia glanced up.

"Where do you think they're taking us?"

Danya shrugged. "Wherever it is, it looks muddy."

The bus slowly wound its way down the muddy road, which was longer and darker than Danya thought possible. Finally, it slowed to a stop, and the engine sputtered off. The door screeched open, and flashlights flicked on as the performers began to file outside.

A shadow with big, bushy hair made its way to the back of the bus. Once it was standing in front of Pia and Danya, a light flicked on, illuminating Penn's face.

"Hey there, reptiles," she said, holding the flashlight under her chin. "We're all heading out to put up our tents. Think you two can handle this one? We're just going to the clearing up ahead. You can't miss it."

She handed Pia a blue canvas and a bundle of metal poles. Danya assumed those things came together to form some sort of tent-like structure, though she had no real idea how.

"We're supposed to do this in the rain?" Pia asked.

"And in the dark. The dark rain." Danya poked at the pile of tent, half hoping it would leap from Pia's arms and build itself.

"Oh, this is for you, too," Penn added, motioning to the flashlight. "When you get off the bus, just turn left and follow the dirt path for about a hundred feet. Do you think you'll need help?"

Danya was just opening her mouth to say yes, of course they needed help, when Pia interrupted her.

"Nah," she said. "Looks easy."

"Cool." Penn flicked off the flashlight and tossed it to Danya before scurrying back out into the dark.

"I could have used help," Danya said under her breath. Pia didn't seem to hear her.

"I guess we should—" Before she could finish her sentence, Pia was interrupted by a crack of thunder so loud it shook the bus. Sancho woke with a start, snorting as he struggled to his feet.

"—go?" she finished. Danya glanced out the window and shivered.

By the time the two girls and Sancho negotiated their bodies (and tails) out of the bus, there was a small circle of tents set up amid the trees. Flashlights blinked on and off behind the canvas walls.

"Looks like we're on our own," Danya said. Sancho whinnied and nudged her forward with his nose.

Together the girls dragged themselves through the mud (Danya lost one scaly foot and her left, clawed glove) and found a dampish, flattish area of land beneath a dripping tree.

Pia dropped the tent onto the ground, and the girls knelt next to it. Danya picked up two poles and tried to get them to stand in the mud. Sancho held them steady with his nose, and for a moment, they kind of seemed like they would balance . . . but then a particularly large raindrop fell from the sky and knocked them over. Sancho scurried out of their way, his hooves making hollow plomping sounds in the mud.

"There are these short, kind of pointy stick things," Pia said, holding up a wooden stake. "I think we're supposed to, like, tie them to the poles using the edges of the tent."

"That makes sense," Danya said.

The girls worked together in silence trying to ignore the rain that plastered their hair to their foreheads, and dripped down the backs of their costumes, and the way their scaly legs sank low into the mud, so they had to stop every few minutes to yank them out. Even Sancho looked miserable. He tried to help by holding the flashlight in his mouth, but mud stuck to his mane and tail and hooves, making it hard for him to move.

Danya kept thinking about her and Pia's secret fort back home, with its twinkly Christmas lights and stacks and stacks of books lining the walls. But the muddy, wet tent was nothing like her hideout, and thinking about how cozy and warm she'd be if she were home right now just depressed her.

"At least we don't have to worry about anyone recognizing us," she muttered under her breath. In the dark, rainy night, not a single person alive would've been able to tell that Pia and Danya were the girls from *Runaway Watch*. That thought made Danya feel a little better . . . until another crack of thunder burst through the sky, making her jump.

Finally, after over an hour of tying and pounding and yanking and balancing, the pile of canvas and poles had taken on a tent-like shape. The girls stood back to survey their handiwork.

"It's done it's done it's done!" Pia said, her teeth clattering together in the cold. She waved her arms in the air and did a funny alligator dance that involved tapping her feet, wiggling her shoulders, and spinning in a circle. Sancho tried to dance, too, but he couldn't really move his legs, so it just looked like he was wiggling his bottom.

"Finally!" Danya said. "It's *freezing*!"

A clap of thunder sounded, and Sancho whinnied, rearing back. "Easy, buddy," Danya said, grabbing his reins. Pia kept dancing. She added a new move where she clapped while doing a leaping spin.

"Wait!" Danya said as Pia spun to perform the move again. Her long, scaly alligator tail swept into the tent, knocking the canvas and poles back into the mud.

For a long moment Danya couldn't move. She stared, frozen, at the ruined tent as water dripped down the back of her costume and thunder rumbled in the distance. Sancho whickered under his breath, pawing at the mud sadly.

"Whoops . . ." Pia said, quickly moving to pick up the muddy pile of canvas and poles. "I can fix this. . . ."

Danya shook her head. She couldn't remember a time she'd been more wet or cold or miserable. Pia shuffled over to Danya, her tail making slapping noises as she dragged it through the mud.

"I can fix this," she said again. "It'll be up in no time. And don't make that face, Snap. We'll just have to make the best of things until I—"

"Make the best of things?" Danya's voice was louder than usual and squeaky, like she might break into tears at any moment. "How are we supposed to make the best of things? Things are awful!"

"Danya . . ." Pia frowned. "Look, I know I messed up, but yelling at me isn't going to help. . . ."

"Maybe I don't *want* to help," Danya yelled. "You think it's easy cleaning up your messes all the time? While you're running around causing trouble and breaking everything you touch, someone has to be responsible. This was supposed to be about saving Sancho, but all I've been doing this entire trip is rescuing *you*."

"Maybe you don't remember," Pia said, her words short. "But this whole trip was *your* stupid idea. I wouldn't even be here if—"

"If *what*?" Danya interrupted. Anger clawed at her chest and her heart thudded. "You said you wanted to help me, Pia. If you hate all of this so much, why did you come at all?"

"Because I couldn't stay at home!" Pia snapped. She was crying now, and her words were interrupted by hiccups that shook her skinny shoulders. "My parents are getting divorced, Danya. That's why they sent me to stay with you and your family."

Danya opened her mouth, then closed it again, not sure what to say. "Pia, I didn't . . ."

"My dad isn't just visiting his sister," Pia continued. "He's living there because he and my mom can't even be in the same room together anymore. They've spent so much time fighting and yelling they barely even notice I'm there."

Danya swallowed. Her mouth was suddenly dry. She thought back on the last few days. How Tía Carla was crying. How Pia told the woman at the edge of the river that her parents didn't care about her. How insistent she was that they run away. How happy she'd been since they'd been gone.

How had Danya never noticed that things had been so bad when they left? How had she missed something so big?

Pia let out another hiccup. "You remember how Petey offered us that job at Gatorville?" she said, sniffing, and Danya nodded. "I really wanted to take it, Danya. There's no reason for me to go home, and I'm good with the alligators. Maybe . . . maybe things would be better if I really did run away. For real."

"Pia, no!" Danya didn't know what to say. It was like a low ringing started in her ears, making everything around her seem far away. "Pia, you can't."

"Why not, Danya? You don't need me for this stupid adventure. I might as well go back. At least there would be a place for me there," Pia said.

"There's a place for you *here*, Pia. With me. Who's going to make a pillow fortress with me when I'm sick? Or sleep next to me after my dad has told a scary story?

You're my best friend, no matter what happens with your parents."

"You really mean that?" Pia sniffed.

"Of course!" Danya insisted. "You're like a sister to me, Pia. I could never have made it this far without you. I *need* you, Pia. Every day."

Pia hiccupped again and Danya waddled over to her, ignoring the way her tail stuck in the mud. She wrapped her arms around her cousin as Pia hiccuped and sniffled and tried to keep herself from crying. Sancho nudged his nose between them, wanting to be part of the hug, too.

The girls and Sancho stood like that for a long time, even as the rain poured around them and thunder rumbled in the distance.

CHAPTER SEVENTEEN

The Sunnyside Cul-de-Sac
Rebel Motorcycle Club for Grandpas

The next morning the circus performers helped Danya and Pia pack up and dropped them off at the Kissimmee train station.

"We really wish we could take you farther," Penn said as Pia and Danya stepped off the bus. Her brown curls puffed up around her, making her head look several sizes larger than a normal head.

Penn had found the girls that morning, crouched down inside their costumes like turtles while Sancho burrowed under the canvas tent, shivering. After making them each eat a stack of the apple pumpkin pancakes Lion Tamer Eddie made on his camping stove, she helped them strip the reptile skins off, and she even gave them some new clothes to wear from the circus school costume closet. Pia wore a rhinestone-encrusted purple-and-pink spandex trapezist costume, and Danya was dressed in a pair of the smallest clown's polka-dot pants and rainbow-colored suspenders. As silly as the costume looked, Danya was just glad to be wearing something clean, that didn't have a tail.

The clowns had all gotten together and even managed to clean the mud off Sancho's fur by squirting him with water from the flowers attached to their jackets at the same time.

"You've helped so much already," Danya said, adjusting the strap of her suspenders. "I'm sure we'll be able to figure it out."

And she found she actually *meant* that. She'd felt so desperate and lost the night before, standing in the rain with Pia. But together they'd gotten through it. That made Danya feel like they could get through anything.

Pia and Danya waved as the circus bus pulled away. It was mid-afternoon now, but last night's rain still covered the ground and the train station benches, making the grass beneath their shoes all soggy. The summer sky was all pink and blue and hazy from the lifting fog.

The damp air seemed to have a good effect on Sancho. He galloped in circles around the station before stopping near a patch of dandelions. He snorted and pawed at the dirt, then lowered his head and started to munch on the weeds and flowers.

Pia shuffled over to the train station bench and sat down.

"What do you think we should . . ." she started, but before she could finish her sentence, the girls heard a rumble in the distance, like the roar of thunder. Danya lifted her arms to cover her head, worried it would start raining again. But the sky above was blue and empty of clouds.

"Danya, look!" Pia said, pointing to the road.

A dozen or so men on motorcycles appeared in the distance. They wore leather jackets and black sunglasses, and they had on helmets decorated with pictures of dragons and bones and what looked like flaming swords. The men rode closer, and the rumbling roar of their engines grew louder, making the ground beneath Danya and Pia tremble.

"That doesn't look good," Danya said, shouting to be heard over the roar of the motorcycle engines. She sat down next to Pia and grabbed her hand. Even Sancho crouched behind the girls, shivering as the motorcycles came closer.

They won't stop here, Danya thought. *They'll keep going. They won't even see us. . . .*

But the men on the motorcycles didn't keep going. They slowed as they approached the train station, and like a flock of birds, they turned down the road together and pulled to a stop just a few feet from where Danya and Pia and Sancho huddled.

The man wearing the flaming sword helmet turned toward them and revved his engine. Then, placing one foot on the road to steady himself, he pulled the helmet off and put it under one arm.

Danya had to clench her lips together to keep her mouth from dropping open in shock. The man wasn't menacing at all—he was *old*. Wrinkles creased his face, and what little hair he had was pure, snowy white.

"Hi there, ladies," he said, smacking his lips. He had big, blue eyes, and his face looked kind. "Don't mean to bother you, but we're just stopping for a snack break. My name is Hank."

Once they'd all taken off their helmets, Danya realized none of the motorcyclists were terrifying. In fact, they were all pretty old—just like Hank. One had a long, hooked nose and droopy ears, and another had wild, bushy eyebrows that took up most of his forehead, and another had a WORLD'S BEST GRANDPA sticker on his helmet, covering up half a picture of a skull shooting lasers from its eye sockets. His motorcycle had a sidecar with a child's seat inside. All of the little old men, Danya noticed, had large, kind eyes and happy, crooked smiles.

The man with the crazy eyebrows wore a purple-and-yellow fanny pack strapped to his waist. "Who wants something to drink?" he said, pulling out a few juice boxes. "I have cran-apple and grape."

All the other old men shuffled over to him and took a juice box. Neither Danya nor Pia asked for one, but one of the old men walked over to them anyway.

"The name's Max," he said, handing each of the girls a juice box and giving them a gummy smile. Christmas had been months and months ago, but Max wore a reindeer sweater over his leather motorcycle pants. Rudolph's blinking red nose flashed on and off while he talked. "Now where are you ladies off to?"

Unable to look away from Max's sweater, Pia plucked the straw from her juice box and unwrapped it. "Where are *you* going?" she asked.

"Where *aren't* we going?" Max glanced at the other little old men and laughed. "You ladies are looking at the Sunnyside Cul-de-Sac Rebel Motorcycle Club."

"For grandpas," added the man with the WORLD'S BEST GRANDPA sticker on his helmet. He had dark skin and eyes, with a pair of tiny rectangular bifocals balanced on his nose. "My name's Dave. See, we're all retired, so we decided to ride cross-country on our bikes. We're meeting our grandchildren at Disney World."

"For Christmas!" Max added, puffing out his chest proudly.

Pia turned to Danya and raised an eyebrow.

"*Half* Christmas," Hank corrected. "We do it every year."

"Didn't you hear them, Snap? They're going to *Orlando*." To the grandpas Pia said, "We're going to Disney World, too."

Danya frowned. She had a feeling she knew what Pia was trying to do, but she couldn't be serious. These men were on *motorcycles*! There was no way they could accept a ride from them. And besides, they seemed a bit goofy, and maybe a little senile. That was pretty good news as it meant Danya didn't have to worry they'd be recognized, but she wasn't sure how safe it was to get on the back of a motorcycle with them.

"Pia . . ." Danya said in a warning voice. "I don't think . . ."

Before she could finish, Max spoke up. "What's that now?" he said, holding a wrinkled hand up to his ear. "Did you ladies say you *work* at Disney World?"

Danya stared at Pia pointedly. Max couldn't even see that they were only eleven years old. He probably wouldn't be able to see stoplights, either, or road signs, or other cars.

"This isn't *safe*," Danya hissed. Pia shrugged, slurping up some of her juice box.

"My grandmother is the same way, and I ride with her all the time," she muttered.

Max frowned. "What's that, dearie?" he said. "My hearing's not what it used to be."

"I said you're right," Pia answered loudly. "We do work at Disney World. We're actors in the . . . um, Small World ride. Because we're so short, you know."

Max nodded. There was a strange, faraway look in his eyes. "You know, I had a job once," he said. "I worked at a shoe store. I polished all of the shoes." He shook his head and glanced around the train station, frowning. "You probably won't be able to get a train from here. According to our maps, this hasn't been a working station for nearly ten years. But you could always ride with us."

Danya sucked the remaining juice from her box, squeezing the cardboard to get every last drop. She glanced over her shoulder at Sancho, who was still nibbling on dandelions. Even if this wasn't totally insane, there was no way Sancho would fit on the back of a motorcycle.

But maybe . . . She glanced back at the motorcycle with the sidecar attached to it, thinking.

"Do you think we could fit our pony in there?" she asked Max. Max narrowed his eyes at Sancho.

"Oh, your little dog would definitely fit. My son had this car made special so my dogs could ride with me, you know. I have two mastiffs who love motorcycle rides, and your little dog is much smaller than either of them."

Danya bit down on her lip to keep herself from correcting Max. He really *was* pretty confused. Sancho *was* smaller than a mastiff . . . but anyone could see he was a pony and not a dog! Still, Max had all these fancy harnesses and stuff—Sancho would probably be pretty safe.

"What do you think?" she whispered to Sancho. Sancho trotted over to the sidecar and flicked an ear—his way of saying, "Let's do it!" Grinning, Danya tickled him beneath the chin. He was getting so brave.

That's how Danya and Pia ended up on the backs of two motorcycles with Sancho strapped into the sidecar of a third. Since the Sunnyside Rebels were a grandpas' motorcycle club, they had special seat belts designed to keep the girls safe on their bikes.

Still, Danya kept her arms wrapped tightly around Max, not entirely able to convince herself that she wasn't going to fall off. They were going so fast, and the road was so bumpy, but Danya still managed to remain in her seat.

The grandpas slowed to take a sharp turn, driving up alongside a silver SUV. Danya stared through the windows, her eyes locking on a black-haired head in the front passenger seat. She faced away from the window, but Danya could just make out the edges of a red scarf sticking out at the figure's neck.

She held her breath, feeling cold all over. Short black hair—a red scarf! It was Violet, Danya was sure of it. She knew she should hide her face or duck down inside the motorcycle jacket Max had given her to wear so she wouldn't get cold. But all she could do was stare at the figure in the car, her heart thudding. She wrapped her arms tighter around Max, wishing he would drive faster.

The black-haired head turned to look out the window— and licked the glass with her big, pink tongue. It wasn't Violet at all. It was a black Lab wearing a red bandanna.

Danya exhaled, finally beginning to relax. She loosened her grip on Max and leaned back just a tiny bit to look around. Traveling by motorcycle wasn't a terrible way to go. The road and trees and grass flew past in a blur of colors and shapes, and the wind blew back her hair and filled her nose with the smells of the road and the outdoors and the lavender-scented laundry detergent Max used on his jean jacket. Every time the bike went a little faster or took a turn, Danya's heart leapt and she felt a rush of adrenaline.

They drove for over an hour, stopping only for bathroom

breaks and a quick lunch of strawberry-banana-broccoli smoothies and granola bars. (All of the motorcyclists were on special diets to keep their cholesterol down.)

Eventually the sun dipped low in the sky and afternoon shadows stretched out across the highway. It was still hours till nightfall but, one by one, the motorcyclists began flipping on their headlights. The sun was still bright enough that you could barely see the white beams on the road.

"Safety first," Max said to Danya over his shoulder. Danya nodded, and her stomach rumbled. She was not on a diet, and the smoothies and granola bars hadn't really filled her up. Luckily Max put on his turn signal, and the motorcyclists pulled into an old gas station.

While Max and the others stopped at the pumps to fill their bikes with gas, Danya and Pia ducked into the station with the last of their casino winnings. A teenage boy was reading a comic book at the register. Behind him was a television turned to some news channel.

"What do you think we should get?" Pia asked, poking at a bag of lime-flavored tortilla chips. "There aren't a lot of dinner things here."

Danya considered the stacks of candy and chips. "We should probably get something kind of healthy," she said eventually, pulling down a peanut butter candy bar and some real-fruit-flavored gummy bears. "That way we don't get sick or anything."

Pia agreed, and the girls grabbed a few other things— corn chips and pretzels and cookies made with milk chocolate because Danya remembered her mom saying that milk made your bones grow strong.

They took their food up to the counter to pay. The teenager put his comic book down on the counter and started to ring it up.

"Paper or plastic?" he asked. Danya didn't answer. She stared at the television behind his head. The news program had been interrupted by an emergency broadcast. The words MISSING CHILDREN flashed across the bottom of the screen, and above them were four people Danya recognized. Her mouth dropped open, and she grabbed Pia's arm.

"Pia . . . look!" she hissed. Pia glanced up at the television, and her eyes grew wide.

Their parents were on the TV screen—all four of them together. They were saying something into the camera, but the volume on the television was turned down so low that Danya couldn't hear what it was. A message flashed across the bottom of the screen: CONFIRMED SIGHTING OF MISSING GIRLS IN FLORIDA! AMBER ALERT IN EFFECT.

Danya swallowed and glanced at the teenage clerk, hoping he didn't get the sudden urge to turn around and glance at the television. Violet's mother must have called the cops after all—that's the only way they'd know she and Pia were here.

"Hey," the gas station clerk said. "Did you hear me? Paper or plastic?"

"Oh, um, plastic." Danya's hands were sweaty as she pulled a bunch of quarters out of her pocket and started to count them for the clerk. Twice, they slipped from her fingers and clattered to the floor. She felt time closing in on her—they'd already spent most of their very last day on the backs of motorcycles. What if they didn't make it to her grandmother in time at all?

Pia wasn't paying attention. Her eyes were glued to the television.

"Danya, they're together," she said, and a smile spread across her face as she watched her parents on the television. "They haven't been in the same room together in months!"

"They're probably worried about you," Danya mumbled under her breath, fumbling for a quarter that had rolled beneath a stand of car fresheners. She plopped her change on the counter, and the clerk scooped it up and started ringing something up on the register. Danya allowed herself one last glance up at the television while his face was turned, just as the image of her parents disappeared, replaced by a photograph of her and Sancho and Pia. Cheeks growing red, she pulled the collar of Max's motorcycle jacket up around her neck.

"Do you really think they miss me?" Pia asked. Danya shot another worried look at the clerk, but he was bagging their food and didn't seem to be paying them any attention.

Once Danya looked back at Pia's face, something inside her melted a little. Pia looked happier than she had in days.

"Of course they miss you!" Danya said. As she spoke the words, a little hole opened up in her gut. Her parents probably missed her, too. They must be so scared. They even went on television to find out where she was. . . .

Shaking her head, Danya grabbed their bag of food and pulled Pia out of the gas station. The grandpas helped them onto the backs of the motorcycles, and once her harness was tightly fastened, Danya tossed Sancho the Little Debbie oatmeal cookie from her pack (oatmeal was healthy, right?). Sancho caught it between his teeth and swallowed the whole thing in one bite.

The motorcycles rumbled on in unison, and soon Danya and Pia were off. Cool wind blew through Danya's thick curls, and she shivered, ducking deeper into Max's motorcycle jacket. While they rode, she replayed the emergency broadcast over and over in her head. Violet told the cops where they were—now even Danya's parents knew she was headed to Florida. A chill crept down her back, and she felt cold all over despite her heavy leather jacket. It was just a matter of time before they were found.

The motorcycles zoomed down the highway in a great flock, like birds. Danya and Max were in the lead. Danya peeked around Max's shoulder and that's when she saw it—a flashing orange sign by the side of the road:

MISSING: TWO 11-YEAR-OLD GIRLS AND PET PONY. IF SEEN, NOTIFY AUTHORITIES IMMEDIATELY.

CHAPTER EIGHTEEN

The Duke and Duchess of Deception

As the motorcycles roared closer to the sign, Danya's chest clenched, and her palms began to sweat. Any moment now Max and the other grandpas would figure out that she and Pia were the missing girls the country was searching for. She popped her head out of Max's leather jacket and shot her cousin a wild-eyed look.

Pia looked terrified, too. She scanned the highway, and Danya knew she was trying to come up with a last-minute plan to save them.

"Hey, Hank," Max said, his voice rising over the roar of the motorcycle engines. "Can you read that sign over there? I'm having a hard time with it."

Danya's heart sank as Hank rode up next to them, motorcycle rumbling. "Messing . . ." he read out loud, squinting beneath the motorcycle visor. "I mean . . . monsoon . . . Michigan!" Hank said. "I think it says there's a monsoon in Michigan. Wait, no, that doesn't make any sense."

"It says Mickey Mouse!" Pia interrupted. "We're getting close to Disney World. The sign says that Mickey Mouse welcomes you to Florida!"

Danya watched Max carefully, wondering if he'd really believe that. For a long, terrible moment Max and the rest of the motorcyclists were quiet, staring at the sign.

"It's, um, time to start your half-Christmas celebration," Pia added. *"Rudolph the red-nosed reindeer . . ."* she sang. She shot Danya a look and, clearing her throat, Danya started to sing along. *"Had a very shiny nose . . ."* Even Sancho tried to whinny in tune to the song—though he was a little off-key . . .

"Everybody now!" Hank called from behind him. *"And if you ever saw him, you would even say it glows!"*

One by one the rest of the motorcyclists joined in, their voices echoing through the early evening as they drove down the highway, leaving the flashing orange sign far behind them.

A little over an hour later, the Sunnyside Cul-de-Sac

Rebel Motorcycle Club for Grandpas rolled up to the gates of Disney World in a cloud of dust, filling the air with the heavy scent of motorcycle grease. The deafening roar of their motors cut through the night, scaring the crows from a nearby tree.

Max placed a heavy leather boot on the concrete and shuffled around inside his fanny pack, pulling out a brown paper bag. "Here's a little care package we all put together for you," he said, handing the bag over to Danya. "There are some juice boxes and protein bars in there."

"Thanks, Max!" Danya said, climbing down from the back of the motorcycle. "That's really thoughtful of you all."

Max shrugged, grinning. Sometime in the night his Rudolph light burned out, and now the reindeer's nose was dark. "Are you sure this is where you want to be dropped off?"

Danya looked around. She could see why they were confused. Since the park was closed now, Max and the others were parked next to a big, empty parking lot, surrounded by trees. She could see the edges of rides peeking out in the distance, but there were few people around.

"Yup," Pia said, climbing down from her own motorcycle as Danya hurried over to unlatch Sancho from the sidecar. "See, look, there's our manager!"

She pointed to an older woman strolling the streets just

past Disney World's main gates. The woman was dressed like a duchess, in a red-and-black floor-length gown and lacy black parasol, her shoulder-length gray hair intricately curled. Danya watched her, remembering the princesses and royal ladies Ferdinand sometimes met in all the stories. She stared at the elegant woman, imagining what it would be like to wear a gown like that. The duchess looked over her shoulder and, seeing Pia pointing, she waved daintily.

"How do you know her?" Danya whispered under her breath, turning her attention back to Sancho. She unclicked the last of Sancho's safety harness buckles. Poor guy! He looked so cramped inside the motorcycle sidecar. Danya ruffled his mane.

"You were really brave," she told him, kissing him on the forehead. Sancho snorted and leapt from the sidecar. He raced around the girls in circles, happy to finally stretch his stubby little legs.

Max and the other grandpas waved and smiled at the duchess. "Did I tell you I had a job once?" Max asked.

"I think you did mention that," Danya said, laughing. Max had told them about the shoe store at least six different times during their trip.

"Be sure to write, you two!" Hank added. Halfway through the trip, Pia insisted she was going to get her own motorcycle and had peppered Hank with questions about his own until, finally, Hank gave her his e-mail address, making her promise to let him know when she decided to buy her own motorcycle so he could tell her what model to get. The girls agreed to do both and waved as the motorcyclists rode away.

"Well, what now?" Pia said, plopping down on the sidewalk once the grandpas were out of sight. Danya stifled a yawn, pulling out her map. After spending so long in her pocket it was as creased as one of the old men's faces, and there was a tiny rip along one of the seams. Danya ran a finger along the edge of the paper. Just looking at it made her think of how far they'd come—how exhausted she felt.

"You feeling okay?" Pia asked, nudging Danya with an elbow. Danya shrugged. She felt . . . strange. She was tired, but buzzing with a kind of restless energy. She was terrified of what her grandmother might say but excited to meet her. It was like her emotions couldn't make up their minds.

"Hopefully my grandmother's house is within walking distance," was all she said, not sure how to explain how she felt to Pia.

"Yoo-hoo!"

The voice came from behind the girls, and they whirled around, confused. The duchess stepped outside the park gates, lifting her red skirts so they wouldn't drag along the sidewalk. She wiggled her fingers at Danya and Pia. She was rather old, her face deeply wrinkled and gray streaks shooting through her thick, auburn hair, but she flashed the girls a beatific smile that made her look years younger. A dapper older gentleman followed close behind her. His carefully curled white hair was tied back in a ribbon, and he held a walking stick.

"Oh. Hi," Pia said. Sancho stopped trotting around the parking lot and headed for Danya's side. When he saw the duke and duchess, he snorted protectively and stepped between them.

"Oh. Why, hello, good sir," the duchess said to Sancho. She dropped into a low curtsy, spreading her skirts out with her hands. Danya and Pia shared a look, giggling. The Duke, too, gave a stiff, gentlemanly bow, winking at Danya as he straightened again. Sancho pawed the sidewalk and shook out his mane, unimpressed.

"How do you do? We were wondering whether you fine ladies needed an escort?" the duke said. "We work at Disney World, and our shift has just ended. It would be unmannerly to allow you to set off alone."

Danya giggled again. He sounded so old-fashioned! Like someone out of a storybook. Sancho grabbed her sleeve with his teeth and tried to pull her away. Danya yanked her shirt out of his mouth.

"Don't be rude, Sancho." She wiped his slobber onto her skirt, grimacing. "We just need directions," she said to the duke and duchess. "We're looking for a retirement community called the Palace. Have you heard of it before?"

"It's where her grandmother lives," Pia added. The duke and duchess shared a look.

"We know the Palace quite well." The duchess twirled her parasol over her shoulder. "It's only a short walk away, but the route can be confusing. We'd be happy to take you if you like."

"That'd be great," Danya said quickly. Pia gave her a look, but Danya shrugged. Sure, they usually traveled alone (unless they were looking for a ride). But if the route was tricky, they probably did need an escort. Besides, Danya thought, stealing a glance at their escorts, she was kind of hoping the duchess might let her hold her parasol.

Sancho stomped a hoof on the sidewalk and shook out his mane. Danya sighed and tried to tickle him under his chin, but he just pulled away.

"I think he thought we were going inside the park," Danya explained when Sancho let out a loud, aggravated snort. "Sancho, we have to find my *abuelita* first. Maybe we can come back to the park later."

"Poor little guy," the duchess said, wrinkling her nose. "He'll feel better once you've reached your destination.

"Come along now, ladies," the duke added. He pointed toward the sidewalk with his cane. "The Palace is just ahead."

Danya, Pia, and Sancho followed the duke and duchess down the street. With every step, Danya's heart rose higher and higher. She'd daydreamed of meeting her grandmother so many times. Now they were finally here, and so much relied on what happened. Silently, Danya counted back the days in her head, though she didn't need to. It was Thursday night—and tomorrow morning her parents were finalizing the paperwork to sell Sancho to that horrible man. Would they have time to get all the money before the papers were signed? And would Danya's grandmother really give her the money to pay her father back?

She was so caught up in her excitement and nerves that she hardly noticed Sancho's distress as he clomped along next to her. He shook out his mane, whinnying loudly. When that didn't get Danya's attention, he trotted in a circle around her and began chewing on the edge of her sweater again.

"My, my, what a spirited pony you have there," the duchess said. Her voice wasn't nearly as courteous as before. Sancho snorted at her, his nostrils flaring.

"Sancho!" Danya hissed. "Stop being so rude."

Sancho dropped her sweater and shook his mane irritably.

Pia stopped next to her, lowering her voice. "Hey, Snap—you think he might be trying to tell us something?"

Danya frowned, staring down at Sancho. There was no way *Pia* could've guessed what he was trying to say when she didn't. Was there?

"What do you mean?" Danya asked.

"Look around! That look like a retirement community to you?"

Danya blinked, and for the first time she really looked at her surroundings. They didn't seem to be heading for a residential area at all. On the contrary, they'd turned down a busy street lined with shops and businesses. Fluorescent signs cast pink and orange lights over the sidewalk, and cars roared past them.

Danya swallowed. She had to admit, this wasn't how she'd pictured her grandmother's place, but she had no way of knowing what it looked like. She'd never seen a photograph or anything. The duke and duchess could be taking her anywhere.

"How much farther do we have to go?" Danya asked. The duke glanced back over his shoulder and smiled. Danya studied him carefully. When she looked past his cool clothes and the fancy way he talked, she noticed a few things: the edges of his jacket were frayed, for instance, and there was a gold cap on one of his teeth.

"It's just ahead," the duchess said. She, too, was a little worn around the edges. There was a tear in the lace on her gown, and the gray in her hair made her curls look brittle. "Around this corner."

The duke and duchess paused beside a narrow driveway that curved into a parking lot, motioning for Danya and Pia to walk ahead. Nerves pricked Danya's arms as she took a hesitant step forward. Pia stiffened next to her.

Sancho was right. Something *was* wrong. The driveway didn't lead to a palace at all—instead it opened into a parking lot filled with police cruisers. Danya froze at the sight of them, and every single hair on her body stood on edge. She felt like she'd just walked into a cave of sleeping bears. Every cruiser was empty, its blue and red lights dark. Beyond them sat a squat, gray building with bars covering the windows, next to a sign that read POLICE STATION.

"No." Danya took a step back and immediately collided with someone—the duke.

"Grab the other one, sweetie!" he snarled. The duchess snatched Pia's sweater sleeve. Pia slipped her skinny arms out of the sweater and, now wearing only her T-shirt, she raced across the parking lot. Her long legs made it easy for her to outrun the duchess in her heavy skirts and heels.

"Come on, Snap!" Pia called. Danya twisted and pulled, but the duke's grip on her arms only tightened. Sancho let out a furious whinny and pawed at the sidewalk. Then he charged—head-butting the duke on the back of his legs, just above his knees. The duke's legs buckled, and he collapsed onto the ground. His grip on Danya's arms never loosened, and he brought her down with him. She scraped her knee on the parking lot as she fell.

"Pia, go!" she yelled. "Save yourself! Find my grandmother!"

"She isn't going anywhere," the duchess said. She crept forward slowly, cornering Pia on one side of the parking lot. She smiled, but it no longer looked lovely—it looked manic, desperate. "This is nothing personal, little girlies. We just need that reward money!"

"You think we make any money working at an amusement park?" the duke grunted from the ground.

Just then a gray sedan pulled into the parking lot, and before it could even park, the passenger-side door flew open and Violet climbed out. She looked a little more rumpled than she had before, with a beanie pulled over her unwashed hair and a cardboard cup of takeout coffee in one hand.

"You let go of her!" she shouted at the duke, kicking up pebbles with her sneakers as she raced across the parking lot. She popped the lid off her coffee and threw the steaming liquid in the duke's direction, drenching his head. The duke screamed and dropped Danya's arms. Danya quickly wriggled away.

"What are you doing?" the duchess yelled, whirling around. "These are the missing girls! They've been on the news every day. We're trying to help them."

"You're scaring them!" Violet shouted.

Pia slipped out of the parking lot, motioning for Danya and Sancho to follow her.

"It's time to run," she said. Nodding, Danya climbed on Sancho's back and tugged on his ear. They darted forward as Pia sprinted next to them.

"Danya, you're making a mistake!" Violet called as the three of them ran away. "You have to turn yourself in! You don't know, but—!"

Before Violet could finish her sentence, the duchess swung at her with her parasol. Violet ducked out of the way, falling to the ground with an *oof*!

CHAPTER NINETEEN

Learning to Forgive

Danya froze. She couldn't let Violet take the fall for her. The duchess could hurt her! But before she could race back, Violet pushed herself to her feet and spit her wad of gum into her hand. When the duchess made another grab for her, Violet mashed the gum into the duchess's hair.

"Take that!" she yelled.

The duchess shrieked and grabbed for the gum as the police station doors flew open and several officers raced into the parking lot.

"We've gotta go, Snap," Pia said, tugging on Danya's arm. "The duke will tell."

"Yeah," Danya said, and started to run. But as they

made their escape, she couldn't help turning everything that had just happened over in her head. Violet just saved them from the duke and duchess. But that didn't make any sense. . . . She'd been planning to turn them in for the reward money before! She'd only helped them in the first place to get a story.

Pia skidded to a stop in front of a gas station and grabbed hold of Sancho's reins, pulling him to a stop as well. "I think we lost them," she said, huffing as she caught her breath.

Danya frowned, chewing on her lower lip. "Did you hear what Violet said?"

"I'm confused, too," Pia admitted. "But at least we got away."

Danya nodded. "I guess we should figure out how to get to the real Palace now."

"Smart move. I'll go inside and see if they can give us directions. You should stay out here with Sancho, but maybe you should hide or something in case Violet comes past. They could still catch us."

Danya climbed down from Sancho's back and pulled him around to the side of the gas station, which was hidden from the street by a couple of dumpsters. As Pia pushed open the door and disappeared inside, she patted Sancho's neck.

"Thanks for the warnings, buddy," she said. "Sorry I didn't listen."

Sancho huffed and pushed his nose into her curls, tickling her neck.

Still, there was one thing that Danya couldn't get out of her head. *Why* had Violet helped them? It didn't make sense. And that thing she'd called after them—turn yourself in, there's something you don't know. What had that meant?

Pursing her lips, Danya pulled Sancho back around to the front of the gas station, where there was an old pay phone next to the sliding glass doors. She pulled a few quarters out of her pockets and stuck them in the slots, then quickly dialed her parents' number.

She held her breath as the phone rang and rang and rang. Then there was a click.

"Hi, you've reached the Ruiz residence," said her mother's recorded voice. "We're not home right now, but if you'd like to leave your name and number . . ."

With a heavy heart, Danya hung up the phone. Sancho licked her cheek.

"Where are they?" she asked him, sniffling. She'd so wanted to hear her mother's *real* voice, to say she was okay and she'd be coming home soon. And what about her dad? Had the bald man already come looking for Sancho?

Danya wanted to promise him she'd pay him back—that he wouldn't have to worry about the bald man's money after all.

Sancho shook out his mane and pawed at the parking lot. Danya buried her face into his mane, wondering where her parents could possibly be and what on earth Violet knew that she didn't.

Danya had started to wipe her eyes on her sleeve when the gas station door swung open and Pia stepped onto the sidewalk, carrying two hot dogs and balancing a bright blue Slurpee in the crook of her arm.

"What's the matter?" Pia said, seeing Danya's tearstained face. "Didn't I make it the way you like? Double mustard and relish, no ketchup."

"It's not that." Danya's voice cracked, and another tear formed in the corner of her eye. She'd made a mistake by running off with Sancho—a really big one, she could see that now. She would still do anything and everything to save Sancho, but in trying to protect him, she'd hurt everyone else. She'd hurt her parents by running away, and she'd hurt Pia by being so focused on her own problems that she hadn't seen what was going on with her best friend.

And Sancho . . . Danya looked down at her pony. He sat in the middle of the sidewalk, swishing his tail like a happy puppy and staring up at her with those big brown eyes. Sancho trusted her, and what if, after all of this, she wasn't able to save him? What if she'd made so many people unhappy and it was all for nothing?

The thought tugged on her heart, making her feel painful and raw. She clenched her eyes shut, trying to push the bad feelings away. But as the darkness closed around her, all she saw was black smoke against the blue sky. She heard fire crackling in the distance and Jupiña's terrified whinny.

"Danya, you're trembling!" Pia grabbed Danya by the shoulders. Danya's eyes flew open, but the smell and feel of the fire stayed with her. Why couldn't she shake that memory? Was it because she felt just as lost and helpless now as she did then?

"What is it? What's wrong?" Pia demanded, her eyes wide with concern.

"There's something I've never told you," Danya answered in a quiet voice.

Pia narrowed her eyes, waiting.

"Remember . . . remember when Sancho's mom died?"

Pia frowned. "Of course. It was just last summer when it was so hot, right? There was a wildfire. Danya, what's wrong?"

"It was my fault." Danya stared down at her sneakers, unable to meet Pia's eyes. "I'd been playing with this magnifying glass in the backyard. Sancho and I were looking for tiny villages, you know, like in *Gulliver's Travels*? When I held the magnifying glass up to the sun, it burned a hole in the grass, so I stopped. But then I left it there, and Sancho and I ran off into the woods to play.

"I didn't realize anything was wrong until . . . until I smelled the smoke." Danya's eyes watered, and she wiped at them with the back of her hand. "Sancho and I tried to make it back in time, but when we reached the pen, the fire had spread and it was . . . it was burning."

Danya sniffled, squeezing her eyes shut so she wouldn't see the disappointment in Pia's face. "It was my fault that Sancho's mom died. If I hadn't left my magnifying glass, nothing would have happened to her. I tried to get back to the stable in time to get her out. But I couldn't."

Sancho made a sniffling noise, flattening his ears against the back of his head. He leaned against her leg, but Danya just stared at her sneakers. She couldn't bring herself to look at him.

Pia reached for Danya's hand and gave it a squeeze. "Danya, you don't know the magnifying glass started that fire. It was so hot that summer that fires started all the time. My mom said one started near the highway because it was so hot the grass burst into flames. And if you'd been by the stable, you probably would have been hurt, too," Pia said.

Danya looked up. She hadn't thought of that before.

"You don't think it was my fault? But the magnifying glass . . ." Pia shook her head before she could continue.

"Your fault? It was a horrible accident. It was nobody's *fault*."

In order to get the fortune you seek, you must forgive yourself. . . . Danya still wasn't sure the fortune-teller was right about that. She didn't know if she could *ever* forgive herself for what she'd done to Jupiña. But after revealing her big secret to Pia, Danya felt light in a way she hadn't since before Sancho's mom died. Maybe she could try telling her parents what happened, too? If Pia didn't think it was her fault, they might not, either. Danya turned the idea over in her head, but even the thought made her feel anxious. Pia could just be trying to act nice, after all.

Danya sighed and scratched Sancho behind his ears. He licked her wrist with his long, scratchy tongue. Maybe she had *reconciled a past harm*. She might start believing in this hero's list after all.

"Maybe," she said. Pia gave her a one-armed hug, handing over the hot dog covered in mustard and relish.

"Well, the evil duke and duchess were right about one thing," she said. "Apparently the Palace *is* right around the corner. The clerk gave me directions." Pia motioned to a napkin poking out of her pocket.

Danya nodded and stared down at her hot dog. She

wiped her eyes with the sleeve of her sweater. "Did you spend the last of our money on these?"

Pia shrugged, taking a big bite of her hot dog, which she'd covered in mayonnaise and rainbow sprinkles. *Gross*, Danya thought. "We have to keep our strength up. And anyway, we're almost there."

Danya took a bite of her hot dog, then tore off a chunk of the bun to feed to Sancho. Pia was right—the money didn't matter right now. Danya no longer had to worry about how much they spent or what they were going to eat next or where they were going to sleep. They'd come all this way, and now they were almost there. Her grandmother's house was right around the corner. Now all she had to worry about was Sancho.

The mustard-covered hot dog turned in Danya's stomach, making her feel sick. What if this was all a mistake? What if her grandmother didn't want to help after all? What if she didn't even want to meet Danya?

Pia noisily sucked Slurpee up through her straw. "Snap?" she asked, her lips and tongue dyed bright blue. Her mouth split into a wide smile, and she hopped in place. "We're going, right?"

Sancho pushed against her arm with his nose, and Danya shook her head, forcing herself to take a deep breath. They'd come all this way. Mistake or not, they had to see the rest of the adventure through. She shoved the hot dog in her mouth and plucked the napkin from Pia's pocket.

"Of course we're going," she said, studying the napkin. "Now where is this place?"

Pia leaned over her shoulder, motioning to a wiggly black line stretching across the napkin. "All we gotta do is follow that road there for half a mile. You think there'll be a drawbridge? Or those, like, pointy things on top of the towers?"

"Turrets?" Danya asked. "No, Pia, it's not a real palace. It's just a condo. It'll probably look like an apartment building." She stared down at the hastily drawn map covering the napkin. It showed a path that cut past the main street and curved onto a tiny road a few blocks over. Danya studied the scribbles, then glanced up to take in her surroundings.

"We need to head that way," she said, pointing to a road lined with manicured bushes and trees that cut through the main street. "According to this, the Palace is two blocks down, on the left."

Pia popped off the lid of her Slurpee and took another gulp. "Onward!" she shouted, pumping a fist in the air.

CHAPTER TWENTY

Problems at the Palace

The girls headed for the Palace with Sancho at their side. Danya insisted she didn't want any Slurpee (her stomach was already fluttery with nerves), so Pia gave the rest to Sancho. It dyed his pony lips and tongue electric blue, and all the sugar made him so hyper he trotted circles around Danya and Pia and chased tiny lizards off the sidewalks into the bushes and up palm trees.

Sooner than Danya expected, they came upon a sign: THE PALACE RETIREMENT COMMUNITY. Taking a deep breath, she focused on moving her feet forward, one in front of the other, until she was standing in front of her grandmother's building.

Danya blinked once, then twice, not sure she could trust her own eyes. The Palace was a pink brick building covered in huge, arched windows. It towered over the houses and apartment complexes around it, overlooking the sparkling lights of downtown Orlando. Lush greenery lined the front steps, and vines and moss spilled over a rocky shore, separating the Palace from a real moat filled with blue water and tiny koi fish.

The only way to reach the front door was by crossing a drawbridge—just like something out of a Ferdinand and Dapple book.

Danya's chest twisted and tightened. Pia grabbed her hand and squeezed.

"Told you so," she said, sticking out her tongue. Danya shoved her playfully, and Pia started to giggle. "What, I *did* tell you. Real life is just like the fairy tales. Anyway, we're right beside you, Snap. You ready for this?"

Danya nodded. "Come here, buddy," she said to Sancho. Sancho trotted up to her side, and Danya pulled herself onto his back. If she was crossing a drawbridge and riding up to a freaking palace, she was doing it in *style*.

Pia grabbed Sancho's reins and led them forward, humming the theme song to some adventure movie under her breath as they approached. The automatic doors whooshed aside, Danya tugged on Sancho's ear, and together they trotted into the lobby, his hooves clomping loudly on the black-and-white-tiled floor. The air conditioning turned the sweat on the back of her neck cold, making her shiver.

Plush leather couches were scattered across the lobby, and a bank of glass elevators lined the far wall, blocked by the largest security guard Danya had ever seen. The sleeves of the guard's uniform were stretched so tight over his muscled arms they look painted on, and his head was shiny, smooth, and roughly the size and shape of a bowling ball. His plastic name tag read RALPHIO.

Gathering all her courage, Danya led Sancho up to the front desk. "Hi, Mr. Ralphio. We're here to visit Angie Ruiz," she said.

"Ms. Ruiz doesn't accept visitors." Ralphio didn't look up from the paperback romance novel he was reading. The words LOVE and HATE were tattooed to his knuckles—one letter for each finger.

Danya glanced at Pia, her confidence fading. "Um, can't you make an exception? I'm her granddaughter, and we came a really long way."

"The Palace Retirement Community doesn't make exceptions," the guard said, flipping a page. "That's why we're the best."

"Oh." Danya glanced down at the desk. A framed photograph of a little girl with curly blond hair and big blue eyes sat next to a jar of pens. Sancho nudged the bag where she kept the Ferdinand and Dapple book, and suddenly Danya had an idea. . . .

"Is that your daughter?" she asked. For the first time, the guard looked up from his book.

"Yeah." He glanced at the photograph and the hard lines of his face softened. It wasn't quite a smile, but it was close. "Amy. She's nine."

Danya brightened and turned to Pia, winking. Her way of saying, "Follow my lead." Pia's eyes widened, and the corner of her lip twitched into a proud smile.

"Does Amy like to read?" Danya asked.

Ralphio snorted—it almost sounded like a laugh. "Yeah, she does. She reads so many books I have a hard time keeping up."

"Has she read this one?" Pia pulled the Ferdinand and Dapple book out of her bag and slid it over Ralphio's desk.

Ralphio set his own novel down on the desk and picked up the Ferdinand and Dapple book, opening to the first page. "I don't think so."

"It's really good," Danya said. As she watched Ralphio hold her favorite book, she felt a pang of sadness in her chest. Still, she forced herself to continue. "There's this one scene where Ferdinand gets into a sword fight with a conquistador, and when he loses his sword, he pulls off his leather boot and uses it to fight the conquistador away." Danya made a slashing move with her arm, like she was holding an invisible sword. "And there's this scene where Dapple gets locked away in a cave, and Ferdinand thinks she's a goner, but she digs her way out and finds Ferdinand at the last second." Danya stopped and looked down at Sancho. "See, Ferdinand and Dapple are the very best of friends," she said, scratching Sancho behind the ear. "Almost like soul mates."

Ralphio started flipping through the pages. "That actually sounds pretty good. Amy loves all that adventure stuff."

"You can take it if you want." Danya shrugged, trying to act like this wasn't a big deal even though handing over the book made her heart hurt.

"Really?" Ralphio raised an eyebrow.

"*If* you let me up to see my grandmother," Danya added. "She wrote it, you know. Maybe I could even get an autograph. For Amy."

"Angie Ruiz is some big-time author, eh? Well, isn't that something." Ralphio shook his head, a smile playing on his lips as he turned the book over in his hand. Finally, he set it back down on the desk. Danya was sure he was going to slide it back over to her and tell her to leave, but instead he reached beneath the desk and pushed a button she couldn't see. One of the elevator doors behind him slid open.

"She's on the twenty-first floor. Tell her you snuck past me, okay?" Ralphio said with a wink. "And the pony has to stay down here."

"Wait, Sancho can't—" Danya started, but before she could argue, Pia took Sancho's reins, ruffling the pony's mane.

"Danya, I think this is something you need to do on your own," Pia said. "I can watch Sancho."

Sancho swooshed his tail in agreement.

Danya swallowed and slid down from Sancho's back. Pia was right. She was about to meet her *abuelita*, her favorite author, her *hero* for the very first time. She needed to go by herself.

"And hey," Pia added, nodding at the book on Ralphio's desk. "You gave up your favorite book. I think that means you just *made the ultimate sacrifice*. That's number fourteen on the list of hero's tasks."

Danya laughed. "Well, maybe I'll become a hero after all. Hold tight, buddy," she said, tickling Sancho under his chin. "I'll be back soon."

Sancho licked her wrist, and Pia took his reins. Danya crossed the lobby to the elevator waiting at the end of the room. The elevator was made entirely of thick panes of glass, and it glided up so smoothly it took Danya a moment to realize she was moving. She was nervous at first, watching the ground disappear below her, but she quickly forgot her fear as she rose higher.

There was a courtyard below that looked like a grotto, with a small waterfall pouring into a beautiful blue swimming pool. Seniors sunbathed under palm trees and played water polo in the shallow end of the pool. Danya pressed her face against the glass, leaving behind fingerprints and clouds of breath. Everything here was so fancy, so *expensive*. It was like nothing she'd ever seen before. For a long moment she forgot her nerves, too enthralled by the beauty of the Palace.

Then the elevator stopped, and the door behind Danya pinged open. Danya turned. There was only one door on the twenty-first floor — a suite. She stepped off the elevator and rang the bell.

The woman who opened the front door was barely a foot taller than Danya herself. She wore a drapey tunic, scarves, and long beaded necklaces, and gray streaks peppered the dark hair piled on top of her head in a neat bun. Danya gaped at her, amazed. Even though she'd practically memorized her grandmother's photograph in the back of the Ferdinand and Dapple books, she'd never noticed that Angie had her father's kind brown eyes and Danya's upturned nose.

Angie blinked. *"Danya?"* she said.

Danya took a deep breath. "Hello, *abuelita*."

"I saw your photo on the news, but I never really thought you'd . . . I can't believe you're . . ." Angie trailed off, and for a long moment she just stood there, clutching the door frame like she might collapse. She lifted her arm, and for a second Danya was certain her grandmother was going to give her a hug. But then an emotion Danya didn't quite understand flickered over Angie's face. Embarrassment, maybe? Or fear? She dropped her arm awkwardly. As though remembering her manners, Angie hurriedly stepped aside and swung her apartment door open.

"Well, come in, come in," she said with a shy smile. "Family doesn't hover on the doorstep like a stray dog."

Danya followed her grandmother into a narrow hallway. Lining the walls were photographs—some so old they were black and white, and some that looked like they were taken just a few days ago. Angie walked down the hallway without glancing at them, but Danya couldn't help peeking at a few as she trailed behind.

There was her grandmother hang-gliding over a crystal-blue sea, and there was her grandmother standing on top of a rocky red mountain, and there was her grandmother under-water, petting a spotted shark with a lethal-looking fin.

Danya smiled, unable to keep a grin from taking over her face. Everything her father told her about her *abuelita* had been true after all. She really *was* an adventurer. Danya reached out and ran her fingers over a framed photograph of her grandma sitting on top of a stallion that was so big he made Sancho look like a tiny toy pony. A little boy sat in front of Angie, and his wide, deep brown eyes made Danya feel happy and lonely all at the same time.

"Hi, Dad," she whispered to the photograph before following the real Angie around the corner.

The living room was an explosion of color. Brightly painted African masks hung from the walls, and thick Peruvian blankets were piled on worn leather couches. One entire wall was taken up by a Japanese watercolor of a geisha crouching next to a still pond filled with lilies. While Danya turned in place, taking it all in, Angie swept into a small kitchen with blue tile floors and nervously put a kettle on the stove top, switching on a burner. She paused for just a moment and, weaving her fingers together, glanced up, like she needed to make sure Danya really was there. Another emotion flitted across her face, but this one Danya recognized. It was the look her mom got when she watched Danya's school play last year or the look her dad got that time Danya got an A on the math test she studied for all night. It was pride.

"Do you drink tea?" Angie asked. Then, shaking her head, "Well, whether you do or whether you don't, I'm making tea. That's what you do in situations like this. You make tea."

"I drink tea," Danya said. Her mom sometimes let her have sips of her Diet Snapple Peach Tea, and even though she was pretty sure that wasn't what Angie was talking about, Danya told herself she'd drink whatever was placed in front of her to be polite. She scooted onto a bar stool next to a marble island that separated the kitchen from the living room. She sat up tall and made sure to keep her elbows off the counter, remembering how her mother taught her to behave when she was a guest in someone else's home.

As soon as she thought the word *guest*, though, Danya felt a little funny. Did it count as being a guest if the person you were visiting was your own grandmother? Danya wasn't entirely sure.

She watched her grandmother flutter around, pulling teacups and saucers and tiny pots of sugar from her cupboards. Sitting next to the stove was a tiny black-and-white television set with the sound switched off. The words RUIZ RUNAWAY WATCH flashed across the screen, along with Danya's and Pia's photographs.

"Hey!" Danya exclaimed, forgetting her manners as she pointed at the television. "You've been watching the news! You knew I ran away."

Angie stopped fussing with her tea bags and turned around. "Of course I knew! I've had the television on nonstop for the past week, I've been so worried. And then when that tipster told the police you were in Florida . . ." Angie shook her head, wringing her hands. "Well, I just knew you were coming to see me."

She slumped against the counter, like a suddenly deflated balloon. "I've been practicing what to say to you ever since."

Confused, Danya sat up taller on her stool. Tipster? Had Violet told the police they were in Florida? "You know why I'm here?"

"You want to know why I stopped talking to your father. Why I haven't been a part of your life all these years."

"Oh." Danya's shoulders fell. "Well, actually I . . ."

"You don't have to explain." Angie poured hot water into two cups and plunked a tea bag in each. "I'd be furious if I were you. But I want you to know it was never because I didn't like your mother."

"You stopped talking to my dad because of my mom?" Danya asked, frowning.

"I guess you could say that." Angie shook her head sadly and slid a cup of tea over to Danya. "They were nineteen. He wanted to quit school to marry her, and I was so against it. I told him if he did, I'd cut him off."

"But why?" Danya blew on her tea to make it cooler.

"They were just so young," Angie said, taking a sip of tea. "Your mother seemed like a nice girl, but I wanted something different for your father. Something bigger. I didn't have Luis until I was in my late thirties. I got to live so many adventures before he even came into the world. I wanted him to hike Machu Picchu and visit the monasteries in Nepal." Angie sighed, shaking her head. "I guess I wanted him to be exactly like me."

She set the teacup down on the counter and smiled at Danya. "But he told me he had to. I just couldn't understand. And can you believe it took me this long to realize what he knew from the beginning?"

Danya lifted the teacup to her mouth, and a smell like cinnamon and oranges drifted up her nose. "What did he know?" she asked before taking a sip.

"That there is no adventure bigger than making a family. And there's nothing more important."

Danya set the cup of tea back down. Her grandmother's words hit her like a punch in the stomach, and suddenly she missed her parents so much. This was the longest she'd ever been away from home. She was almost surprised by how it hurt—she felt fine one moment, then it hit her all at once, aching so much she could hardly breathe. How had her grandmother managed to stay away from her family all these years?

As though to answer, Angie continued. "I've thought of calling your father so many times, but every time I pick up the phone, something freezes inside me and I can't do it. I even returned all those letters your mother sent me. It was just too painful to open them and see what I'd given up. I almost felt . . . like I didn't deserve to know you, I guess."

Her grandmother didn't deserve to know *her*? Danya turned those words over in her head, trying to make sense of them. All these years her grandmother had been her hero—her role model. How could her grandmother possibly think she didn't deserve to know her?

"I would always want to know you," Danya blurted out, but as soon as she'd said the words, they sounded strange to her. Childish, almost. Her grandmother gave her a sad smile.

"You're so young, Danya. You don't know what it feels like to fail someone you love so completely."

But Danya *did* know what it felt like. She wrapped her

hands around her teacup tighter, remembering the night of the fire. Pia might think it wasn't really her fault, but the memory was still so vivid, so fresh in Danya's mind. She wondered if she'd think of those crackling flames, the dry grass, Jupiña's whinnies every time she closed her eyes, no matter what else happened in her life. Did it feel like that for her grandmother, too? Was there some memory of her father that she could never take back, no matter how badly she wanted to?

"I'm not too young to know what that feels like," Danya said in a quiet voice.

Her grandmother nodded sadly and reached forward, taking one of Danya's hands in her own.

"My sweet girl. How can I ever make up for missing so much of your life?"

Danya cleared her throat. "Well, actually, I might know a way." Gathering her courage, Danya told Angie about Sancho, her parents' financial difficulties, the bank loan, and how she'd come all this way to seek a miracle that might save them.

"I thought," she finished, staring down at the tea growing cold in her cup, "well, I hoped maybe you would want to help. You made so much money off the Ferdinand and Dapple books, and I just thought . . ."

The end of Danya's sentence got tangled up in her

mouth, and she found she had no idea how to finish it. Still, she thought she'd gotten the point across. She glanced up at her grandmother hopefully.

Angie Ruiz's face had crumpled like a tissue. The corners of her mouth pulled down in a deep frown, and when Danya looked up at her, she sighed deeply.

"Oh, *mija*. I'd love to help you," she said. "But there is no money. My fortune is gone."

CHAPTER TWENTY-ONE

Finding the Fortune

"Gone?" Danya's stomach felt full of rocks. "But you're a novel-ist! You're famous!"

"In *Cuba*, I was famous." Angie shook her head slowly and looked down at her hands, still clenching the teacup. "But Americans don't want stories about a Cuban boy and his pony. I spent what was left of my money moving up here and buying this place. It's gone, Danya."

Danya nodded woodenly. A sudden, intense rush of sadness crashed over her. It was over—there was no way of saving Sancho now.

The only other time in her life she'd felt this helpless was the day Jupiña died in the fire. Once again someone she loved was in trouble, and Danya wouldn't be able to save them. When she opened her eyes, tears spilled onto her cheeks.

"Oh, *mija*, don't cry." Grandma Angie set her teacup down and pulled Danya into a hug. Danya wrapped her arms around her grandmother, surprised by how easily they fit together—like two puzzle pieces. She buried her head into her grandmother's soft scarves, breathing in her scent: cinnamon and vanilla and gardenias. Her scarves were silky and soft on Danya's cheek.

"I just thought . . ." Danya said, her voice breaking. "I thought maybe I could be a real hero. That I could save him. Like Ferdinand would have."

Grandma Angie ran a hand in slow circles over Danya's back. "Let's give your parents a call, okay? We need to tell them where you are so they'll stop worrying. Then maybe you and I can make cookies. I'll teach you to make—" A loud *buzz* interrupted her, making Danya jump.

"What was that?" Danya asked.

"The intercom." Angie crossed the room and brushed aside a tapestry to reveal a metal intercom mounted on the wall. She pressed a red button to talk, but before she could say a word, Pia's frantic, staticky voice filled the apartment.

"Mayday! Mayday!" Pia called. "Snap, you better get down here *fast*."

Danya's chest clenched. "Is it Sancho?" she shouted, and leapt from her chair. She raced to the intercom, but when she pressed the big red button, all she heard was static. "Pia? Pia, what's wrong?"

No one answered. Danya ran to the door, Grandma Angie at her heels. During the ride down to the first floor Danya pressed her face up against the sides of the glass elevator, but she didn't see Pia or Sancho in the courtyard below. Had the evil duke and duchess followed them here? Had the police found them at last?

"I'm sure they're fine," Grandma Angie said, squeezing Danya's shoulder. Danya nodded, but she couldn't ignore the heavy feeling of dread that had washed over her. The elevator opened and Danya stumbled into the lobby. The front doors whooshed apart as she ran toward them. Once outside she froze.

"*Mom?*" Danya said, blinking. "Dad?"

Her parents stood on the moat, crowded around Sancho. Maritza scanned the grounds while her dad scratched the top of Sancho's head. Just behind them Pia's parents were on their knees, wrapping their daughter in a hug. All Danya could see of Pia was the spiky tips of her hair.

"*Mija!*" Maritza ran at Danya, lifting her off the ground and into a hug. Danya wrapped her arms around her mother's neck and buried her face in her hair, breathing in the familiar oranges and coffee smell of home. She couldn't believe her mother was *here*, that she'd found her. All of the emotion of the week caught up with her, and Danya let out a choked sob, tightening her arms around her mother's neck. Maritza squeezed right back.

"We thought we'd lost you," Maritza said in a shaky voice. "Oh, Danya, we were so scared."

Luis wrapped his arms around them both, pulling them close. Her father's cheeks were wet. She'd never seen her father cry before. Sancho nudged the back of her knee with his furry nose, and Danya grinned down at him.

"My girl!" her dad said. "My Snap!"

"Daddy, Mom, I missed you both so much." Danya sniffled, leaning down to scratch Sancho on the head. "How did you know I was here?"

"The police called. Someone tipped them off. She said you—" Before Maritza could finish her sentence, the lobby doors whooshed open again and Grandma Angie stepped outside. She didn't say a word, just folded her hands in front of her and watched from a distance. The wind played with the ends of her scarf and blew a strand of hair from her bun.

Maritza set Danya down on the sidewalk. Danya watched her family, and it was like all the relief and gladness froze inside her chest, waiting to see what would happen next. Luis stepped back, wiping his cheek with the back of his hand. His expression was cold, and Danya had never seen his shoulders go quite so stiff.

"Mom," he said. His mother shifted uncomfortably.

"I'm sorry to interrupt," she said.

"You're not interrupting!" Maritza put a hand on Luis's shoulder and pulled him closer to Angie. "This is a family moment. You've always been our family, Angie."

Angie nodded, and a sad smile crossed her face. Looking at Luis, she said, "Can you forgive me? For being a stubborn old woman all these years?"

Sancho nuzzled Danya's hand, and Danya absently scratched him behind his ears, not able to look away from her dad. The muscles in his jaws had gone tight, and Danya couldn't help wondering if it was too late, if her father wouldn't be able to forgive Grandma Angie for everything that had happened. The moment seemed to stretch forever, and Danya found herself holding her breath.

Then Luis's eyes shifted to his daughter, and his expression softened. He took a step forward and pulled his mother into a hug.

"Of course," he said, burying his face in her hair. "I forgive you, Mama." Angie pulled her son closer, squeezing her eyes shut as a tear slid down her cheek.

"Looks like everyone is having a magical family moment

over here, too," Pia said, coming up behind Danya. Her parents were right behind her. Pia's dad even ruffled her spiky hair. Pia had a big grin on her face.

"Are your parents getting back together?" Danya asked. Sancho perked up his ears, but Pia shook her head.

"No, Danya," Tía Carla said. "But we did tell Pia that we'll always love her and we'll always be a family. No matter what changes."

"They already have a plan for how I'm going to spend time with both of them," Pia explained. She was trying to keep her voice casual, but Danya could hear the relief in her words. "I don't know. Maybe things will be okay after all."

Danya grabbed her cousin's hand and squeezed. For the past week, it was like the world had been spinning wildly out of control and now *finally* it was right-side up again. Everything was the way it was supposed to be—she was here, with her family, and everyone was hugging and crying and happy.

Danya closed her eyes and laughed out loud, letting the warm Florida wind blow against her cheeks. She felt warm and content and really, truly *happy* for the first time in days.

Then Sancho snorted and leaned his head against Danya's hip. Danya opened her eyes, looking down at him, and all at once the feeling disappeared. She hadn't managed to save Sancho. She hadn't even gotten *close*. Danya wrapped a protective arm around her pony, pulling him close. Tomorrow was Friday, and as soon as they all got back to Kentucky, Sancho would have to go live with that horrible bald, sunglasses man. This moment might feel perfect, but it was the last perfect moment Danya would ever spend with her entire family. It was the very last time they would be together, *whole*.

Danya's mother and father were speaking with Angie in Spanish. Maritza smiled down at Danya, but when she saw the look on her daughter's face, the smile faded.

"Baby, what's wrong?"

Danya swallowed her tears, trying to be brave. She didn't want to ruin her family's perfect moment, but suddenly everyone was quiet, their faces turned to her. Danya sniffed and looked down at Sancho. He closed his eyes and leaned his head against Danya's hip.

"We still have to sell Sancho," she said in a small voice. "All this was for nothing."

Maritza blinked back tears as she stared down at Danya. Luis put a hand on his wife's arm and squeezed. Silence stretched between them, interrupted only by a muffled snort as Sancho dropped to the ground next to Danya and buried his nose beneath his hooves.

Danya looked down at her sneakers, not sure she could

continue to meet her parents' eyes without bursting into tears. This wasn't their fault. She knew there was nothing either of them could do to save Sancho, but still her heart ached. It had been up to her to find the money, and she'd failed.

"This is just like what happened with Jupiña," she said in a whisper. Her father frowned and crouched on the sidewalk in front of her. He took her chin in his hands and gently lifted her face so she'd meet his eyes.

"Snap?" he said. "What do you mean this is just like Jupiña?"

"I can't save Sancho, just like I couldn't save Jupiña," Danya said. She sniffed again, but she couldn't help it— tears stung her eyes and poured over her cheeks.

"*Mi querida niña.*" Maritza shook her head as she knelt on the sidewalk next to Danya. "That was not your fault."

"It *was* my fault," Danya insisted. Maritza and Luis spoke at once, and their voices tangled together like yarn as they tried to convince Danya it wasn't true. Taking a deep breath, Danya explained about the magnifying glass and how it'd lit the grass on fire.

"I started that fire. It's my fault Sancho's mother isn't alive anymore. I thought that if I saved Sancho, it would be almost like making everything better. That I could make life like a story again, and this time I'd be a real hero." Her voice cracked.

"Danya, sweetie," Luis said. "The stable didn't burn down because of your magnifying glass. We talked to the firefighters after it'd been put out. It was an electrical fire. One of the porch lights sparked around midday, and the grass was so hot it caught fire and spread too quickly for anyone to do anything about it. What happened to Jupiña was not your fault."

Danya stared at her father, shocked. "The firefighter said that? Really?"

"Really, really." Her dad pinched her nose affectionately. "And as much I love Jupiña, and as much as I miss her, I'm so glad you didn't run into that stable to try and save her. I love your grandmother's books, but I think they may have given you the wrong idea of what it means to be a hero. Real heroes don't always win, and they can't always save everyone. Real heroes know right from wrong, and they are willing to risk everything for the people they love." He smiled up at his mother. "I haven't always been able to do that, Snap."

Angie stepped up behind him and placed a hand on his shoulder. "Neither have I," she added in a quiet voice.

"But *mija*, you do that every day. For Sancho, and for Pia." Maritza smiled at her daughter—a wide, proud smile. "Now *that's* heroic."

Sancho nudged her sneaker with his nose. Danya wiped

the tears from her cheek with the back of her hand. Pia wrapped her arms around Danya's neck and rested her head on her shoulder.

"Told you, silly. Not your fault. You were a real hero all along."

Danya hugged Pia back, and for the first time since Jupiña died, she actually believed her. It really wasn't her fault. The knowledge of that lit in her head like a firecracker. She didn't have to feel guilty anymore. She wasn't to blame after all.

A siren blared, interrupting Danya's thoughts. She looked around for the source of the noise. And just beyond the row of palm trees surrounding the Palace Retirement Community, she saw flashing red and blue lights.

The police! Danya grabbed Pia's arm, and her muscles tightened before she remembered that the danger was over. Her parents had found her. She didn't need to run anymore.

"What do you think they want?" Pia asked as the police car pulled to a stop in front of the Palace. Danya shrugged. The cop driving the car leaned back in his seat, pulling out a newspaper, but the cruiser's back door flew open and Violet stumbled out.

"Danya! Pia!" Violet raced across the drawbridge, clutching a sleek silver laptop in one hand.

"Violet?" Pia narrowed her eyes and put her hands on

her hips. "What are you doing? You betrayed us. Why would you think we'd want to see you?"

Violet was out of breath when she reached them. "Look," she pleaded. "It's not what you think. I never told my mom you were on the ship. I guess one of the cleaning ladies saw you when she was washing one of the East Wing bathrooms. My mom's the one who called the cops, not me."

"But we heard you," Danya said, confused. "You were talking to your mom the day we left the ship—you told her you'd betrayed us."

Violet took a deep breath and pulled a sheet of paper out of her pocket.

"That's because I did," she said, handing the paper to Danya. "I stole this from you. And I put it on my blog. I know I shouldn't have, but . . . Danya, it was just so beautiful."

Danya took the piece of paper from Violet and unfolded it. It was a page torn from her writing notebook, the one she'd written on about stories and heroes the night she'd spent on the cruise ship. She thought Sancho had eaten it, but here it was. Violet must've snuck into her room and stolen it somehow.

Sancho nudged her leg with his nose, and Danya smiled down at him. "Yeah, okay," she muttered. "I'm sorry I blamed *you* for this."

He wiggled his bottom, tail swishing. His way of saying, "Told you so."

Danya's parents and grandmother crowded behind her, and Danya could feel them reading her words over her shoulder. Her cheeks reddened, and she started to fold the story back up, but Pia snatched it out of her hands.

"This is really good, Danya," she said, holding the page up so that Maritza, Luis, and Angie could see it, too.

"Oh, Danya," Angie said, smiling. "You're a natural."

"I'll say," Violet added. "Danya, thousands and thousands of people read your story on my blog. Look—they even wrote to me to see if there was any way they could help."

Violet showed Danya the screen. Alongside Danya's story were photographs Danya didn't know Violet had taken. There was one of Danya and Pia fighting alligators at Gatorville and one of them talking to the circus school performers in the parking lot. There was even a photo of Sancho and Danya standing on the balcony of the *Sailing Swan*, looking wistfully out over the ocean. Danya's family crowded closer to the screen to look at the photographs, too. Seeing the photograph with the alligators, Maritza gasped and raised an eyebrow at her daughter.

"You have some explaining to do when we get home," she said.

"And look," Violet continued, scrolling down. "Look at all the comments people left for you."

Danya took the computer from Violet's hands and started scrolling. She couldn't believe her eyes. So many people had wished them luck and encouragement. There were even a few familiar names.

Stay free, girls! — Karina and Simone

Never stop singing — the King

If you need luck, try a moon jar. Found one in my truck and it changed my life. — Turtle

Business has been booming since your appearance! Can we book you for next summer, too? — Petey

. . . and then,

Only those with true friends are truly rich. — Circe

The comments went on and on and on. Danya read them until the words blurred before her eyes.

"Wow," Luis said, reading over Danya's shoulder. "Danya, your words really inspired those people."

"I can't believe there were so many people rooting for us," Pia added.

"That's not even the best part," Violet said. "Look, I put a donation button on the page so people could give a few bucks to help you save Sancho. Danya, you made over five thousand dollars!"

For a moment Danya wasn't sure she'd heard that correctly. "I *what*?"

"Your story made enough money to save Sancho," Pia said with a squeal. "Danya, we did it!"

The words swirled through Danya's head, hardly making sense. She handed the laptop to her dad and dropped to her knees, holding Sancho's happy pony face up to her own.

"Did you hear that, buddy! We get to keep you." Sancho licked her nose, and giggling, Danya looked back up her parents. "Mom, Dad, we can, right?" she asked. "That's enough money for us to keep him?"

Maritza took her husband's hand, beaming. "We're so proud of you, Danya," she said. Then, glancing at Violet, she asked, "You're sure you don't mind parting with it?"

"It was never mine," Violet insisted. "The people donated it because of Danya's story. She earned it." Violet crouched next to Danya. "And that's not all," she added. "Your story was so moving that I was wondering if you'd want to be a regular contributor."

Danya blinked. "You mean like a *writer*?"

"Yup!" Violet said. "The readers love you. You can be a junior reporter. I'll teach you everything I know."

Grandma Angie knelt next to her, taking her hand. "You'll make a fantastic writer, Snap!" she said. Behind her, Luis and Maritza smiled.

"I always thought we needed another writer in the family," Luis said. "But no snorkeling with sharks or climbing Mount Kilimanjaro, okay?"

Angie winked at her. "We'll see about that," she whispered, too low for Luis to hear.

Danya turned to Violet and shook her hand. "You've got yourself a deal!" she said. Pia grabbed Danya's shoulders and squeezed, so excited she did a kind of leaping, tapping dance around her.

"Snap, you did it," Pia said. "You finished the list from the book! You're a real hero now. You won the coveted treasure!"

Sancho snorted and whipped his tail against the sidewalk. Grinning, Danya leaned forward, planting a wet kiss on his forehead.

"I really did," she said. And looking around her, at her *abuelita*, who was hugging Luis, and her mother, who was shaking hands with Violet, and Pia, who was standing between her parents, and then back at Sancho, who was grinning his horsey grin at her . . . Danya knew it was true, what the prophet had told her. That the treasure had been with her all along.

Acknowledgments

A big ol' heartfelt thanks to Rhoda, Lexa, Laura, and the whole team at Paper Lantern Lit for making me feel like a rock star every day. An equally big thanks to Gillian and everyone at Razorbill for making my book all shiny and perfect. I could NOT have done it without you!

This book is about friendship, so I have to say a special thanks to my friends Maree and Becca—for throwing a truly amazing book party—and, also, Wade, Julia, and Lucy, for asking how the writing was going (even when you were probably tired of hearing about it!), cheering me on, and basically just making me feel like a star. I love you guys!

My family has been there for me from the beginning, so thank you mom, Steve, Bill, and Alex for being so supportive all the time. Thanks, also, to Bill, Lorraine, Jon and Christine, and to Carrie (for reading the first book to your sons, even though it was about a little girl), and to everyone who bought and read *Zip* and showed up to the book reading in the middle of a BLIZZARD. I have the best family ever!

And, of course, biggest thanks to Ron, for helping me through the hard parts and never doubting I could do it.

Loved Snap and Pia's adventure?
Try zipping along with Lyssa in: